**"You feel the heat, don't you, Zoe?
The fire. You feel it."**

Oh, yes, she felt it all right. His heat. Her heat.
Their heat. It scorched her nerve endings, setting
her whole body ablaze with desire. She bit back
a moan.

"I know," Reed murmured soothingly. "It burns,
doesn't it? It makes you ache inside."

The words were spoken a hairsbreadth away from
her lips, so close she could feel the warmth of his
breath against her skin. "But we have to wait to put
the fire out. It will be better that way. When we
finally give in to it and come together, we'll know
why."

"Why?" Zoe breathed. The word was little more than
a whimper.

"Lust," he growled. "We're going to burn each other
up and it's going to be glorious. But until that time
comes—" with superhuman effort he pushed away,
releasing her from the spell he'd woven with his
words and his body and the hot, dangerous look in
his eyes "—we aren't going to take any chances."

Blaze™

Dear Reader,

Harlequin Blaze is a supersexy new series. If you like love
stories with a strong sexual edge, then this is the line for
you! The books are fun and flirtatious, the heroes are hot
and outrageous. Blaze is a series for the woman who wants
more in her reading pleasure....

This month, *USA Today* bestselling author JoAnn Ross
brings you #5 *Thirty Nights,* a provocative story about a
man who wants a woman for only thirty nights of sheer
pleasure. Then popular Kimberly Raye poses the question
of what women really expect in a man, in the sizzling
#6 *The Pleasure Principle.* Talented Candace Schuler
delivers #7 *Uninhibited,* a hot story with two fiery
protagonists who have few inhibitions—about each
other! Carly Phillips rounds out the month with another
SEXY CITY NIGHTS story set in New York—where
the heat definitely escalates after dark...

Look for four Blaze books every month at your favorite
bookstore. And check us out online at eHarlequin.com
and tryblaze.com.

Enjoy!

Birgit Davis-Todd
Senior Editor & Editorial Coordinator
Harlequin Blaze

UNINHIBITED

Candace Schuler

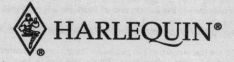

HARLEQUIN®

TORONTO • NEW YORK • LONDON
AMSTERDAM • PARIS • SYDNEY • HAMBURG
STOCKHOLM • ATHENS • TOKYO • MILAN • MADRID
PRAGUE • WARSAW • BUDAPEST • AUCKLAND

To my editor, Susan Sheppard,
who has the patience of a saint

ISBN 0-373-79011-2

UNINHIBITED

Visit us at www.eHarlequin.com

Printed in U.S.A.

1

REED SULLIVAN ASCENDED the wide brick steps of his great-grandmother's Beacon Hill mansion with nearly the same trepidation as he had shown the first time she had summoned him to share her afternoon tea.

The weekly ritual had started as a lesson in deportment, a continuation of the Wednesday afternoon torture known as Miss Margaret's Dance Academy for Young Ladies and Gentlemen. Moira Sullivan had seemed ancient to his eight-year-old self, with her snowy hair swept up into what he now knew was a Gibson girl topknot, and her elegant afternoon suits, which he now knew were Chanels. He'd been tongue-tied and uncomfortable at first, painfully aware that he was supposed to be on his best behavior, and itching for the whole ordeal to be over as soon as possible.

His great-grandmother had graciously invited him to stuff himself with frosted petits fours without regard for how they might ruin his dinner, all the while skillfully encouraging him to vent about the indignity of actually having to put his arms around a girl and attempt to waltz her around the room in front of his giggling friends. And then she'd rolled back a corner of the Aubusson carpet covering the gleaming parlor floor, placed a small needlepoint pillow beneath her knees and beat him in a hotly contested game of ringer.

He'd lost his prized Indian lutz to her, the one he'd traded two peppermint swirls and a blue clearie for.

After that, the visits to his great-grandmother became, if not the highlight of his week, then an eagerly anticipated part of it—if only because they offered him the ongoing opportunity to reclaim his Indian lutz. Even during his teen years, when girls and cars and being cool were the focus of his existence and marbles were the last thing on his mind, he still found time for the weekly visits. In the nearly two decades since then, all through the time he spent earning both a law degree and an M.B.A. from Harvard, through the long days spent toiling at his first lowly job in the family firm to the even longer days required by the high powered position he now held, through schoolboy crushes, discreet love affairs and the very public embarrassment of a broken engagement, the weekly ritual had endured. Sharing tea and conversation with his great-grandmother was still one of the highlights of his week.

They were an unlikely pair, perhaps, the oldest living Sullivan and the thirty-three-year-old heir apparent. Although they were separated both by gender and generations, with nearly sixty years of living between them, they clicked on some instinctive level that had nothing to do with experience or age. Sitting in Moira Sullivan's front parlor, sipping tea, trading benign gossip and bits of personal news, Reed wasn't the senior vice president in charge of international investments; he wasn't the head of any high-profile committee; he wasn't the heir to the vast fortune and responsibilities of the Sullivan business empire. He was simply Moira's favorite great-grandchild. And there was nothing that great-grandchild wouldn't do for his beloved granny.

Or almost nothing.

Lately, she'd been testing the limits of his affection and forbearance.

Well, forbearance, anyway, he amended, absently fingering the smooth Indian lutz marble in the trouser pocket of his navy, worsted flannel suit. There were no limits on his affection for her.

With a sigh, he slipped his hand from his pocket and lifted it to press a well-manicured index finger against the bell on Moira Sullivan's front door. It opened before the sound of the chimes had drifted away on the cool September air.

"Good afternoon, Eddie," Reed said, handing his briefcase and gym bag to the strapping young man who'd answered his summons. "Is she alone today?"

Eddie grinned and shook his head. "Got a luscious little redhead in there with her."

Reed groaned.

"Wait till you see her before you start complaining, man," Eddie counseled as he skillfully relieved Reed of his camel hair overcoat before Reed could do it for himself. "She's better than the last three, for sure."

Reed raised an eyebrow, then lifted his hand in response to the twinge of discomfort that accompanied the motion, absently smoothing the small butterfly bandage bisecting his brow with one finger as if to make sure it was still secure. "Better how?" he asked.

Eddie's grin turned into an appreciative leer. "Big brown eyes. Soft, sexy mouth. Lots of wild, curly hair hanging halfway down her back. *Killer* body. She's got style, too. Dresses real funky."

"Funky?"

"Think Annie Hall meets Pamela Anderson," Eddie said over his shoulder as he hung the overcoat in the hall closet. The briefcase and gym bag were neatly stowed on the floor beneath it.

"Annie Hall meets..." Reed shuddered at the thought. His taste ran toward the sophisticated Grace Kelly type. Cool, understated and elegant—that was his kind of woman. Badly dressed waifs with untidy hair, no matter how well endowed, were not his cup of tea.

"Pamela Anderson," Eddie said helpfully as he curled his meaty fingers around the curved brass handles on the elaborately carved double doors leading into the parlor. "You know, the blond babe with the prodigiously fine hooters." He pushed the doors open with a flourish. "Mr. Sullivan has arrived, ma'am," he intoned sonorously, bowing slightly toward his employer, as stiff and proper as if he had never uttered the word *hooters*—nor even knew what it meant.

The two women sitting on the pale blue brocade Victorian settee looked up expectantly. Moira Sullivan appeared much the same as she had the first time Reed had taken tea with her, nearly twenty-five years ago. She was wearing one of her elegant afternoon suits, a deep wine-colored bouclé that was immensely flattering against her pale skin and soft white hair. A triple strand of milky pearls adorned her neck. A large, square-cut sapphire sparkled on her right hand, complement to the impressive sapphire-and-diamond wedding set on her left. But it was her eyes that caught and held Reed's attention. Bluer than the sapphires she wore, they were full of warmth and welcome, as always, with an undisguised hint of excitement and anticipation lurking in their depths.

"Hello, Gran," he said cautiously, his gaze shifting to the young woman who sat beside his elegant, aged, *conniving* relative.

The redhead's eyes were as big and brown as Eddie had said they were, wide set and heavily lashed beneath thick, sharply arched auburn brows. Her hair was a riotous mass of corkscrew curls that tumbled well past her shoulders. Her clothes were a colorful hodgepodge of fabric and style.

More gypsy than waif, Reed decided in that first comprehensive glance.

She wore a man's soft white tuxedo shirt with a wing collar and an intricate Celtic brooch at the throat. Fanciful earrings of twisted metal and shiny stones dangled from her ears, glittering through the mass of springy curls. Dark forest-green, velvet pants were tucked into purple suede half-boots. A knitted mohair shawl in deep, rich shades of gold, brown and aubergine slipped off one shoulder to pool on the brocade settee beside her, its soft, nubby folds spilling over the edge toward the floor. Reed couldn't tell anything about her alleged killer body because of that shawl and the large tapestry bag she held open on her lap, but her mouth was... well, soft and sexy didn't even *begin* to describe it, he decided after a moment's absorbed reflection.

Her lips were full and beautifully sculpted, as pink and glossy and moist as if she'd just finished eating a raspberry Popsicle. It was the kind of mouth made for heated, heedless kisses and breathless promises whispered in the dark across a satin pillow. Not a waif's mouth, but a gypsy's.

And he didn't date gypsies—not even gorgeous, sexy gypsies—any more than he dated waifs. He dated nice, normal, conventional, well-bred women; the kind of women the men in his family had been dating and marrying for generations; the kind of women who were exactly like the last three women he'd met in Moira's parlor over the past couple of months. The kind of women, in fact, who were exactly like the kind of woman he thought he'd been engaged to a couple of years ago.

It had turned out that his ex-fiancée hadn't been all that conventional, after all, when it came right down to it. After a five-year engagement, she'd more or less left him standing at the altar and run off to New Orleans to work in a friend's lingerie shop while she decided whether or not she really wanted to get married. She decided she did—to a laid-back New Orleans hairdresser rather than Reed's illustrious self.

He'd put a good face on it—Sullivans always put a good face on things—but it had been quite a blow. To his pride, if nothing else. And truth be told, after all the dust had settled, he'd realized it *was* only his pride that had suffered any real damage; his heart had remained completely unscathed. In retrospect, he realized that Katherine had been absolutely right to run out on him because what he'd felt for her—what they'd felt for each other—had been nothing more than lifelong friendship coupled with a desire to satisfy family expectations. Reed still intended to satisfy his family's expectations, and his own, as well. Eventually.

So what in hell was his dear granny up to?

It certainly couldn't be matchmaking, not with *this* woman.

Could it?

"Shall I get the tea cart now, ma'am?" Eddie asked, his voice jolting Reed out of his absorption with Moira's flamboyant guest and the likely reason for her presence in his great-grandmother's front parlor.

"Yes, please, Eddie." The whisper of an Irish lilt enhanced Moira Sullivan's voice, adding piquancy to her upper-crust Boston accent. "And remind Mrs. Wheaton that there should be plenty of scones on the tray, won't you?" She flashed a warm smile at the young woman sitting next to her. "I promised our guest a traditional tea with scones and clotted cream and strawberry preserves."

"Yes, ma'am." Eddie bowed again and backed out of the room, pulling the doors closed behind him.

Moira lifted her hand, extending it toward her great-grandson. "Reed, dear," she said, her voice overflowing with delight. "Come and meet my new friend. This is Zoe Moon." She flashed a warm, approving smile at the young woman sitting beside her. "*Miss* Zoe Moon," she added, beaming like a proud mother showing off her new baby.

Reed stifled a sigh. No doubt about it now. As unlikely as it seemed, he'd just been introduced to yet *another* candidate for the position of Mrs. Reed Sullivan IV. It had been almost three years since his aborted trip down the aisle, and obviously his dear old granny was getting desperate to see him take that walk again. After all, he'd be thirty-four soon and no other Sullivan male in documented history had made it past thirty unwed. For him to have crossed that benchmark still a bachelor was looked upon as not quite proper—suspect, even—by the more conservative members of the family. Which was nearly all of them.

Plastering a polite smile on his face, Reed moved across the carpet to take his great-grandmother's outstretched hand, resigned to enduring the next two hours of her relentless matchmaking efforts with all the charm and good grace at his command.

"How are you, sweetheart?" he said, bending to kiss

Moira's cheek. He nodded at the young woman sitting next to her as he straightened. "Miss Moon."

"Call me Zoe, please," she said as she extended her hand to him.

The scent of violets, incongruously sweet and old-fashioned, drifted up to meet him as he reached out to shake her hand. Her palm was cool and small against his, the fingers long and tapering, delicate but not fragile. Her nails were painted a gleaming coppery color and she wore several narrow rings of various metals, some with glittering stones like the ones in her ears.

Reed had a brief, heated image of those slender, bejeweled hands on his bare back, the gleaming nails pressing into hard muscle as she arched under him and begged for more. He withdrew his hand from hers.

"Reed Sullivan," he murmured politely, wondering if she was available for anything other than the matrimonial bliss his great-grandmother was so dead set on.

"It's a pleasure to finally meet you." Zoe Moon's voice was throaty and melodious, as seductive as the rest of her. The look in her eyes as she smiled up at him was friendly, curious and just slightly speculative, as if she were sizing him up.

As possible husband material, no doubt, he thought cynically.

"Moira has told me so much about you," Zoe Moon said.

"Really?" He shot a cool, amused glance at his great-grandmother and seated himself in the wing chair opposite the settee. A low piecrust table, its gleaming surface decorated with an arrangement of golden button mums in a crystal bowl, occupied the space between them. "She hasn't said a word about you to me."

"That's because Zoe and I only just met this past Monday," Moira informed him.

Oh, great, he thought, *now she's parading complete strangers under my nose!*

"Zoe's an entrepreneur."

"Really?" Reed murmured, polite but not encouraging. "In what field?"

"Cosmetics," Moira said before Zoe could answer. She gestured at the table between them. "She was just showing me a few of her wonderful products."

Reed glanced at the table. Half-hidden behind the arrangement of mums were several small jars and bottles. At least half of them were open, perfuming the air with the faint, fresh scent of flowers and aromatic herbs. He'd noticed the fragrance when he came into the parlor, but hadn't thought anything about it, unconsciously assuming it came from the crystal bowls of potpourri Moira always kept scattered around the house.

On the settee next to Moira were a couple of shoe boxes he hadn't noticed before, either, and a large Betsey Johnson shopping bag on the floor between the two women's feet. Either Miss Moon had made a stop on Newbury Street before she called on Moira, or she was carting her wares around like a well-heeled bag lady. Whichever, someone really ought to tell her how unprofessional it made her appear.

"Then Miss Moon is...what?" He arched an eyebrow, ignoring the accompanying twinge as the butterfly bandage tugged at the fine hairs. "An Avon lady?"

"No, she's not an Avon lady. She's an *entrepreneur.*" Moira stressed the word as if he might not have understood it the first time. "She doesn't sell other people's cosmetics. She sells her own."

"Well, not cosmetics, exactly," Zoe Moon demurred with a smile. "Just lotions, body oils and sachets. So far, at least."

"They're not *just* anything," Moira objected. She plucked a slender, frosted-green-glass bottle off the table. The words *New Moon* were hand-lettered in elegant calligraphy across the label, superimposed over a line drawing of a pale crescent moon. "Zoe makes them herself, right in her own kitchen, using only the purest, most natural ingredients." Moira twisted the top off of the bottle and held it across the table toward Reed. "Try this," she ordered. "It's the most exquisite hand lotion I've ever used. Makes your skin feel as soft as water."

Zoe extended her hand and intercepted the bottle before Reed could stir himself to reach for it. "I'm sure Mr. Sullivan—" she gave him a slanting, sideways look as she said his name, both her expression and her tone letting him know she'd noticed and was…amused, he decided, by his insistence on the formality of address "—doesn't want to go back to the office smelling like a flower garden."

Both puzzled and just a bit disgruntled by her attitude, he watched her recap the bottle and set it on the piecrust table. As one of Boston's wealthiest and most eligible bachelors, Reed was accustomed to a great deal of respect, even awe, from the opposite sex. Women didn't usually laugh at him, not even silently.

"Oh, Reed won't go back to the office from here, will you, dear?" Moira said, apparently oblivious to the byplay between her guests.

Which was decidedly odd, Reed thought. Despite her advanced age, his great-grandmother prided herself on knowing exactly what was going on at all times.

"He always heads off to rugby practice after tea." Moira smiled in the direction of her great-grandson without actually taking her eyes off Zoe. "So I'm sure he doesn't care what he smells like."

Zoe Moon slanted Reed another glance, taking in the small white bandage on his eyebrow, skimming the width of his shoulders, sweeping the length of his legs beneath the worsted flannel of his navy slacks as if assessing his fitness for the sport...or something else. Only sheer strength of will kept him from squirming like an inexperienced adolescent under her frank, unabashed scrutiny. He managed to meet her gaze, when she brought it back to his, with a cool expression and an elegantly raised eyebrow, the epitome of masculine aplomb.

She didn't even have the grace to blush at being caught checking him out so blatantly. She simply smiled and looked away, turning her attention back to her hostess.

"I don't imagine his teammates would appreciate the scent of lavender in the middle of a..." Her gaze flickered back to Reed. "What do you call that group hug in the middle of a game?"

He scowled at the teasing note in her voice. She was definitely laughing at him! "A scrum," he growled, all but biting off the word in irritation.

Zoe Moon didn't seem to notice the warning edge in his tone. "A scrum. Thank you." She nodded, smiling, and turned her gaze back on Moira.

His scowl deepened.

If she was vying to become a candidate for the position of Mrs. Reed Sullivan IV, she was sure as hell going about it the wrong way. Not that she was in the running, anyway, of course. Not that *anyone* was in the running. But still… Didn't she know that bank presidents and highly placed corporate executives had been known to tremble in fear when he scowled at them?

"I don't think his teammates would appreciate the scent of lavender in the middle of a scrum," she said to Moira, completely oblivious to Reed's growing annoyance. "It would interfere with the smell of fresh blood and manly sweat."

"Well…perhaps you're right," Moira agreed, not seeming to notice Reed's annoyance, either. "But, still, it's important that he be familiar with the products, don't you think?"

"He could look at my formulas."

"Yes, of course. That's a splendid idea." Moira picked up one of the shoe boxes near her hip, removed the lid and began shuffling through the contents.

Not shoes or cosmetics, Reed noted sourly, but papers. Untidy stacks of papers, shoved every which way into the shoe box.

"Now, where are they?" Moira murmured, half to herself. "I had the one for your wonderful lotion in my hand not more than ten minutes ago."

"Why the he—" Reed caught himself before he uttered the profanity in front of his aged relative. "Why in the world would I need to look at the formula for some hand lotion?" he asked. "I'll look at it, of course, if you want me to," he amended when Moira glanced up with a delicately raised eyebrow that showed their kinship more clearly than the brilliant blue of their eyes, "but why would you want—"

The parlor doors opened. "Tea, ma'am." Eddie rolled the two-tiered cart into the room.

"Oh, wonderful." Moira beamed at her butler. "I'm sure everyone must be as parched as I am. All this talk of business has worked up a thirst in all of us, I'm sure."

"Business?" Reed said. Had he missed something here? "What bus—"

"Put it right there, please, Eddie." Moira motioned to a spot in front of the Adams mantel, halfway between Zoe's end of the settee and the wing chair where Reed sat. "You can just leave it," she instructed when Eddie began to fiddle with the delicate cups and saucers. "We'll serve ourselves today."

"Very good, ma'am." Eddie bowed himself out of the room.

Moira gestured toward the tea cart. "Zoe, dear, would you mind pouring, please? I'm afraid my wrists aren't up to managing that heavy teapot these days."

"Yes, of course. I'd be glad to." Zoe shifted the tapestry bag from her lap to the floor, shrugging the enveloping shawl from her shoulders as she rose to her feet.

The question Reed had been about to ask about his great-grandmother's supposedly weak wrists died on his tongue due to a sudden and complete lack of moisture.

Killer body, indeed.

Zoe Moon was built like a goddess...an Amazon...a Playboy Playmate of the Year.... Hell, of the decade!

She was all lush, tempting curves and intriguing hollows: high, round breasts swelling luxuriantly against the front of the mannish tuxedo shirt; an impossibly tiny waist set off by a narrow, gold leather belt; sleekly rounded hips and slender thighs lovingly outlined beneath the caress of forest-green velvet.

What was the word Eddie had used to describe her? *Luscious.*

Reed actually felt his mouth begin to water as he watched her pour tea into one of his great-grandmother's delicate Spode cups.

He swallowed.

Twice.

"Sugar? Lemon?" Zoe asked, her limpid, brown-eyed gaze fixed attentively on her hostess. "Milk?"

Moira glanced up from the open shoe box on her lap. "Oh, nothing in the tea, thank you. But I will have one of those butter cookies on the side, if you'd be so kind," she answered. "You can just put it on the table there." She indicated a spot on the piecrust table in front of her with a nod. "There's a dear," she said approvingly before returning her full attention to the papers in the shoe box. "I know it's here...." she murmured vaguely as she rifled through them.

"Just what are you looking for, Gr—"

"And you, Mr. Sullivan?" Zoe asked, turning to him with an empty cup in her hand. "What would you like?"

You, he thought in that split second before he could censor himself. *Naked. In bed. Under me. Moaning my name in mindless ecstasy.*

Zoe smiled and shook her head. "In your tea," she chided softly, as if he'd spoken his desire aloud.

Reed Sullivan IV, scion of the Sullivan empire, financial wunderkind, experienced man of the world, suddenly felt exactly the way he had the time he'd been caught by Sister Madeline Marie, trying to look up Patsy Flannery's dress on the jungle gym during recess. Now, as then, he opened his mouth to answer, but the words got stuck in his throat. He could only hope he wasn't blushing, too.

"Mr. Sullivan?" Zoe prompted, as she stood holding

a cup of tea in one slender, beringed hand and the silver sugar tongs in the other.

He had a sudden, searing vision of her standing there naked, in exactly the same position. No...not naked. In his mind's eye she was wearing stiletto heels and a frilly little apron made of sheer net and black lace, and—

"Mr. Sullivan," she said sharply, as if she had read his thoughts.

Or maybe it was just his guilty conscience that made her sound so much like Sister Madeline Marie had that day on the playground.

"One sugar, please," he croaked.

"One sugar it is."

She bent her head to her task, using the silver tongs to pluck a sugar cube from the bowl and drop it into his cup, lifting a tiny teaspoon to stir the hot liquid and melt the sugar, tapping the spoon lightly against the rim of the cup before placing it gently back on the silver spoon rest. The back of her hand brushed against a frosted petit four and she lifted her hand to her mouth, absently licking at one knuckle.

Reed sat mesmerized, watching every precise, delicate movement. Her tongue was nearly as pink as the frosting. *And probably sweeter, too...*

"Your tea, Mr. Sullivan."

He snapped out of a brief, delicious fantasy of licking frosting off of her fingers—and various other places—to find her standing in front of his chair, the cup of tea held practically under his nose. He tried not to picture her naked again—he really did—but it was a hopeless endeavor; she was the kind of woman who inspired lustful fantasies. He wondered how she'd look in one of those skimpy bits of satin and lace that graced the pages of the Victoria's Secret catalog. Something black with garters, he thought, decorated with little rosettes the color of the frosting on the petits fours.

"I hope it's the way you like it," she said.

"I'm sure it is," he managed to answer suavely, years of good manners and lessons in deportment coming to his rescue despite the lascivious pictures forming in his mind. "Thank you."

Their fingers touched.

Heat sizzled up his arm and straight into his brain cells, frying untold millions of nerve endings and sending alarm signals to points south. Her gaze lifted to his, eyes widened, startled, as if she felt something, too. And then she released her hold on the saucer and turned away. His fingers were suddenly so unsteady he had to reach up with his free hand to anchor the fragile cup in its saucer to keep from spilling hot tea in his lap.

"Ah, here it is!" Moira's voice was triumphant. "I knew I'd seen it in this box."

"Seen what, Gran?" Reed asked, without taking his eyes off of Zoe.

She stood with her back to him now, calmly pouring out her own cup of tea, as if that charged moment had never happened. Her wild tumble of hair was so long it brushed against the wide leather belt encircling her impossible waist.

"The formula," Moira said.

"The what?" he murmured, wondering how all that glorious hair would look cascading down Zoe Moon's naked back...wondering how it would feel if he reached out and grasped a handful...wondering if the curls between her slender thighs were the same flame-hot color as the ones on her head.

"The formula I want you to look at, dear," Moira said. "I found it."

Reed managed to tear his eyes away from Zoe long enough to glance at his great-grandmother. "What formula is that, Gran?"

"For Zoe's wonderful hand lotion. Haven't you been paying attention? Reed?" Her voice rose slightly in reprimand. "Reed, are you listening to me, young man?"

"I'm sorry." He turned his head toward his great-grandmother, refocusing his attention with superhuman effort. "You have my full attention." Or she would when Zoe sat down beside her again so he didn't have to strain to keep her in his peripheral vision. "What do you want me to look at, sweetheart?"

"This formula, for starters." Moira tapped the side of the shoe box with the tip of one finger. "And the rest of the papers, too, of course."

"The rest of the papers?" His glance darted sideways as Zoe reseated herself in the corner of the settee.

She brushed a long, springy tendril of hair back with one hand, casually sweeping it behind her shoulder, and crossed her legs—her long, slender, velvet-sheathed legs—balancing her teacup and saucer on her knee.

"What, ah..." Reed swallowed and forced himself to look back at his great-grandmother. "What kind of papers?"

"Oh..." Light glittered off the sapphire on Moira's right hand as it fluttered through the air. "Receipts and bills and things," she said vaguely, finally claiming her great-grandson's attention completely.

Moira Sullivan was never vague about anything. Ever.

"Zoe brought all her files as well as her formulas."
She smiled approvingly at the younger woman. "You
did bring everything with you, didn't you, dear?"

"Everything I thought might be useful to the discussion." Zoe gestured at the tapestry bag on the floor.
"What's not in shoe boxes is in there."

"Useful to what discussion?" Reed leaned forward
and carefully set his teacup and saucer on the little
piecrust table so he could give his full attention to the
conversation. He had the uneasy feeling that he'd
missed something vitally important in his libidinous
preoccupation with the luscious Miss Moon. "Just
what are we talking about here?"

"Well, my goodness, Reed," Moira admonished
him, "haven't you been listening? I want you to look
at Zoe's papers for me."

"Yes, I got that part. Why?"

"Because I'm going to give her the money to expand
her company, that's why. And I want you to tell me
the best way to do it."

2

"YOU STAY RIGHT WHERE YOU are, Gran." Reed rose to his feet as he spoke. "Miss Moon and I can see ourselves to the door."

Moira relaxed back onto the settee without even a token murmur of protest. "Thank you, dear. I'd appreciate that. These old bones of mine are a bit creaky and uncooperative these days." She held her hand out to Zoe. "I'm looking forward to getting started on our project," she said when Zoe reached out and clasped her fingers. "It's going to be *so* exciting. As soon as Reed gets all the paperwork done we'll have a little party to celebrate." Her eyes twinkled at the thought. "A sit-down dinner, I think, with the men in black tie so we ladies can get all gussied up. And lots of champagne. Do you like champagne, Zoe?"

"I love champagne." Impulsively, obeying her instincts as she always did, Zoe bent and kissed her hostess's cheek. It was soft and papery beneath her lips, and smelled sweetly of expensive face powder and Chanel No. 5. "Thank you," she whispered, and gently squeezed the fragile hand in hers.

"No, thank *you*." Moira returned the squeeze with surprising strength from someone with creaky old bones. "I haven't looked forward to anything half so much in a long time. It's going to be *such* fun." She smiled up into her great-grandson's face, her own alight with an almost childlike joy. "Isn't it going to be fun, dear?"

Zoe didn't think *fun* was exactly the word Mr. Reed Sullivan IV would have used to describe the situation. Unless she was very much mistaken, he hadn't been the least bit amused when he finally realized what his great-grandmother was planning to do. He'd been...well, *appalled* was the only word for the look that had flashed, ever so briefly, in his cool blue eyes.

"We'll see," he said stoically, confirming Zoe's supposition. "It's a little too early in the game to be making predictions."

He reached out as he spoke, touching his fingers to the small of Zoe's back as if to hurry her along, then drew back sharply. Zoe felt a small jolt and her skin rippled, chill bumps racing up her spine. She took a half step to the side, glancing uneasily over her shoulder. "Lots of static electricity in the air this time of year," she said with a tight little smile.

"Yes," Reed agreed as he took a step back from her. "That must be it. Static electricity. You should have Eddie check the setting on your humidifier, Gran. It might need to be turned up a notch or two. Miss Moon?" He extended his hand in a gesture that indicated she should precede him toward the double doors.

Though he was excruciatingly polite about it, the man obviously couldn't wait to get her out of his great-grandmother's parlor...away from his great-grandmother's wallet. Oh, he hid his impatience behind a patrician air and the same sort of bland, noncommittal smile she'd seen on the faces of half a dozen bankers over the last couple of months, but she knew exactly what he was thinking. If it were up to him, she wouldn't get the money. Thank goodness it wasn't up to him.

"I hope," she muttered.

"I beg your pardon?"

Zoe shook her head at him. "Nothing. Just thinking out loud."

"Then." He extended his hand again, polite, implacable, expecting to be obeyed. "After you."

Zoe abruptly decided it would do him good to be forced to hold his horses for a minute or two. She got the impression that he wasn't often required to wait for much of anything, and patience *was* a virtue, after all. She dropped her heavy tapestry bag to the floor and unhooked one of the handles of the Betsey Johnson shopping bag from the crook of her arm, letting it swing open.

"Why don't I leave a sample of my hand cream with you," she said to Moira as she dug through the bag. "That way you can compare the two—the lotion versus the cream." She extracted a small, squat, green glass container from the bag and presented it to Moira on the flat of her hand. "Use one on each hand for a week or so and see which you like better. Sort of our own form of, ah..." she glanced over her shoulder at Reed with a wide, guileless smile "...market research?" she said, all but batting her lashes at him. "Is that the right term?"

He gave her a slight nod. "It is," he said civilly.

She had to hand it to him. The man really did have lovely manners and truly impressive self-control. He stood there in his understated silk tie and his expensive navy blue suit—custom-made, no doubt—looking all cool and unconcerned, as debonair as James Bond at the baccarat table, while underneath she knew he wanted nothing more than to grab her by the scruff of the neck and toss her into the street. She'd been aware of his gaze on her all during their oh-so-civilized tea, sensing the disapproval lurking just beneath the surface of his cool, unruffled calm even *before* he realized what his great-grandmother meant to do.

Which didn't make any sense.

Zoe was well aware of her effect on most men. Just the sight of her was often enough to turn the weak-minded among them into slobbering, adoring idiots. Not that she thought Reed Sullivan was weak-minded but...well, even strong-minded men were usually inclined to look favorably on her, at least at first sight. It wasn't something she exploited—not often, anyway, not unless she really had to—but it *was* something she counted on to be there, kind of like the sun rising in the east every morning. Fair or not, her looks gave her an edge she had come to depend on in her dealings with men.

Instead of looking favorably on her, though, Reed Sullivan had been suspicious and disapproving from the minute he walked into the cheery, sunlit parlor and saw her sitting on the settee beside his great-grandmother. Her initial offer of friendliness—"Call me Zoe, please"—had been rebuffed in no uncertain terms. Very politely, of course, and oh-so-charmingly, but rebuffed nonetheless.

His attitude had puzzled her at first, even beyond his lack of a favorable response to her physical self. What could she, a stranger, have done in those first few moments that he could possibly disapprove of? Maybe he was having a bad day and the disapproving air didn't have anything to do with her, she'd thought charitably. Or maybe she'd intimidated him; it wasn't unknown for a certain type of man to get shy and tongue-tied in her presence. Although, admittedly, Reed Sullivan didn't strike her as either shy or inarticulate, she was willing to give him the benefit of the doubt. So she'd tried teasing him, gently, smiling to let him know she was harmless. Most men, strong-minded or not, went a little slack-jawed when she gave them her slanting, sideways glance, that whisper of a smile that tacitly invited them to share the joke. Reed Sullivan had narrowed his brilliant blue eyes and looked down his aristocratic nose at her, as if she were an impertinent employee who'd overstepped her bounds.

Zoe had distinctly felt her hackles rise. How dare he disapprove of her! Just because he was wealthy and pedigreed, and belonged to what she was sure were all the right clubs, and she was...well, okay, she was there with her hand out, more or less, hoping for a loan from his great-grandmother. But that was no reason for him to look at her as if she were some kind of panhandler who'd accosted him in the street. Moira Sullivan had invited her to tea specifically to discuss the possibility of investing in New Moon.

Zoe began to needle him subtly, mocking his pretensions with a provocative little smile, using her expressive eyes and her centerfold body in an effort to make him squirm, trying to find some way to pierce that polished facade of urbane civility. A couple of times there, she'd thought she'd succeeded. Almost. He'd looked distinctly guilty at one point, as if whatever he was thinking at that particular moment probably wouldn't have borne the light of day. And then, a minute or two later, there'd been a certain betraying light in his eyes as he'd looked at her—not disapproving just then at all, oh no, but speculative, absorbed...fascinated, almost. She'd handed him his tea, wondering exactly what was going on behind that distant, glazed look, feeling the tiniest bit triumphant at having rattled him at last.

And then their fingers had touched.

And their eyes had met.

And she'd felt as if every nerve ending in her body had been scorched.

She'd had to turn away, trying not to fumble as she poured her own tea, taking several slow, calming breaths while she tried to compose herself. And as she regained her composure, the budding feeling of triumph returned along with it. He'd shaken her, yes, but she'd shaken him, too. She was sure of it. He wasn't as cool as he pretended. As unaffected. Not if that hot, glittering look that had flickered in his eyes when his gaze met hers was anything to go by.

Telling herself to be satisfied with that small victory, she'd reseated herself on the settee with what she felt was a convincing nonchalance, managing, finally, after a long, fidgety moment, to glance casually toward Reed to see how he was reacting to whatever it was that had flashed between them.

Mr. Nose-in-the-air Stuffed Shirt Reed Sullivan IV was leaning forward in his chair, his teacup on the gleaming piecrust table, his eyes focused intently on his great-grandmother, calmly talking business! New Moon business, true, but still...

Zoe wondered if *anything* had ever ruffled that insufferable, infuriating poise of his for more than a second. Wondered, too, what that anything might be. It certainly couldn't have been a woman! Money, maybe. No, probably, she decided peevishly. He was obviously the bloodless, cold-fish type who couldn't get worked up about anything *except* money.

Well, she could oblige him there.

"Why don't you just take all my samples," she said to Moira, as if the idea had just occurred to her. Which it had. "Use them yourself. Give them to all your friends and female relations." She continued to dig through her shopping bag as she spoke, putting small jars and bottles and plump satin sachets back on the piecrust table from where she had picked them all up a few minutes ago. "That way we can expand our research and make it a real survey. After all, it's women like you and your wealthy friends who have the money to spend that will make New Moon profitable."

She glanced at Reed out of the corner of her eye to see how he was taking it. His countenance hadn't changed except for a slight narrowing of his eyes and a too-tight something about his jaw, as if he were clenching his teeth. Encouraged, Zoe rattled on.

"Maybe we could hold a sort of informal market focus group," she said recklessly, tossing ideas out off the top of her head. "You know, invite your friends over some evening and let them sample the products and tell us what they think about each of them. I could even give minifacials or—oh, I know!" She snapped her fingers as inspiration struck. "How about massages with my scented body oils? My friend Gina is a massage therapist and she'd lend me her table. We could set it up right here in the parlor. Gina might even come along to give the massages herself, if she's free. She's very good. Very much in demand. In fact, she has scads of clients right here on Beacon Hill. Probably some of your friends, even. Maybe you've heard of her? Gina Molinari? No? Well, anyway, I'm sure she wouldn't charge *too* much, as a favor to me. Although, with your money, I don't guess you'd worry about that.''

Zoe tossed another quick look over her shoulder. Reed Sullivan was still standing there, a bland look on his face, seemingly at ease as he patiently waited for his great-grandmother's guest to be ready to leave...but a tiny, telltale muscle in his chiseled jaw had begun to twitch, ever so slightly. Zoe smiled brightly and plunged ahead.

"If that goes well, we could do something more formal. Well, not exactly formal, but more, um..." she tapped a forefinger against her chin, parodying someone deep in thought "...businesslike," she decided, the word forming on her lips as if she wasn't quite sure of its pronunciation, or exact meaning. "We could widen the survey. You know, pay different people to come in off the street to try the products, with questionnaires afterward to see what they like and don't like. I've participated in dozens of focus groups like that when I've been between jobs, and they're all pretty much run the same way," she said confidingly. "I even worked as a researcher myself once, on one of my temp jobs, so I know how it's done. So. How does that sound to you? Just to start, I mean?"

"Well, ah..." Moira's gaze flickered from Zoe's flushed face to her great-grandson's stony countenance and back again. She smiled. "That sounds like quite an ambitious plan, my dear." She nodded emphatically. Approvingly. "Quite ambitious."

"Oh, I'm ambitious, all right." Zoe slanted another quick glance at Reed. The muscles in his jaw were bulging now, as if he'd gone beyond clenching his teeth to grinding them. Zoe felt a surge of pure adrenaline and went in for the kill. "*Extremely* ambitious."

She leaned over slightly, reaching out to clasp one of Moira's hands in both of hers. "Why, with all your lovely money behind me there's no telling what I can—'' She broke off, startled, as Reed's long fingers wrapped themselves around her biceps. She dropped Moira's hand as he pulled her upright with something very close to a jerk.

"We can talk about what you can or can not do with all Gran's lovely money at some other time," Reed said quietly, through his teeth.

Zoe's protest was automatic. "But I haven't fin—"

"I hate to rush you, but I'm running late, Miss Moon." He glanced pointedly at his watch, turning his wrist without letting go of her. "If you want a lift home, we'll have to leave right now."

"Late for what? Oh. Your rugby practice," she said, realizing belatedly that her hostess's great-grandson was actually teetering on the edge of losing his cool. He'd never have laid hands on her, otherwise. "Well, don't worry about me, then." She gave him a bright, saccharine smile meant to push him clean over the precipice. "I can take the T home when I'm ready to go." She shrugged dismissively, trying to dislodge his hand. "Moira and I have lots more to discuss and—"

His fingers flexed on her arm. "I really must insist, Miss Moon."

"No, thank you. I appreciate the gesture but—"

"I didn't want to mention it, but I'm afraid Gran is getting tired." The look he turned on Moira was one of filial concern. "Aren't you, Gran?"

"Nonsense. I'm not the least—" Moira began.

"She'll never admit it, of course," Reed continued smoothly, talking over his great-grandmother's protest, "but it's been a long afternoon for her. She usually takes a nap right after tea, and we're keeping her from it.'' He lowered his voice, putting his lips very near Zoe's ear as if to keep Moira from overhearing. ''She *is* ninety-two, you know.''

''Oh. Oh, yes. Of course. How thoughtless of me.'' Guilt pierced Zoe's tender heart, instantly chasing away all thought of goading Reed. ''I'm so sorry. I wasn't thinking. You've been so kind to me,'' she said to Moira, ''and here I am, keeping you up when you should be resting. Just let me grab my purse and—''

''Got it.'' Reed bent down, scooped the tapestry bag off the floor by its braided leather straps with his free hand and swung it toward her.

Zoe grabbed at it awkwardly, fumbling to hold on to it without upending the precariously gaping shopping bag hanging from her arm. She felt her shawl begin to slip, and hunched her shoulder, trying to boost it back into place.

''Dinner here after practice?'' Reed said to his great-grandmother as Zoe grappled with her belongings.

''Dinner? Well, actually, I—''

Reed stared down his nose at her and waited.

''Yes, of course, dear. Dinner here,'' Moira agreed demurely. ''If you like.''

''I like.'' He bent and pressed a quick kiss on her cheek. ''I'll be back around eight-thirty, if that's all right with you?''

Moira nodded. ''Eight-thirty will be fine.''

''Good.'' He nodded, once. ''That's settled, then.'' His hand tightened on Zoe's arm. ''Miss Moon?''

Zoe braced herself against the pressure. ''Thank you for a lovely tea, Moira. I really enjoyed it.''

''So did I, dear,'' Moira said. ''Immensely. I'll call

you about the market research party early next week and we can discuss the details at more length.''

Reed mumbled something that sounded suspiciously like ''Over my dead body'' under his breath.

''What was that, dear?'' Moira asked. ''I didn't quite hear you.''

''I said, I'll take care of all the details.'' He looked down at Zoe, smiling at her through gritted teeth. ''Ready, now?''

Without waiting for either assent or refusal, he propelled her into motion, steering her around the piecrust table and across the Aubusson. It was either stumble along beside him as best she could or fall flat on her face and let him drag her. Zoe stumbled along, the shopping bag dangling from her arm, her purse clutched to her chest, her soft, knitted shawl slipping farther and farther off her shoulder. She had to quick-step to keep up with his long-legged, no-nonsense stride as he headed toward the tall double doors. The doors opened outward just as they reached them, and Eddie stepped back, bowing them into the foyer with a nod of his head.

''Sir?'' he said in the same formal, sonorous tone he had used before. The word and the tone contrasted incongruously with the bright red shorts and red-and-yellow color-block rugby shirt he was wearing. No one paid any attention to the fact that he must have been listening at the keyhole to have opened the doors so promptly.

''Grab my things, please, Eddie,'' Reed said he marched across the marble foyer, towing Zoe in his wake. She was nearly on tiptoes now, and the shawl had slipped entirely off of one shoulder and was dragging on the floor. ''I'm running late.''

Eddie already had Reed's things laid out in readiness, the overcoat draped across the top of a tufted velvet Victorian bench, the briefcase and gym bag side by side on the floor in front of it. He grabbed them up along with his own gym bag and fell in step behind the two scurrying figures.

"I take it you're not going to change here as usual?" he asked pleasantly, as if the sight of his employer's great-grandson quickstepping a guest out of the house wasn't anything out of the ordinary.

"No," Reed said shortly. "No time. We have to drop Miss Moon off at her apartment on our way." He yanked the front door open with his free hand before Eddie could maneuver around to do it for him. "I'll change at Magazine Beach."

I really ought to let him drive me home, Zoe thought vindictively as he all but dragged her over the threshold and out onto the front steps. Considering his final destination, a detour to the North End during rush hour traffic would make him *really* late. But it would make Eddie late, too, and Eddie wasn't the one giving her the bum's rush. And besides, she wasn't in the mood to go *anywhere* with Mr. Stuffed Shirt!

"You don't have to drop Miss Moon at her apartment," she said between her teeth, digging in her heels and rearing back as he reached for the door handle of the sleek black Jaguar XJ6 parked—wouldn't you just know it!—at the curb directly in front of the house. "You don't have to drop Miss Moon anywhere, because Miss Moon will take the T. Now let go of my arm!"

She yanked her arm out of his grasp and turned to face him, there on the sidewalk in front of his great-grandmother's Beacon Hill mansion.

"Boy, I sure don't know what your problem is, mister." Huffily, head down, Zoe wrestled with the handles of both shopping bag and purse, settling them securely over her arm. "And I don't particularly care." She hitched her shawl up over her shoulder with a jerk, draping the excess over her forearm. "But I definitely do *not* appreciate being treated like some kind of two-bit street hustler who's out to make a quick buck off a sweet old lady."

"If a quick buck was all you were after, there wouldn't be any problem, would there?" Reed said mildly, his tone as urbane and civil as if he hadn't just dragged her out of his great-grandmother's house by the scruff of the neck.

Zoe found it *really* annoying that he could sound so cool, as if that mad dash across the marble foyer and down the wide brick steps hadn't happened, while she was left feeling frazzled, put-upon and decidedly ill used. "Then just what *is* your problem?" she demanded.

"My problem is your brazen effort to bilk a sweet old lady out of a small fortune to finance some fly-by-night cosmetic company."

"Fly-by—" Zoe's mouth gaped open and she stared at him like a hooked fish for a full five seconds. "New Moon is not fly-by-night!" she exclaimed furiously, and then clamped her mouth shut. Shouting at the top of her lungs might be all well and good in the North End, but Beacon Hill called for a little more decorum. Besides, if she lost her temper, Mr. Stuffed Shirt would win. And she'd implode before she'd let that happen. "I've been selling New Moon products to individual clients for over three years, and commercially, on a commission basis, for almost two," she said with quiet dignity. "I have steady retail customers in two shops in the Faneuil Hall Marketplace and several locations in the Back Bay, including one in a very exclusive boutique on Newbury Street, which, for your information, is where I met your great-grandmother. I'd hardly call that fly-by-night."

"Regardless of what you'd call it, Miss Moon, you're not getting any money from my great-grandmother to expand your little...enterprise." His slight hesitation made the word sound distinctly unsavory.

"Why not?" Zoe demanded, truly puzzled by his attitude. "Moira told me she invests in all kinds of businesses. And with your blessing, too. So just what have you got against me and New Moon?"

"Let's just say I have a constitutional aversion to con artists and leave it at that, shall we?"

"Con artists!?" She had to fight to keep her voice even. "But I just told you, I'm not trying to con any— Moira's the one who invited me to tea and I— Oh, forget it! It's obvious you've already made up your mind," she accused, ignoring the fact that her little act in his great-grandmother's parlor might have had something to do with his poor opinion of her. "And you aren't about to change it, are you? No matter what I say."

Zoe lifted her chin. "All I can say is that you're cheating your great-grandmother out of a wonderful investment opportunity. New Moon is going to be worth hundreds of thousands of dollars some day. Millions, even." She picked up the end of her shawl and tossed it across the opposite shoulder, haughty as an affronted queen. "It's going to be bigger than Estee Lauder. And you're going to be very, very sorry."

With that, she turned and stomped off down the street, her mass of fiery, corkscrew curls swaying against her back, her purse and shopping bag bouncing against her hip, the heels of her purple suede boots clicking like castanets against the venerable old Boston street.

For once in her life, she had come up with the perfect exit line. Perfect! She hadn't said too much, or too little. She hadn't lost her temper. She'd been cool, calm and composed. It took all of her willpower not to ruin it by turning around and rudely thumbing her nose at Mr. Stuffed Shirt Reed Sullivan IV.

"Well," Eddie said. "That was certainly interesting."

"Yes," Reed said slowly, his eyes on her retreating back. He rubbed a hand over the back of his neck, wondering why it felt so hot and…twitchy. "Wasn't it."

3

"BUT I WANT TO INVEST in Zoe's business, Reed."

"Gran, sweetheart, be reasonable. Whatever New Moon is, it can hardly be called a business. She doesn't have a business plan. Nor a P&L. Not even a simple, basic set of books to track income and expenses." He dug his hand into one of the shoe boxes on the table between them and grasped a sheaf of papers to illustrate his point. "Just this disorganized mess." Which, he noted, smelled disconcertingly of violets. He lifted them halfway toward his nose before he realized what he was doing, and stuffed them back into the box with a disgusted snort. "You can't run a business, let alone expect people to give you money to expand it, if you don't keep decent records."

"Well, there, you see." Moira smiled at him approvingly. "That's just the kind of advice Zoe needs. I *knew* you could help."

"Gran, you can't really be serious about this." He looked at her over the top of his reading glasses. "Can you?"

"Dead serious," she assured him with an emphatic little nod of her regal head.

"Well, I'm dead set against it." He took his glasses off and tossed them down on the table like a gauntlet. "I don't approve of the idea at all. Not at all."

Moira's brows lifted at his tone. "May I remind you,

young man, that it happens to be *my* money we're discussing, not yours. And as I have been legally of age for quite some time now and am in full possession of my faculties, I am perfectly free to do as I please with it." She lifted her chin and looked down her elegant nose at him. "Whether you approve or not."

Reed abandoned his high horse. It never worked with his great-grandmother, anyway; nobody had ever been able to dictate to Moira Sullivan, not even her dear departed husband.

"But *why,* Gran? Can you at least answer me that? Why on earth do you want to invest in that woman's business?"

"Her products are wonderful," Moira said promptly. "And I like her."

"You hardly know her," he countered. "You said yourself you only met her this past Monday and—" He broke off as a thought occurred to him. "How exactly did you happen to meet her, anyway?"

"She didn't maneuver an introduction or try to ingratiate herself in any way, if that's what you're thinking," Moira chided him gently. "I overheard her talking to the proprietor of The Body Beautiful about the difficulties she's been having getting financing to expand her business, and I interrupted their conversation and introduced myself to her."

"And you say she didn't maneuver it," he scoffed.

Moira stiffened ever so slightly and her chin came up again. "Despite my advanced years, I am not some poor senile old lady who doesn't know which end is up," she said with quiet, reproachful dignity.

Reed was instantly contrite. "I'm sorry, Gran. I didn't mean that the way it sounded. I never meant to suggest that you—"

"Neither am I gullible or easily misled," Moira went on, as if he hadn't spoken. "I know very well when someone is trying to pull the wool over my eyes. And when they aren't. And I assure you, my dear Reed, Miss Moon had no idea I was listening to her conversation in that shop until I interrupted her."

"I'm sure you're right," Reed agreed. "You know I have the utmost faith in your judgment. I always have and always will. I just..." He paused and reached for his discarded glasses, twisting one stem as he searched for the words to say what he meant without insulting his great-grandmother again. "All question of how you met aside, the fact remains that you've known her—and I use that term loosely!—three days. Barely. And yet you say you like her. Three days isn't enough time to make that kind of decision about a person. It's not enough time to make *any* kind of decision about a person, especially if you're contemplating lending that person a great deal of money."

"You've known her—and I also use the term loosely—less than a day, and you've already decided you *dislike* her. Why is that, I wonder?"

"I don't dislike her," Reed objected, which was the strict truth. His reaction to the luscious Zoe Moon was a little more complicated than mere like or dislike. It was...well, he didn't know what it was exactly. "And this isn't about me, anyway. It's about you. So quit trying to change the subject and answer my question. Please," he added when she raised an eyebrow at him. "Give me a *little* insight into why you decided it's a good idea to lend money to a woman you've known for barely three days."

Moira sighed. "I decided I wanted to marry your great-grandfather after only an hour in his company."

"That's hardly the same thing."

"True," Moira agreed. "Marriage is a much more serious matter. With much more serious consequences if you're wrong. But the basic principle is the same. Trust."

"Are you telling me you *trust* Zoe Moon?"

"Yes, I do. She appears to me to be an eminently trustworthy young woman."

"Good Lord, Gran!" Reed just barely managed to keep his voice at a reasonable level. One didn't shout at Moira Sullivan with impunity. Not if one wanted to get anywhere with her. "Didn't you hear a word she said this afternoon?"

"I'm not deaf, dear. Certainly I heard her. She has a lovely, soothing voice, don't you think?"

"Oh, lovely," he agreed with a snort. Soothing, however, it was not. Now, if she'd said arousing... He deliberately veered away from that line of thought. "But that's not what I meant, and you know it."

"What did you mean, dear?"

"'Women like you and your wealthy friends'," he quoted. "'All your lovely money...' 'With your money, you wouldn't worry about that....' The woman obviously came to tea today for one thing and one thing only."

Moira gave a little gurgle of laughter. "Well, of course she did! For goodness sake, Reed, I asked her to tea specifically to talk about the possibility of lending her the money to expand her business. I expected her to talk about it. That was the whole point."

Reed remembered Zoe Moon trying to tell him something along the same lines, out there on the sidewalk in front of the house. But he hadn't bought it then, and he wasn't buying it now. "It's the *way* she talked about it that I object to."

"The way?"

"As if it were a done deal and the money were already hers. Good manners, if nothing else, should have kept her from acting as if you'd already signed on the dotted line."

"Well, perhaps, but..."

Reed jumped on her hesitation. "Come on now, Gran," he cajoled. "Admit it. Didn't she sound like a greedy, money-grubbing little mercenary out to take you for all she could get?" And why was he attracted to her, despite that?

"Really, dear." Moira shook her head. "Isn't that a bit harsh?"

"A bit, maybe," he conceded, disposed to at least try to be fair now that he could see his great-grandmother starting to come around to his way of thinking. "But I notice you didn't deny it."

"She was nervous," Moira said. "It made her babble and say things awkwardly, is all. She's really a lovely, gracious young woman. And very sweet, too."

"Nervous?"

"Well, anyone would have been, with you glowering at them across the tea table."

"I don't glower."

"You're glowering right now, dear," Moira informed him. "If I were a sensitive young woman like Zoe, I'd be babbling, too."

"You've never babbled in your life," Reed scoffed.

She laughed softly. "Oh, I babbled a bit more than I like to remember in those early days with your great-grandfather." The laughter faded into a fond smile. "You're very like him, you know. It quite takes me back sometimes, just to look at you. He could be very intimidating, too, when he chose.''

''Are you saying *I* made her nervous?'' Reed asked incredulously. The mere thought was almost laughable. The bold, red-haired gypsy who'd looked him up and down with that provocative gleam in her big brown eyes didn't strike him as the nervous type. Lovely, yes, he'd grant her that. But gracious? Sweet? Nervous? His eyes narrowed. ''Now wait a minute here, Gran. You're not suggesting...'' He leaned across the mahogany table, his expression wary and accusing, wondering if he'd been right in his first assessment, after all. ''This isn't some kind of crazy, harebrained matchmaking scheme, is it? Because if it is, you're barking up the wrong tree.''

''Matchmaking? You thought I was matchmaking?'' A soft gurgle of laughter bubbled up and was quickly suppressed. ''Well, really, Reed.'' The look she gave him was full of amused indignation. ''At least give me credit for having the sense God gave a goose. I know perfectly well Zoe isn't even remotely your type.''

Placated, Reed leaned back in his chair. ''I'm glad you realize that.''

''Nor are you hers, I might add. Zoe is the kind of woman who would be drawn to someone with a little more...'' one soft white hand fluttered through the air as if groping for the words ''...joie de vivre.''

''I enjoy life,'' Reed objected.

''Oh, I'm sure you do, in your own way. I don't mean to suggest otherwise. It's just that I'm afraid you're a bit, oh...staid, shall we say?...for someone like Zoe.''

''Staid?'' he murmured, vaguely insulted by the word.

"Dignified. Proper," Moira clarified with a fond smile. "You're a credit to the Sullivan name, Reed. I've always thought so, ever since you were a baby."

"Well, thank you. I think," he said, wondering why he suddenly felt like a priggish, self-satisfied boor. His great-grandmother had just complimented him, hadn't she? "Now, if you don't mind." Reed rapped a knuckle against the papers on the table. "Could we get back to the subject at hand?"

"Certainly." Moira folded her hands on top of the table, like an eager little girl at lessons. "What's the next step?"

Reed sighed. "Do you really mean to pursue this, Gran? No matter what I say?"

Moira nodded. "I do."

"And if I refuse to have anything to do with it?"

"I'll be disappointed, of course. But I'm sure I can find someone else to handle the paperwork for me."

"Not at Sullivan Enterprises, you won't," he warned her, his financier's scowl firmly in place. "Not if I advise against it. And, be assured, I will."

But Moira Sullivan wasn't easily intimated, especially not by her own great-grandson. "Well, then, I'll just have to go outside the family business, won't I?" She tilted her head, giving him a considering look from under her lashes. "I've heard young Andrew Hightower is making quite a name for himself in financial circles these days."

Andrew Hightower was Reed's ex-fiancée's youngest brother. A nice enough kid, but... It galled Reed to realize that the mere mention of the Hightower name struck a sore spot he hadn't known he had. "You wouldn't."

"Yes," Moira said. "I most definitely would. I intend to arrange for Zoe Moon to have the funds she needs to expand her business. I'd like for you to help me find the best way to do that, so that everyone's interests are properly looked after. But if you can't or won't, well...'' she lifted her shoulders in an eloquent little shrug ''...I'll find someone who will, be it Andrew Hightower, or someone else entirely. Or maybe I'll just give her the money outright,'' she said consideringly. ''It might be simpler all around that way.''

Reed knew when he was beaten. ''All right, Gran. You win. I'll see what I can do about getting Miss Moon her financing.''

IT WAS NEARLY NINE-THIRTY that night before Zoe heard her next-door neighbor banging around outside in the hallway. Zoe put down the glass of pink grapefruit juice she'd just poured for herself and rushed toward the front door, nearly bursting with the need to vent.

A petite, slender young woman with a short, sleek cap of dark hair and even darker eyes looked up and smiled as Zoe all but exploded into their mutual hallway. ''Ciao, Zoe. How's it goin'?''

''Gina! I thought you'd never get home. Where on earth have you been this late?''

''Same place I've been every Wednesday night for the past couple of months. That new client with the arthritis, remember? I told you about him.'' She set the edge of her massage table on the floor and let go of the handle, tilting it toward Zoe. ''Hold on to this for a minute while I get the rest of my stuff. I left it at the bottom of the stairs.''

''You aren't going to believe what happened today,'' Zoe hollered at her friend's retreating back. ''I had tea with Moira Sullivan. Remember, the woman I told you about? The one I met at The Body Beautiful on Monday?''

''The one who's going to lend you the money for New Moon, right?'' Gina said as she came back up the steps with her equipment bag slung over one shoulder and a bulging sack of groceries in her arms.

Zoe leaned the massage table against the wall and reached for the grocery sack, freeing Gina so she could unlock her front door. ''Well, she *was* going to lend me the money.'' Zoe's lush mouth screwed up in a grimace. ''But I think we can kiss that idea goodbye.''

''Oh, no.'' Gina turned in the open doorway, automatically reaching out to offer comfort. ''She turned you down, after all? I'm so sorry.'' She squeezed Zoe's arm, her sympathy swift and sincere. ''I know how much you were counting on this.''

''Oh, *she* didn't turn me down.'' Zoe moved past her friend into a small studio apartment that was the exact duplicate of her own floor plan, except in reverse, and dropped the grocery sack on the kitchen counter. ''He did.''

''He who?''

''Mr. Stuffed Shirt Reed Sullivan IV, that's who.''

''Her husband?''

''Her great-grandson.''

''What does he have to say about it?''

''Plenty, apparently.'' Zoe leaned back against the counter and crossed her arms, waiting while Gina deposited her equipment bag on the sofa bed and retreated back into the narrow hall to retrieve her massage table. ''And none of it good,'' she said, when the other woman came back into the room and deftly slid the folded table into its accustomed place behind the sofa.

"Tell me what happened while I put my groceries away," Gina said, moving toward the kitchen area without bothering to close the front door.

Directly across the hall, Zoe's door stood wide open, too. Theirs were the only two apartments above the family-owned Italian restaurant on the first floor. The bottom of the stairway was protected by a tall iron security gate that blocked any unauthorized access to the second floor apartments.

"Out." Gina flapped a hand at Zoe, waving her away as she began to help unload the groceries. "It's too crowded in here with two of us."

Zoe moved to one of the two stools on the other side of the counter and plopped down with a dejected sigh. "Things were really going great at first," she said morosely, watching Gina as she moved around the tiny kitchen. "Moira Sullivan is a wonderful old lady. Very charming and elegant, but really sweet and down-to-earth, too. Not snobbish or stuck-up in the least. She was interested in everything I'd brought her and was talking about what I could do *when* I had the money, not *if*. And asking how much and did I think it was enough. And then he walked in."

"He being the stuffed shirt?"

"Yes. And right from the first...from almost the *second* he walked in and saw me sitting there next to his great-grandmother...I could tell he didn't like me."

Gina turned to face her, a package of spaghetti in one hand, eyes rounded in disbelief, her lips parted in astonishment. "He didn't like you?"

"Nope."

"But, Zoe, men always like you. They can't help it. It's—" she extended her free hand, palm up, moving it in an expressive gesture that encompassed the half of Zoe's body that was visible above the counter "—hormonal."

"He didn't."

"Well. My goodness," Gina murmured, momentarily at a loss for words. She opened a cupboard and put the package of spaghetti away, then turned around with a thoughtful expression on her face, her hand still on the cupboard door. "Is he gay?"

"Definitely not," Zoe said, shivering a bit as she remembered the way he'd looked at her, and the spark, or whatever it was, that had sizzled between them. She'd had a good long time to think about it, sitting alone in her apartment, fuming, as she waited for Gina to get home so she could discuss it with her. The conclusions she'd drawn left her almost as angry as she'd been when she'd stomped away from him that afternoon. Almost. "I'm pretty sure he's got the hots for me."

"The hots? Well, then..." Gina's eyebrows rose into spiky bangs on her forehead. "You've lost me."

"He likes my body—a lot—but he disapproves of *me*."

"Aaah." Gina nodded her head knowingly. "One of those."

"Yes, definitely one of those. He practically undressed me with his eyes. Oh, very politely, of course—the man could give etiquette lessons to Miss Manners—but his eyes were anything but! Polite, I mean," she clarified when Gina just stood there, staring at her. "They're like blue laser beams. Very cool on the surface, but intense underneath, like a volcano. Very focused, you know? He gave me this one look that practically scorched me all the way to my toes."

"Scorched?"

Zoe chose not to respond to the question in Gina's voice. "And then he had the nerve to call me a con artist—me! a con artist!—and accused me of trying to swindle that sweet old lady out of a fortune."

"In front of her?"

"No, not in front of her. Well," she amended, "the hot looks were in front of her, but I don't think she noticed. She's ninety-two, you know. He waited until we were outside before he started calling me names. That's when he called New Moon a fly-by-night operation—" her voice rose indignantly at the remembered slur on her company "—and said I could just forget getting any money from his great-grandmother to finance my little *enterprise*." She curled her upper lip, giving the word the same unsavory implication he had.

"Jeez." Gina folded the grocery sack and bent down to put it under the sink. "That sounds a little extreme, even for the repressed type. They usually content themselves with blaming you for arousing their libido, and let it go at that." She reached for the bright red teakettle on the stove, then hesitated, head tilted as she considered her friend. "Wine or espresso? I've got some plain biscotti that would go with either."

"Espresso," Zoe said. "Wine would only make me get all weepy and maudlin."

Gina nodded and turned on the faucet, her gaze lowered as she watched the kettle fill. "What on earth made him think you were some kind of con artist?"

Zoe shrugged. "Beats me."

Gina lifted her gaze from the kettle to Zoe's face.

"Honest, I have no idea why he would think that."

"You want to look me in the eyes when you say that?"

Zoe sighed, knowing she was caught. "Okay. So maybe I, um...influenced his opinion in that regard. A little."

Gina set the kettle on the stove and turned the heat on. "Influenced?" she murmured encouragingly.

"Well, he made me so darn mad. Staring at me as if he were imagining me naked one minute, and then looking down his nose at me the next, all superior and disapproving, as if it were my fault he was having lewd fantasies in his great-grandmother's parlor. But I swear, Gina, I didn't do one thing—not one darned thing—to encourage him. Not at first, anyway," she admitted, making a clean breast of it. Gina would know if she lied, anyway, just by looking at her. "It was only *after* he made me so mad that I, well..." She shrugged. "You know how I get sometimes when I lose my temper."

"I know, sweetie, and it's not your fault this time. Some men are just pigs," Gina said sympathetically. "You aren't responsible for what goes on in their tiny little minds." She reached across the kitchen counter and patted Zoe's hand. "So, tell me what you did to make him think you were after his dear old granny's fortune."

"Well, Moira had told him she wanted to lend me the money for New Moon, and he was looking at me like he thought I was going to steal the silver on my way out or something, so I sort of—" she shrugged, her lips turning up in a little shamefaced grin "—lived down to his expectations, you might say. You know how I get sometimes, putting my mouth in gear before I've engaged my brain."

Gina nodded sagely. "And what did he do then?"

"He clamped his hand around my arm and hustled

me out of there so fast you'd have thought the house was on fire. And then he called me a con artist and said New Moon was a fly-by-night cosmetic company and accused me of trying to bilk—bilk!—his great-grandmother out of a fortune.''

"Cazzone cafone."

"Yeah, well, he was kind of a jerk, but..." She shrugged again, and the shamefaced look was back. "I guess I can't really blame him completely."

"Zoe! He acted like a pig."

"Oh, I blame him for the pig part," she assured her friend, "but not what came after. I mean, at the end there, I *did* act like all I was interested in was the money. And you can't really blame a guy for trying to protect his sweet old granny from being taken to the cleaners.''

"I can," Gina said loyally.

Zoe smile at her. "I appreciate that. I really do. But I've got to face facts. I lost my temper and blew it, big time. There's no way Moira Sullivan's going to be investing in New Moon. Not if her great-grandson has anything to say about it. And it's my own darn fault."

"You'll find another investor. There's bound to be someone out there who has the vision to see what a great investment New Mo—" Gina cocked her head, listening. "Is that your phone?"

ZOE WAS BACK in her friend's apartment less than ten minutes later. "You'll never guess who that was."

Gina didn't look up from the tiny cups she was filling with thick, black espresso from the coffee press. "Who?"

"Mr. Stuffed Shirt himself."

Gina put the coffee press down. "And?" she said carefully, her eyes on Zoe's face.

"And he apologized for what he said this afternoon." A big grin turned up the corners of Zoe's mouth. Her eyes sparkled with anticipation and renewed hope. "He wants to meet with me as soon as possible to discuss investing in New Moon."

4

"WHICH ONE'S THE STUFFED shirt?"

Zoe brushed the blowing tendrils of her hair out of her eyes with one hand, scanning the rugby field as they approached the sidelines. "There," she said, unerringly zeroing in on him among all the identically clad men. "The tall one with the dark hair in the second row of that huddle." She pointed at him with the straw sticking out of the top of her iced latte. "On the red team with the number five on his shirt."

"Scrum," Gina corrected, standing on tiptoe to get a better look. "It's a scrum, not a huddle." She sank back onto her sneakered heels as the men lowered themselves into an interlocking mass of humanity and started to move like some kind of giant multiheaded crab as they scrambled for possession of the football. "You didn't tell me he was gorgeous."

"Is he?" Zoe shrugged and poked her straw into the bottom of her drink cup. "I didn't notice."

"And when did you start losing your eyesight, Ms. Moon?"

"Well, I didn't," Zoe said defensively. It wasn't *exactly* a lie; last Wednesday she'd been more concerned with the look in his eyes than his looks. Not that she hadn't noticed those, too, but… "I had other things on my mind, if you'll recall."

Gina snorted inelegantly. "Don't waste that big-eyed

innocent look on me," she advised dryly. "I haven't got enough testosterone for it to work."

"Fine." Zoe jabbed her straw into the ice at the bottom of her cup again. "Think whatever you want."

"He's really got you rattled, doesn't he?"

"Well, of course he does. He's only holding the future of New Moon in his hands."

But it was more than that.

Her cheeks were flushed and warm, despite the cool September breeze blowing across the field from the Charles River. Her palms were damp. Her nerve endings tingled, making her feel jittery and on edge, almost expectant, like a child sitting in front of the fireplace on Christmas Eve waiting for something wondrous to happen. And it had absolutely *nothing* to do with what he could mean to the future of New Moon.

Zoe sighed.

She wasn't usually stupid about men. She was, in fact, *never* stupid about men. She'd learned early that a woman who let herself get all excited and moony-eyed over a handsome face or a charming manner invariably ended up paying for her gullibility in heartache and broken dreams. Her mother, who'd been married and divorced as many times as any Hollywood movie star, had taught by unwitting example what *not* to do in relationships with men, and Zoe had taken the lessons to heart. She knew, all too well, that to let herself start weaving silly little romantic fantasies about Reed Sullivan was stupid in the extreme.

Oh, sure, he'd apologized for what he'd said out there on the sidewalk in front of his great-grandmother's house, but that didn't negate his attitude while they were inside. As Gina had so wisely remarked, his attitude and actions identified him as "one of those," meaning the kind of man who based his opinions of women on how they looked.

It wasn't that Zoe minded being thought of as attractive, or having men think she was sexy or beautiful. Or even having them say so. That *would* have been stupid, because she was all of those things. And she liked being those things. Most of the time. No, what she objected to were men who thought what was on the outside was the sum total of what was on the inside. Or men who thought her spectacular physical attributes constituted a deliberate come-on, and got bent out of shape when she failed to deliver on what they thought she had promised, simply by being.

Not that Reed Sullivan actually fit either of those profiles, precisely. But he'd disapproved of her at first sight, on the basis of her looks alone, and that was enough to condemn him in her eyes.

Or should have been.

It was just the tiniest bit distressing that she couldn't seem to work up the proper contempt for his sexist attitude, not with him running up and down the field in those little red shorts and the bright color block jersey with the word *Bulldogs* emblazoned across his broad chest.

Which meant, Zoe realized, totally amazed at herself, that she obviously had a few sexist attitudes of her own to address.

"What are you standing there looking so pensive about?" Gina asked, breaking into her reverie.

Zoe shook her head. "Nothing," she said, her eyes still focused on the playing field.

Gina followed the direction of her gaze. "He's got great thighs, doesn't he?"

"Mmm," Zoe murmured, absently reaching up to

tuck a blowing tendril of hair behind her ear. "Great thighs." They were long, tanned and heavily muscled, the rock-hard thighs of a dedicated athlete. It was amazing what that expensive navy-blue suit had kept hidden.

"And a really cute little ass," Gina said. "World class, I'd say."

"Oh, yeah, definitely world—" Zoe broke off guiltily. Her hand stilled at the back of her head, and she cut her friend a quick, sideways glance.

Gina smirked. "Gotcha."

"I was talking about that blond Adonis." Zoe gave a final pat to her hair and lowered her hand. "The one with the shoulders and the stubby little ponytail."

Gina's derisive jeer was good-natured. "Sure you were."

"I was. I—"

"Heads up!" somebody yelled.

Both women ducked as the football came sailing over their heads into the crowd where they stood. By the time they'd straightened up and turned backed to the field to see what had happened, men from both teams were rapidly converging in front of the nearest set of goalposts.

"What's happening?" Zoe tried to stay out of the way as players who'd been standing on the sidelines rushed onto the field to join their teammates. "Is it a fight?" she asked, and then realized that no one was swinging fists. Instead, the men formed a loose circle and began to chant.

"Is the game over?"

"Yes, the game's over." Gina laughed. "But that's not what this is about. It's a Zulu dance."

"A what?"

Gina waved at the action on the field. "Watch."

"Watch what? Oh, my goodness. Is he taking his clothes off? He's taking his clothes off!"

The blond Adonis Zoe claimed to have been admiring was stripping down, egged on by the rhythmic chanting of both teams. Shirt, shorts, jockstrap, everything but his cleated shoes and heavy white athletic socks came off in turn. Each garment was grabbed by a teammate as the Adonis discarded it, and flung up over the crossbar on the goalposts. And then, as naked as a newborn baby except for his footwear, the player began climbing up after his clothes. The crowd cheered and clapped, taking up the players' chant.

"Is that some bizarre kind of penalty?" Zoe asked, her eyes on the bare white bottom of the naked rugby player as he wriggled up the goalpost.

"No, it's not a penalty. It means he scored his first try."

"Try?"

"Like a touchdown in the NFL," Gina explained. "The team gets five points when the ball is kicked or carried over the try line and touched down."

"And for that the poor man is publicly humiliated?"

"The Zulu dance is a time-honored tradition. Every player does it after he scores his first try."

"Every player?" Zoe's glance darted over the men in the field. Over one man in particular. "Every time he makes a touchdown?"

"Try, not touchdown," Gina corrected. "And only the first time he does it." She followed the direction of Zoe's gaze and grinned knowingly. "I'm afraid you missed your chance there," she said. "Judging by the way he played today, the stuffed shirt isn't new at the game. He probably scored his first try years ago.

You're going to have to figure out some other way to see him naked.''

"I have no desire to see Reed Sullivan naked," Zoe said, but it was a lie.

And they both knew it.

Any healthy, red-blooded, heterosexual woman in the world would have paid good money to see *this* Reed Sullivan naked, whatever they might have thought of the stuffed shirt. This Reed Sullivan was all-male: tousled and grass-stained and sweaty, his big hands clapping in time to the deep-throated masculine chant, his head thrown back, laughing, triumphant, as he watched his teammate struggle to climb out onto the crossbar and retrieve his clothes. Blood trickled down the right side of Reed's face, evidence that the cut bisecting his eyebrow had come open. One of the shoulder seams of his rugby jersey had been torn and the sleeve was hanging down, exposing his arm from the rounded bulge of his shoulder to the swell of his heavily muscled biceps.

That tailored blue suit, Zoe found herself thinking again, had covered up a *lot,* including a good deal of his...uh, personality. This Reed Sullivan wasn't poised and polished. He certainly wasn't repressed. He didn't even look quite civilized. He looked basic and elemental and male, like a man who'd know how to appreciate a beautiful woman. Or any woman at all, for that matter. A man who'd know exactly what to do with one if he ever got his hands on her.

He turned his head just then, catching her staring at him, staring back, registering no surprise at seeing her there even though they weren't scheduled to meet again until Monday morning at his office in the Sullivan Building. Even with half the width of the field between them Zoe could see the change in his eyes—the laughter fading, the heat slowly building, the blatant, unabashed, purely masculine speculation in his gaze. It was a scorching, searching look, akin to the one he'd given her when she'd handed him his tea in his great-grandmother's parlor, only more so. And this time she had no trouble reading it.

What was she doing here?

Was she available?

Would she let him take her?

When?

Zoe couldn't look away. She didn't even want to. She'd never been the focus of that much heat before, the center of that much concentrated sexual intensity. It was as if the world had suddenly narrowed down to only two. Him and her. Man and woman. Everything else faded into insignificance. She forgot all about the laughing, cheering crowd. Gina. New Moon. His disapproval of her. His perfunctory, albeit charming, apology over the phone. Her own doubts and misgivings about what she might be getting herself into. She forgot everything except the look in his eyes and the thrilling, exhilarating, frightening sense of anticipation and excitement it generated in her.

Then the men turned, seemingly en masse, and headed for the sidelines. He was coming right toward her, that heat still in his eyes, his eyes still on her face, purpose in every step.

Hail the conquering hero, she thought inanely, fighting the urge to shrink back behind Gina like some trembling Victorian virgin.

What had happened to the stuffed shirt?

She could handle the stuffed shirt with one hand tied behind her back.

She couldn't handle *this* man with a whip and a chair.

Zoe managed to look away, finally—to the ground first, and then, panicked, at Gina. But Gina wasn't any help. She was staring at Reed, too. Or at least in Reed's direction.

"Who's the yummy Italian stallion with him?" she asked.

Zoe ducked her head, her lashes protectively lowered, sucking air and melted ice from the bottom of her cup as if getting the last drop of creamy iced coffee was the most important thing in the world at the moment. "Him who?"

Gina rolled her eyes. "The stuffed shirt. Who's the guy with him?"

"How should I know?" Zoe mumbled, without looking.

"Well, he seems to know you," Gina said. "He just waved."

Zoe darted a quick glance from under her lashes without lifting her head. "That's Moira Sullivan's butler. Eddie something."

"The stuffed shirt plays rugby with his great-grandmother's butler?" Gina's expressive eyebrows lifted like twin arches. "How democratic of him. I guess maybe he's not quite so stuff— Hi, there, fellas. Great game."

raspberry lips pursed   Reed automatically checked his stride to avoid running into the brunette who suddenly stood in his way. "Thanks," he murmured absently, his gaze still riveted on the object of his rampaging...affections.

Apparently oblivious to his presence, she was standing half-hidden behind her pint-size friend, her lids lowered, her lusious raspberry lips pursed around the straw protruding from the plastic lid of a paper cup. No one looking at her would believe she'd just been staring at him as if they were gazing at each other across the width of a rumpled bed rather than a rugby field. He almost didn't believe it himself except there was something just a bit *too* studied and deliberate about the way she stood there, not looking at him. Something that told him she was as aware of him as he was of her. Something that made him think... hope...wish...that if he reached out and wrapped his arms around her, she'd melt against him in total surrender and beg him to take her. Repeatedly.

"I'm Gina," the brunette said. "You must be Reed."

"Uh...yeah." Reed tore his gaze away from Zoe's averted face, gathering himself together with a Herculean effort. The rugby field was no place to indulge in ridiculous sexual fantasies. "Yes, I'm Reed." Belatedly, remembering his manners, he extended his hand to her. "Reed Sullivan," he said politely, somehow managing to sound as calm and unaffected as if they were standing in his penthouse office. As if his blood wasn't roaring through his veins like an out of control locomotive on a downhill grade. As if he weren't still fighting the insane urge to toss the luscious Miss Moon over his shoulder and keep right on walking—preferably straight to the king-size bed in the master bedroom of his Back Bay town house. "And you're Gina..." he did a quick scan of his memory banks "...Molinari, isn't it?"

"Yes, I'm Gina Molinari." She grinned at him. "And you're bleeding."

"Bleeding?"

"Over your right eye."

"Oh, that." He touched his fingers to his forehead, feeling for the cut over his eye, then looked at the smear of blood on his fingers. "It's nothing." He grabbed the hem of his jersey and pulled it up to wipe at the blood.

The movement exposed a taut, rippling six-pack of muscles bisected by an arrow of dark silky hair. The small intriguing well of his navel, the hard curve of a hair-dusted pectoral, a tiny male nipple, visibly contracting as the cold air hit it...

Zoe bit down on her straw, hard.

"You're the massage therapist, right?" Reed said as he dropped the hem of his shirt, blood-smeared now, letting it fall back into place, covering up all that glorious masculine pulchritude.

Zoe stifled a sigh.

"Yes, I am." Gina tilted her head, eyes narrowed as she gazed up at him. "You in the market for a massage?"

"No, thanks," he said easily, passing her test without even knowing he'd taken it. "I've got a standing weekly appointment at a gym over near the Hancock Building with a big Swede named Gunnar. He gets jealous if I go anywhere else."

"Me, on the other hand, I've got this *really* sore shoulder," said Eddie.

Reed took the hint. "Eddie DiPasquale," he said by way of introduction. "Miss Molinari. Eddie's the Bulldogs' hooker."

"Just call me Gina, please," Gina said, smiling as she reached out to shake Eddie's hand. "The nuns at Sacred Heart Elementary School used to call me Miss Molinari." She gave an exaggerated shiver. "Usually right before they sent me down to the Mother Superior's office.''

"Sacred Heart, huh?" Eddie said as he took her hand. "My youngest sister went there. Christina Di-Pasquale. Maybe you knew her?"

"Chrissie is your sister? Well, isn't it a small world...."

And they were off and running, happily tracking down the acquaintances they had in common, leaving Reed and Zoe all alone in the crowd.

Zoe fiddled with her straw, poking it into the ice in the bottom of her cup, then reached up to brush at her hair and tug at the collar of her quilted vest, trying to think of something intelligent to say. Trying to think of *anything* to say. It was an odd, disquieting sensation to find herself tongue-tied; she was rarely at a loss for words.

Reed stared at the top of her bent head, equally silent, wondering if he'd imagined that bold, hypnotic stare that had drawn him to her like a magnet. This fidgeting young woman certainly didn't look anything like the femme fatale who had summoned him from across the field with her hot come-hither gaze. She didn't even remotely resemble the woman who'd brazenly looked him up and down in his great-grandmother's parlor last Wednesday, either. Nor was she the greedy little opportunist with great big dollar signs in her eyes.

No, *this* woman was as shy as a schoolgirl.

She looked like a schoolgirl, too. No snug velvet pants and high-heeled boots now; no soft, curve-hugging white shirt; no wild cascade of tumbling corkscrew curls. Instead, she wore black Converse high-tops, faded jeans and a bulky butter-yellow turtleneck sweater under a quilted brown velveteen vest that hid all semblance of her centerfold body. Her glorious red hair was plaited in a long, loose braid that allowed only a few unruly tendrils free to dance in the breeze around her face. Simple gold metal hoops pierced her ears. Golden-brown freckles he'd somehow failed to notice at their last meeting peppered her straight little nose and unpowdered cheeks. Only her hands were the same—long slender fingers tipped by shiny copper nails, decorated with half a dozen narrow rings. Her hands, and the faint, sweet scent of violets that perfumed the air around her.

No wild gypsy this, no bold seductive temptress with come-hither eyes, but a quite ordinary woman, after all.

"Well," Reed said finally, his disappointment cloaked in automatic good manners. "This is a surprise."

"Oh?" she murmured, still staring down at her cup. "How so?"

"I didn't know you were a rugby fan."

"I'm not. Gina is." The tiny stones in her rings flashed in the sunlight as she fiddled with her straw. "A couple of her cousins play—for the Wolfhounds, I think she said—and when I mentioned that you played, too, well..." one shoulder lifted in a shrug "...she suggested it might be fun to come down and watch."

A lie, but a necessary one, Zoe felt. The suggestion had been hers, not Gina's. She'd thought it would be a good idea to see another side of the man who, if all went well, would soon become her financial advisor. It hadn't been. A good idea, that is.

She would have been infinitely better off not to have seen this particular side of Reed Sullivan IV because it was going to be a lot harder to think of him as a stuffed shirt now. A *lot* harder. Stuffed shirts didn't have world class butts and rippling torsos. They didn't stare at a woman as if they wanted to drag her off to a cave somewhere. And they certainly didn't make a woman's fingertips itch to touch—

"And was it?" he asked.

"Was it what?" Zoe replied, having lost the thread of the conversation. She seemed to be doing that a lot these days. Whenever she saw him, or thought of him, or—

"Fun," he said.

"Fun?" she murmured, looking up into his eyes at last.

And he was caught anew, his gaze trapped and tangled in the wide brown eyes staring up at him. They *were* the same eyes that had laughed at him in his great-grandmother's parlor. The same eyes that had so wantonly assessed him, then glanced away disdainfully, as if she'd found him wanting. The same eyes that had summoned him from across the rugby field with a look that had been both a challenge and a promise, as provocative as a lover's breathless demand in the dark. The same, and yet intriguingly, maddeningly different.

Now she simply stared up at him, the mocking laughter gone, the challenge nonexistent, the promise revoked as if it had never been. The expression in those fascinating, fathomless eyes was puzzled and searching, as if she were trying to work something out. There was a bit of anxiety there, too, as if she didn't quite know what to make of him, and wasn't sure she wanted to find out.

She was a chameleon, changing colors while he watched. Gypsy temptress, money-hungry opportunist, tongue-tied ingenue...which one was the real Zoe Moon?

And why was it suddenly so important that he find out?

"...invite the ladies to join us?" Eddie asked, punching Reed in the arm with a loosely curled fist as he spoke.

Reed had no idea what he'd just been asked. "Join us?" he said stupidly. "For what?"

"A beer, man. I just suggested to Gina here that the ladies might like to join us for a burger and a brew at Bruno's with the rest of the team."

"Bruno's? Oh, yes." Reed's eyes lit up. "Of course. Great idea," he agreed, wondering why he hadn't thought of it himself.

Every good businessman knew that spending time with people in a relaxed, informal atmosphere was an excellent way to get to know them. And he was a very good businessman. Bruno's wouldn't normally have been his first choice for a getting-to-know-you lunch, especially with a woman and most especially not with all his teammates there—*that* was probably why he hadn't thought of it—but he couldn't very well take her to Maison Robert or the Hampshire House, not dressed in rugby shorts and without a reservation, and not on a Saturday afternoon, in any case. Bruno's would have to do.

"How does that sound to you, Zoe?" he said, as naturally as if he hadn't insisted on calling her Miss Moon up to that point. "Are you up for a burger at Bruno's?"

Zoe hesitated, unsure of what she should do. She knew what she *wanted* to do, but she'd already decided that would be stupid. They were supposed to be developing a business relationship, not a social one. "Well, I...ah..." She glanced at her best friend for help, but Gina had tucked her hand into the crook of Eddie DiPasquale's arm and was smiling up at him as if he were Brad Pitt. Zoe's glance flitted back to Reed. "A burger would be okay, I guess, but..."

"Fine. That's settled, then. Here, let me get rid of that for you." He plucked the empty latte cup out of Zoe's fingers as he spoke, tossing it into a nearby trash can, and cupped his hand under her elbow in one smooth, seamless motion. "You can leave your car wherever you parked it. Bruno's is just across the street and down two blocks. Do you need to put any money in the meter before we go?"

Zoe shook her head. "No car. We took the T over from Haymarket, then walked."

"Even better," Reed said as he gently, expertly, inexorably maneuvered her through the thinning crowd and away from the rugby field. "One less thing for you to worry about." His smile was warm and charming, almost caressing in its solicitude. "And I get to play the gentleman and see you home after lunch."

It was a far cry from the hurly-burly way he'd escorted her out of his great-grandmother's house, but it was just as effective. As he deftly steered her down the street to Bruno's, Zoe felt a bit dazed, like a cartoon character who'd been run over by a steamroller and was still seeing stars.

BRUNO'S WAS COZY, crowded and noisy, its pseudo-English interior filled to overflowing with rowdy men in red shorts and grass-stained jerseys. The yeasty smell of beer predominated, underscored by the aroma of fried onions and the stink of cigar smoke. A college football game flickered on the TV screen at the end of the bar, action at the dartboard was fast and furious, and there was a game of eight ball in progress at the pool table in the back of the room.

Eddie was immediately hailed by one of the dart players, and headed off in that direction, towing a willing Gina in his wake. Zoe made an instinctive move to follow, but was brought short up by the hand still cupping her elbow.

"There are a couple of empty booths over by the far wall," Reed said, his lips so close to her ear she could feel his warm breath against her skin. "We ought to grab one while we still can. Eddie and Gina can join us as soon as he gets beaten at darts. It shouldn't take too long."

Zoe nodded and allowed herself to be maneuvered through the crowded tavern, wondering why she felt like a mare who'd just been cut out of the herd. He hadn't done anything untoward or encroaching. His hand was now resting lightly, politely on the small of her back, well above her rear end. His gaze was focused on the empty booth that was their destination. And yet she had the distinct—admittedly, not entirely unpleasant—feeling that if she suddenly did an abrupt about-face and headed for the door, he'd be right on her tail.

"Hey, Sullivan, you wuss. You finally made it." A very large man with a strip of black electrical tape dangling from his ear hailed them as they passed the small table where he sat facing another large man. Their right hands were clasped, elbows on the table, biceps bulging, as they pitted their considerable strength against each other.

"Some of the guys were beginning to think you were

gonna try to skip out on us to avoid havin' your new
lady friend see your humiliation,'' said the burly guy
who had hailed Reed. His glance flickered over Zoe,
then lingered appreciatively. ''Not that I'd blame ya,
considering.'' He grinned ingratiatingly. ''Hiya, gorgeous.''

Reed's hand flattened on Zoe's back, sliding around
to ride the curve of her waist. She glanced at him,
surprised by the move, but didn't shift away. To do so
would have accorded the sneaky little maneuver more
importance than it warranted. Besides, having the rest
of the men in the pub think she was off-limits was fine
by her; it reduced the possibility of her having to make
the point herself. And she was quite capable of setting
Reed straight later if she needed to. At least, she hoped
she was.

''Zoe, this ugly mug is Bill Larson,'' Reed said
pleasantly. ''He's one of the Bulldogs' props, which,
in case you're wondering, is why he's wearing electrical tape as a fashion accessory. It's supposed to keep
his ears from being ripped—'' he grasped the dangling
end of the tape with his free hand and yanked ''—off
during a game,'' he said, smiling evilly as he dropped
the strip of tape on the table.

Bill didn't flinch, even though the tape had taken
hair with it.

''Bill's our official team badass. He leads the league
in fouls this year,'' Reed informed her.

Zoe couldn't decide whether that was a recommen-
dation or a warning.

''I lead the league in fouls every year,'' Bill said
proudly.

Reed ignored him. ''The quiet one on the other side

of the table is Jake Warner. Jake is our other prop. Guys, this is Zoe Moon. Miss Moon to *you* bozos.''

The one named Jake looked up briefly, nodded a quick, silent greeting, then turned his attention back to the contest between him and his teammate.

Bill smiled like a man who'd just seen heaven. ''So, Zoe, what's a beautiful woman like you doin' hanging out with this—'' he jerked his chin at Reed ''—loser?''

''Oh, we're not hanging out,'' Zoe assured him airily, answering his flirtatious smile with one of her own. She could handle this kind of harmless come-on in her sleep, especially when there was no chance—due to Reed's proprietary gesture—that she'd be taken seriously. And Reed Sullivan IV needed to know he hadn't slipped anything by her...just in case he thought he had.

''Mr. Sullivan is a business acquaintance. I'm considering taking him on as my financial advisor.'' She leaned forward slightly, giving the seated man her full attention, ignoring the one who still had his hand on the curve of her waist. ''Do you mind if I ask how he's going to be humiliated?'' she queried, thinking of the Zulu dance she'd seen earlier.

''I think you just took care of that,'' Reed said dryly, stung by her denial that they were anything more than business associates—even though it was true—and wondering why the hell she was smiling at his teammate as if he were her long lost buddy. She'd certainly never smiled at *him* like that.

Bill gave a short bark of laughter. ''Give me a second to finish this and you'll see for yourself, doll face.'' He turned his attention to his opponent, grunted once—loudly—and slammed the other man's hand to the table. "Someone fill up the plunger," he bellowed as he stood up. "It's time for Sullivan to take his medicine."

Reed Sullivan's "medicine" turned out to be beer. And it was served up in the bowl of a red rubber toilet plunger.

Zoe couldn't help but wonder if his great-grandmother or any of his Beacon Hill friends had ever seen this side of him. She felt sure they hadn't. Moira Sullivan would undoubtedly faint dead away if she could see her elegant, debonair great-grandson swilling beer from a toilet plunger. And his ritzy friends would surely cut him from their guest lists for doing something so tacky and juvenile. Even after seeing him out on the rugby field, Zoe would never have guessed that a man like Reed Sullivan IV, upright, uptight scion of a respected Beacon Hill family, would have a boyish side. Let alone this rowdy, puerile boyish side. Much to her surprise, she found it rather endearing, and just the least bit reassuring, too. How could she possibly be intimidated by a guy who drank beer from a toilet plunger?

"That's really disgusting," she said, watching as Reed tilted his head back and proceeded to swallow the entire plungerful of beer in one long draft while his teammates showered him with good-natured verbal abuse.

"The plunger's clean," Eddie said. "Markus, the bartender, keeps it behind the bar and doesn't use it for anything else. At least—" he shrugged "—that's what he says."

"But why is Reed drinking out of it at all?" Zoe demanded.

"He made the worst play of the game today," Eddie said, and launched into an explanation that left Zoe sitting there with her forehead crinkled up in a frown. Gina just laughed. "...almost cost us the game. Would have if that new guy—" he nodded toward the formerly naked Adonis "—hadn't come out of nowhere and scored just before the whistle."

Zoe shook her head. "I don't get it. For making the winning touchdown—excuse me, the winning try—a guy has to strip naked in public and climb up the flagpole, but—"

"Goalpost," Eddie corrected her.

"Goalpost," she echoed obediently "—but for nearly losing the game because of making a bad play he only has to drink beer out of a plunger. It makes absolutely no sense at all."

"It doesn't have to make sense," Reed said as he slid into the booth beside Zoe. "It's rugby."

He looked so pleased with himself, Zoe couldn't help but smile. "Oh, I see. That explains it. It's rugby." She raised her glass. "A truly manly sport," she said, holding the beer aloft until the others at the table did the same. "Full of blood, sweat and public humiliation."

Reed laughed. "To manly sports." He lifted his glass to his lips, taking a long swallow, his gaze holding Zoe's over the frosty rim of the mug.

Zoe refused to let him fluster her with that look again, refused to look away. She had his number now. He was just a man like any other. Okay, better looking than most. And richer than most. And sexier than most, too. But still, just a man. Nothing she couldn't handle.

"You've got foam on your upper lip," she said prosaically, and handed him a paper napkin.

He took it from her and wiped his mouth, slowly, his gaze never leaving hers.

She quirked an eyebrow at him, head tilted, the corners of her mouth turned up in a teasing little smile. A mocking, challenging, gypsy-temptress kind of smile.

Testosterone surged through his veins. Without thought, without consciousness, without knowing what he was going to do until he'd actually done it, Reed reached out and curled his fingers around the back of her neck.

Zoe had time to gasp, but only just, her smile disappearing as her lips parted in a wordless sound of protest and surprise.

Perfect, he thought, and took her mouth with his.

5

"TRUST ME," Zoe said as Reed slowly cruised Salem Street. "You'll never find a parking space. Just stop anywhere along the street and we'll hop out."

"That isn't exactly what I had in mind when I said I'd see you home," Reed objected.

What he'd had in mind was an intimate little scenario that would end with him getting invited into her apartment for coffee or...something. But Eddie had bailed out on him right after lunch, citing a prior engagement that left Reed with both women on his hands. Gina, instead of residing in a place where he could conveniently drop her off first, apparently lived right across the hall from Zoe. And Zoe herself had been as skittish as a Victorian heiress in a roomful of fortune hunters ever since he'd given in to the irresistible urge to kiss her.

It wasn't like him to misjudge a moment like that. He wasn't the spontaneous type, especially not where women were concerned. But she'd given him that *look,* that challenging, faintly mocking, I-dare-you, gypsy look and he'd... Well, he'd lost his head for a minute there. And it had been glorious. Her mouth was as luscious as it looked. As soft. As warm. As sweet. And it had left him itching—all right, *aching*—to repeat the experience as soon as humanly possible, preferably somewhere more private than a booth at Bruno's, someplace where he could do a thorough job of it and gain her full cooperation in the process. He had an idea her full cooperation would be even better than he could imagine, and his imagination had already proved to be pretty good where she was concerned.

If he could only find a damned parking space! Didn't people ever move their cars in this part of town?

"A gentleman always sees a lady—" he glanced in the rearview mirror "—ladies," he amended, smiling charmingly at Gina "—to their door."

"Maybe on Beacon Hill," Zoe said. "But in the North End a gentleman has to be a bit more practical, and a lady considers the street outside her door close enough. Really, Reed, this is fine. You can stop right here. This is our block." She curled her fingers around the door handle as she spoke and lifted it, causing a discreet red light on the dashboard to alert Reed to the fact that the passenger door was ajar.

He scowled through the windshield and eased the Jag from a crawl to a full stop. Zoe hopped out of the car before he had a chance to do more than turn toward her, hand extended along the back of the leather seat.

"Thanks for the lift," she said, leaning down a bit to look back in at him.

"Yes, thanks," Gina echoed as she scooted across the back seat and got out.

"It was very kind of you to go so far out of your way," Zoe said politely. "I really appreciate it."

"Enough to have brunch with me tomorrow?" The words just popped out. He'd had no idea he was going to say them until he heard himself speak, but dammit he *had* to get her alone. Soon. He couldn't wait until the meeting on Monday.

"Brunch? Well, I, uh—"

A horn blasted impatiently behind them. Reed ignored it. "I'll pick you up at eleven."

"No." Zoe shook her head. "I can't. I've already got a date for brunch."

"Dinner?"

"Sorry," she said firmly, determined not to let him steamroll her again. "I'm booked for din—"

The horn sounded again, longer and louder.

"I'd better let you go," Zoe said, silently blessing the impatient driver. "We're blocking traffic." She straightened, pushing the door shut with the flat of her hand. "Thanks again for the ride," she mouthed through the window, waggling her fingers at him as she backed between the bumpers of two parked cars and stepped up onto the sidewalk.

Reed curled his hands around the steering wheel, barely managing to restrain himself from leaping out of the car and hauling her back inside. What he'd do with her after that he didn't know. Well, he did know, but—

Zoe frowned and shook her head as if to say no. For a second, Reed thought the gesture was aimed at him— she'd certainly say no if she could read his mind at the moment!—but then he realized two things almost simultaneously. She was looking at the car behind him, and the clown who'd been hammering on his horn had stopped. Reed's glance flickered to the rearview mirror. The driver was stretched across the empty passenger seat of his sporty little Miata, hand extended, beckoning to Zoe as if she were a little girl he was trying to entice with candy. Reed's left hand dropped to the door handle, and he'd actually pulled up on it, releasing the catch, fully intending to drag the guy out of his sports car and punch his lights out, when Zoe turned away, dismissing her inopportune suitor with an insouciant little wave.

The guy straightened up behind the wheel, apparently accepting his rejection with good grace. And Reed was left wondering why he was acting like some love-struck, testosterone-ridden adolescent, all lathered up over his new girlfriend. But Zoe Moon wasn't his girl. She wasn't even his friend. In truth, he barely knew the woman. What he did know, he didn't understand. Or trust.

He tried to remember just why he didn't trust her, but couldn't quite bring his reasons—perfectly sound reasons, he was sure—into focus at the moment. The lingering scent of violets was fogging his brain.

There was something about the woman that reached out and touched—*grabbed!*—something almost primitive in him. Something instinctual. Predatory. Possessive. He wanted her. It was that simple. She sent his hormones into the kind of frenzied overdrive he hadn't known since he was a horny teenager, and he wanted her.

Desperately.

The very thought appalled him, suggesting as it did a lack of self-control. He had always prided himself—quite rightly, he thought—on his prodigious self-mastery. And in any case, a thirty-three-year-old man should have progressed beyond desperation where women were concerned. He'd certainly been operating on that assumption. But then Miss Zoe Moon sashayed into his tidy, well-ordered life with her wildfire hair, her pinup body and those hot, laughing gypsy eyes, and he wanted to strip her naked and press his mouth to every inch of—

The guy in the Miata pounded on the horn again,

accompanying the strident sound with a rude hand gesture.

Reed swore but refrained from returning the gesture, and calmly, quietly, being in perfect control, pulled away from the curb.

"So, who are you having brunch with tomorrow?" Gina asked, as they strolled down the street to their building.

Zoe gave her a sideways glance. "You know very well I haven't got a date for brunch," she said, and lifted a hand to wave at old Mrs. Umberto, who was leaning out her third-story window, keeping an eye on the comings and goings in the street below.

By tomorrow morning everyone on the block would know that Zoe Moon and Gina Molinari had been seen getting out of a fancy black car.

"Are you seeing the same guy for dinner, too?" Gina pressed.

The corners of Zoe's eyes crinkled up when she smiled. "Smart-ass."

Gina's answering grin was unrepentant. "You want to tell me why a date with the invisible man is more attractive than going out with a gorgeous not-so-stuffed-shirt who drives a Jag and has a serious case of the hots for you?"

"What makes you think he has the hots for me?" Zoe hedged.

"Oh, please." Gina rolled her eyes. "First of all, you told me yourself he did, remember? Last Wednesday, when you were so pissed about the way he'd acted? And second of all, I'm not blind. The man didn't take his eyes off of you all afternoon. He touched you every chance he got. And, oh my, that kiss..." She placed her right hand on her chest and patted it, miming a wildly beating heart. "It curled my toes, and I was just watching from the sidelines."

Zoe flashed her friend another sideways look. "Can you keep a secret?"

Gina touched two fingertips to her tongue and held them up as if she was a Girl Scout pledging allegiance. "Spit promise," she vowed solemnly.

"It curled my toes, too." Zoe sighed and glanced down at her black hightops. "I think they're still curled."

Gina's mouth all but fell open. "It curled *your* toes? Really?"

"Really," Zoe admitted, her tone halfway between baffled and embarrassed.

"Oh, wow. That is so great. It's about time some guy got to— Are you blushing?"

"No, I am *not* blushing," Gina said, even as her redhead's complexion turned a telltale pink. "And he did *not* get to me. Not the way you mean. He's a good kisser, okay? A world-class kisser. I'll grant you that. And I admit it—I enjoyed kissing him. But it doesn't mean anything more." She wouldn't let it mean anything more than that. "And it isn't going any further."

"Jeez, Zoe, how can you not want it to go any further? The man's a hunk. A rich hunk. He's got a serious case of the hots for you. *And* he made your toes curl with just one measly little kiss. As far as I know, no guy has ever managed that particular feat before. So how can you just blow him off?"

"I didn't blow him off," Zoe said irritably, wishing she'd kept her opinion of his kiss to herself. "I very politely declined his invitation to brunch."

"And dinner," Gina reminded her.

"Yes, and dinner."

"You want to tell me why?"

"Well, for goodness sake, Gina." Zoe stopped short on the sidewalk to face her insistent friend. "I've got a meeting with him on Monday morning, remember? A *business* meeting." She cocked an eyebrow. "You ever hear the one about not mixing business with pleasure?"

"So, don't mix them. Do business at the meeting and jump his bones after."

"Oh, *that* would be real professional, wouldn't it?" She shook her head, forestalling whatever reply Gina might have made. "He's already expressed his reluctance to have anything to do with me. Businesswise," she added, when Gina shot her an incredulous look. "You and I both know he only arranged the meeting on Monday because his great-grandmother pressured him into it somehow. He thinks I'm a con artist, remember? He called New Moon a fly-by-night enterprise and practically tossed me out of Moira's house on my rear."

"And whose fault is that?"

"I didn't plant the idea in his head," Zoe reminded her. "I just reinforced the opinion he already had."

"So, change his opinion. I don't think it would be all that hard to do, considering. The man *wants* to have his opinion changed. Anyone can see that."

"And I'm supposed to do that by jumping his bones? Not a chance. He'd think I was using sex to get him to okay Moira's investment in New Moon."

"Hmm." Gina nodded thoughtfully. "I hadn't considered that."

"Besides, why would I even *want* to go out with a man who thinks I'm some kind of con artist, but still has the hots for me, anyway? It just proves he's shallow and superficial and...and..."

"Yeah, but you've got the hots for him, too, and you think he's a stuffed shirt, so you're even."

"I do not!"

"What? Think he's a stuffed shirt or have the hots for him?"

"He *is* a stuffed shirt and I do *not* have the hots for him."

Gina screwed up her mouth in a disbelieving moue and looked down at the toes of Zoe's black hightops.

"Okay. I'm...mildly attracted, all right?"

"Ha! There's no *mild* about it. I was there, sweetie. I saw your eyes glaze over when he planted that little smacker on you."

"Oh, they did not glaze over. You're exaggerating."

But not by much.

That "little smacker" had rung all of Zoe's bells and set every nerve ending she possessed to tingling in the most alarming way. Quite amazing, she thought, for a kiss that had lasted all of three seconds. He hadn't parted his lips or used his tongue, or touched her anywhere except for where his hand clasped the back of her neck and his mouth covered hers. But when he'd let her go and turned away to give his order to the waitress, Zoe had been very glad she was sitting down. Otherwise, her knees would have buckled.

"I'm not some brainless bimbo at the mercy of my hormones," she said firmly. "So the man is attractive. So what? I don't have to jump every attractive man I meet, do I?"

"Well, you never have before, but—"

"And so what if he's a great kisser? I've kissed better."

Gina rolled her eyes. "Sure you have."

"And just because he apparently doesn't see anything wrong with mixing business and pleasure doesn't mean I have to abandon good sense, too, does it?"

"No, it doesn't but—"

"So what's your point?"

"My point?" Gina shrugged, conceding defeat. "Did I have a point?"

"Apparently not," Zoe said as they turned into the alley between the dry cleaners and the Ristorante Marcella. "So let's not have any more talk about—" A wide smile lit up her face. "Hey, guys. How's it going?"

Three young neighborhood boys looked up at her greeting. "Hey, Zoe. Hey, Gina," they chorused.

One of them rose to his feet, stuffing a piece of white chalk in the pocket of his jeans as he did so. "We just got all set up for a game of potsies," he said, gesturing to the large, powdery white circle on the asphalt, "but we haven't lagged to see who goes first. Do you wanna play, Zoe?"

"I don't think so, kiddo. Last time I played potsies with you pirates, I lost my favorite tiger's-eye aggie to Spencer."

Still on his knees on the ground, Spencer grinned, showing the gap where one of his front teeth had recently gone missing. "I got it right here, Zoe." He patted his marble sack. "But you've got to put your giant steelie up against it if you want to try to win it back."

"That settles it, then. I'm not putting up my biggest steelie just so you can hustle me out of it."

"Chicken," Spencer jeered, and the other two gleefully took up the chant. "Chicken. Zoe's chicken."

"I'll play bridgeboard if you want," she offered slyly, knowing they'd refuse. Bridgeboard was really an indoor marble game, meant to be played on a very smooth surface. There was no knocking another player's marble with your shooter, which seemed to be a requirement of the boys' favorite games and the main reason young Spencer had his eye on her steelie. The marble's weight and size made it an excellent and very effective shooter.

"Bridgeboard's a girl's game," one of them sniffed disdainfully.

"Well, there you go. I'm a girl." Zoe flapped her hand at them when they laughed at her, half a wave, half a gesture of pretended affront. "Ciao, guys. Have fun," she said as she and Gina headed toward the locked gate that led upstairs to the hallway of the two apartments above the Ristorante Marcella.

There was a note taped to her door.

"Mama Marcella wants to see me," she said when Gina tilted her head inquiringly.

"What'd you do? Forget to pay your rent?"

"I don't think so." She looked up. "She wants to see you, too."

"Me?" An expression of trepidation crossed Gina's face. "How come?"

Zoe shrugged. "All it says is that she wants to see me the minute I get in—minute is underlined twice— and that I should bring you with me." She handed Gina the note. "See for yourself."

Gina took the note and read it. "What do you think she wants?"

Zoe shrugged. "Only one way to find out." She slipped the key to her apartment back into the pocket of her jeans without opening the door. "Let's go see Mama."

They trooped back down the stairs.

"Did you change your mind, Zoe?" one of the boys asked hopefully.

"Nope. Sorry. Mama wants to see me."

The three boys looked at each other. Mama Marcella was a legend in the neighborhood. She was related to half of its inhabitants by blood and the other half by marriage. Of the five people standing in the alley, only Zoe had no formal familial tie to her. Not that the lack of official sanction had ever stopped Mama from interfering in anything she deemed her business. And Zoe, by virtue of her long friendship with Gina, was very much Mama's business.

"Whad'ya do?" Jason asked.

"Nothing, as far as I know."

"Must of done something if Mama wants to see you."

Zoe tried to think what that something might have been as she and Gina walked around to the rear of the building like two condemned prisoners on their way to the gallows. Her conscience was clear. She couldn't remember having done anything lately that would require an interview with Mama.

As they entered the *ristorante* through the kitchen, the mouthwatering scents of simmering marinara, freshly grated Parmesan and roasting garlic floated out to greet them. The staff was busy setting up in preparation for the Saturday night dinner crowd. Two waitresses had just finished breaking down the steam table and were lining it up again, changing the pans of sauces and prepared dishes to reflect the more extensive dinner menu. A busboy was refilling salt and pepper shakers.

Mama was standing in front of the stove, tasting spoon in hand, haranguing one of her cooks about the huge pot of sauce that was simmering over a low gas flame.

Apparently, he'd forgotten to add some essential ingredient, the lack of which held the potential to ruin the business Mama had spent the past fifty years of her life building to its present glory. Zoe and Gina stood quietly, just inside the door, waiting for the diminutive restaurateur to run down before they made their presence known.

"It must have sugar in the sauce to bring out the sweetness of the tomatoes," Mama said as she added the ingredient and stirred it in with a big wooden spoon. "There, now. Taste." She lifted a clean tasting spoon to the young cook's lips. "You see that it is better, yes?"

"It is…" He closed his eyes and raised his fingertips to his lips, kissing them in an extravagant gesture of culinary ecstasy.

Mama hit him on the arm with the spoon, leaving a blob of tomato sauce on the sleeve of his white chef's jacket. "Next time, you remember," she said sternly, but she smiled. Fortunately for the cook, Mama had a soft spot for handsome young men.

"It smells wonderful," Zoe said, judging the time was right to make their presence known.

"Ah, you are here. Good. Lucia…" She summoned one of the waitresses working on the steam table with a flick of her wrist. "Bring wine."

She stripped off her voluminous white apron and handed it to the other waitress, who came scurrying forward to receive it. The trim, black silk couture dress Mama wore was set off by a delicate gold chain and a plain gold crucifix. Sleek gold teardrop earrings swayed against her neck, peeping out from beneath the short, stylish sweep of chestnut hair, in which no trace of gray had ever been allowed to show. Mama lifted a hand to pat her hair, then smoothed both palms down the front of her already impeccably smooth dress.

"Come." She gestured to her two tenants, imperiously beckoning them to follow her. "We must talk."

Zoe glanced at Gina and raised an eyebrow. Gina shrugged and shook her head. Whatever it was, it was serious. They were headed for the dining room, and Mama had ordered wine. With Mama that usually meant someone was either about to be formally commended or royally chewed out, and you could never tell by her demeanor beforehand which it was going to be.

"Mama, whatever it is, I'm sure—" Gina began.

Mama held up her hand, forestalling further speech. "Wait. Let Lucia pour the wine first. Then we will talk." She pointed at the table. "Sit."

They sat, as obedient as chastened puppies, hands folded in their laps as Lucia uncorked and poured the wine. They tried not to watch or exhibit any impatience and make the poor girl even more nervous than she already was. Mama Marcella had no such qualms. She observed the entire process with the eagle eye of a general reviewing his troops.

"Very good, Lucia. You are improving," she said when the glasses had been filled exactly halfway and no wine had been spilled on the pristine white tablecloth.

Lucia ventured a relieved smile.

"But you still take too long. My customers will be finished with their dinner before you get the cork out of the bottle." She flicked her hand in a vague but unmistakable gesture of dismissal. "Tell Michael to come back out here, *subito,* and change the linen on table six," she said, as Lucia turned to go. "The tablecloth is stained on the edge. And one of the water glasses on table nine is spotted."

Lucia nodded and retreated to the kitchen to deliver the bad news to the hapless busboy. When Mama said *subito* in that tone of voice, she meant ten minutes ago if not sooner.

Mama turned her attention to the two young women sitting across the table and lifted her glass of wine. *"Cin'cin,"* she said, and sipped.

Zoe and Gina repeated the toast and did likewise.

The formalities satisfied, Mama put her glass down. "Now." She pinned Zoe with her field marshal gaze. "Why does some man come to my restaurant today during the busiest hour of lunch and ask questions about you, hmm?"

"Someone was asking questions about me?" Zoe wouldn't have thought the day could hold any more surprises. Apparently, she was wrong. "What kind of questions?"

"Questions with answers that were none of his business," Mama said. "How long do you live here?" She pointed upward to the apartments overhead. "Do you pay your rent on time? Do you have loud parties? Are you a good girl or no?"

"Someone was asking if I was a good girl?"

Mama nodded. *"Sì."* He asked me if I know where you get your money to live. If you have rich parents or a job or—" Mama's lips thinned "—if you have boyfriends who give you money and expensive presents."

"Boyfriends who give me money?" Zoe's mouth

fell open in astonishment. It took a moment or two for the outrage to kick in. "Who was asking questions about me?" she demanded. "Did he give his name?"

Mama slipped her hand inside the modest V-neck of her black dress and pulled out the business card she had tucked under her bra strap. "He gave me this," she said, handing the card to Zoe.

"'Leland Davies Investigations,'" Zoe read aloud. She looked back up at Mama. "A private investigator?" Her forehead crinkled. "Why would a private investigator be asking questions about me?"

Mama shrugged. "He said you were being considered for a very important job and he was doing a..." she groped a moment for the word "...a background check. But I did not believe him. Those were not the kind of questions that are asked when someone is considering hiring a person for a job. Even I—" she tapped her chest lightly "—do not ask such questions."

"No, of course not," Zoe agreed, her mind racing as she considered possibilities. "Besides, I haven't applied for a job anywhere. I don't even need a regular job now that New Moon is doing so well."

"That's it," Gina said.

"What's it?" Zoe said.

"*Che cosa?*" Mama said.

"New Moon," Gina repeated. "Reed's having you investigated because of New Moon."

"Oh, no. No. Reed wouldn't..." Zoe began in automatic protest, then stopped.

The Reed she'd met that afternoon—the one in the red shorts and the torn rugby shirt, the one who had kissed her in an excess of high spirits and testosterone—wouldn't. But the Reed she'd met last Wednesday in Moira Sullivan's parlor most certainly would. *That* Reed Sullivan would view the hiring of a private investigator to pry into her life as just good business. To him it would be as routine as ordering a credit report, even if he didn't suspect her of being some kind of unsavory character out to fleece a sweet old lady.

"Who is this Reed?" Mama asked, her worried eyes on Zoe's face.

"Reed Sullivan," Gina said when Zoe was too slow to answer. "He's the great-grandson of the woman who might lend Zoe the money to expand New Moon."

"Ah, New Moon. I do not know why you go to strangers for the money, *bambina*," she chided, "when you have family to help you."

Zoe felt a tightening in the region of her heart, knowing Mama meant those words as sincerely as if they'd been spoken to Gina.

The two girls had met when they'd been assigned adjoining desks in Mrs. Tuttle's seventh grade English class. For Gina, it had been her first experience outside the confines of the all-girl Catholic grade school she'd attended since kindergarten. For Zoe, it was the first day at a new school, in a new neighborhood, in the new smaller family unit created by her mother's third divorce. Gina became her best friend. And Gina's large extended family opened its collective heart to the lonely young girl their gregarious young relative had brought home to Sunday dinner.

Once the Molinaris had taken you in, you were in for life. And part of being "in" meant Mama felt perfectly free to poke her nose into any aspect of your life.

Zoe loved it.

"I'm not taking your money, Mama," Zoe said firmly, repeating an oft-voiced refrain.

Mama crossed her arms. "I do not see why not," she said. "It is green like everybody else's money."

"Because I want to do this on my own, that's why. I want to build something that's mine, the way you and Papa Molinari—"

"May God rest his soul," Mama murmured, and all three women crossed themselves, even Zoe, who wasn't Catholic.

"—did," Zoe finished.

"Papa and I did it on our own because we had no family in America to help us. You—" she lifted her right hand chest high, fingertips together and made a quick flicking motion toward Zoe "—have family."

"Yes, I know." Zoe reached across the table and patted Mama's arm. "And I'm grateful for that. I can't even begin to tell you how grateful. But I'm still going to do this on my own."

"But you do not do it on your own," Mama pointed out, with what Zoe was sure the woman considered extreme reasonableness. "You take someone else's money to help you. This Signora Sullivan—" she sniffed disdainfully, in full martyr mode now "—you are willing to take *her* money."

Zoe shook her head in exasperation. "That's business and you know it," she said, refusing to let herself be manipulated by her feelings. "Just like getting a loan from a bank."

"Pah, banks," Mama scoffed. "Usurers. Family is better."

"But, Mama, you got a loan from the bank three years ago when you renovated the apartments upstairs," Gina said sweetly. "Remember? You didn't go to Uncle Nunzio or Cousin Robert for the money, even though they would have been happy to help out.''

''They would have been happy to stick their nose into my busi—'' Mama began huffily, then snapped her mouth shut as she realized what she'd said.

Zoe's eyes sparkled, but she had the presence of mind not to laugh. ''My point, exactly,'' she said, permitting herself a small smile of triumph.

Mama tsked and lifted both hands this time, fingertips together and pointed upward as if entreating the Almighty to give her patience. ''Have it your way, then.'' She sighed loudly and dropped her hands. ''I give up.''

''Thank you, Mama.'' Zoe rose and went around the table to kiss her on the cheek. ''I knew you'd understand.''

''Eventually,'' Gina muttered under her breath.

Mama Marcella narrowed her eyes at her grandniece to let her know she'd heard the muttered remark, then lifted her hands to cup Zoe's cheeks and hold her at eye level for a moment. ''And what are you going to do about this Reed Sullivan and his private detective, hmm?''

''Nothing,'' Zoe said.

Mama let her go. ''Nothing?''

''Not a thing. He's having me investigated the way I assume he would anyone his great-grandmother wanted to loan money to. That's fine. That's business.''

And *only* business, from now on.

She refused to let it be anything else.

6

ZOE CONSIDERED NEARLY every article of clothing she owned before finally deciding what to wear to the meeting Monday morning. Even after she began to dress, though, she wasn't completely sure she'd made the right choice. The problem was she didn't have any real business clothes, no nine-to-five, going-to-the-office, I'm-really-serious-about-this type business clothes. She only owned one suit that even came close to that ideal. Maybe.

It was a deep eggplant-purple in a light-weight gabardine, with a peplum jacket and long narrow skirt, circa 1945. She'd bought it at a little antique clothing store in the South End. It wasn't exactly a business suit, not by current standards, but the more conventional little dress-for-success suits available at mainstream stores just didn't fit her—not her body, not her personality and definitely not her wallet. The purple number had been more in line with what she was willing to spend, and it had been designed at a time when fashionable women where allowed to be considerably curvier than they were today. With very little alteration, it fitted Zoe as if it had been custom-made for her.

In any case, all of her other clothes were even less suitable for a business meeting. Everything in her closet was either a one-of-a-kind flea market find or a funky piece from some out-of-the-way boutique, with an occasional basic from the Gap thrown in just to keep things from getting too predictable. She didn't own a traditional blazer, plain pearl studs or a pair of classic navy pumps, and she wouldn't have worn them, anyway, even if someone had given them to her.

So her only choice, really, was the eggplant suit. She made it more businesslike by wearing simple amethyst drop earrings and eschewing the enameled, pink flamingo pin that would have jazzed up the lapel. She wound her hair into a modified French twist and stepped into her most conservative pumps, which were plain black suede with a deep V-shaped vamp and three-inch heels. A boxy little black lacquered purse with a clear Lucite handle, just large enough for essentials, took the place of her oversize tapestry bag.

As she gazed at her reflection in the mirror, she had to admit the outfit looked pretty darn good, even without the flashy jewelry she usually wore with it. The jacket lay smoothly over her breasts without any puckering or pulling around the row of tiny jet buttons that ran, single file, down the front. It nipped in neatly at the waist, formfitting without being the least bit tight, then flared slightly to cover her hips. The straight skirt fell to midcalf with a discreet slit up the back to make walking possible. The ensemble cried out for seamed stockings, of course, but that would have been a bit much for Boston at nine o'clock on a Monday morning. Zoe had settled for sheer black hose, instead. If she had a briefcase and a jaunty little hat with a feather, she thought, she'd look like Joan Crawford or Rosalind Russell in one of those classic forties career-woman films—ready to take on the world and any man who dared get in her way.

With a final approving nod at her reflection, she exited her apartment, head high, purse firmly in hand, confidence soaring. Nineteen-year-old Tony Umberto at the dry cleaners next door whistled at her when she emerged from the alley between the two buildings, confirming her opinion.

"Lookin' good, Zoe," he hollered. "Lookin' real good." He kissed his fingers to her. *"Bellissima!"*

She grinned and sent him an airy wave, then turned and hurried on down the street at a brisk, confident clip to hail a taxi at the corner.

THE SULLIVAN BUILDING WAS located on Commonwealth Avenue in the Back Bay section of Boston, just one block from the Public Garden. Unlike many of its neighbors, with their Italian marble, French friezes or fussy Victorian trim, the building boasted a plain brick facade with no gargoyles or fancy ironwork to distract from its stolid, substantial lines. It reeked of wealth, respectability and chilly good taste, a monument to puritan restraint and well-bred Brahmin affluence.

If she had been more easily intimidated, Zoe would have turned tail and run. But she was Rosalind Russell today, so she lifted her chin and made her way across the wide Parisian-inspired sidewalk and up the steps to the double doors. A uniformed security guard opened them for her, bowing smartly when she smiled her thanks.

As financial institutions went, it was certainly impressive and even quite attractive in its own formidable, banklike way. The hum of commerce was very low-key and highbrow. Rockefeller would have felt right at home. Zoe felt like a stranger in a strange land. She took a deep, steadying breath, squared her shoulders beneath the fine wool of the eggplant suit and walked over to the information desk, determined to behave as if she trod the hallowed halls of high finance every day of her life.

"Could you tell me where I can find Reed Sullivan's office?" she inquired jauntily, still pretending she was the imperturbable Rosalind Russell.

"Take the elevator, over there." The clerk smiled and pointed to a little nook hidden behind a lush, potted palm. "All the way up to the top floor. The receptionist will direct you from there."

Predictably, the executive floor was even more impressive than the lobby had been. The marble floors became gleaming hardwood covered with gently worn Persian rugs. Glossy, hand-rubbed mahogany wainscoting ran halfway up the walls, then gave way to pale blue watered silk that had faded just enough to avoid being ostentatious. A tasteful grouping of small watercolor landscapes graced one wall. A larger oil depicting Boston Harbor at the turn of the century hung opposite them. Decorative brass wall sconces, neither too plain nor too fanciful, provided ambient light. A shaded Tiffany lamp sat on a corner of the receptionist's rosewood desk. The receptionist herself, in a gray cashmere twin set and a single strand of pearls, was as classy and elegant as the room.

"May I help you?" she asked in dulcet tones, as subdued as the pastel carpet under her desk.

Zoe's confidence slipped a notch, but she tightened her fingers on the Lucite handle of her lacquered purse and told herself to settle down. She'd made it this far without disaster; it would be silly to let nerves get the best of her now.

"Zoe Moon," she stated in her firmest, most businesslike manner. "I'm here to see Reed Sullivan. The fourth," she added hastily, in case numbers one through three were still around somewhere.

REED PACED THE WIDTH of his office, waiting for his secretary to buzz him. When she did, he nearly jumped out of his skin. "Steady there, Sullivan," he admonished himself. "Get a grip." He leaned across his desk from the far side and pushed a button on the phone. "Yes?" he said, as calmly as if he'd been sitting there, reading the month-end reports for the various Sullivan business concerns.

The voice on the other end wasn't the one he expected.

"This is Karla, sir. At reception? I'm sorry to bother you, but Mary Ellen isn't at her desk at the moment and I was instructed to let your office know the minute Ms. Moon arrived. She's here, sir. Shall I send her to your office or should I wait for Mary Ellen to come back or...?"

Sullivan company policy clearly stated that no visitor was to be left to wander the halls alone. It also stated that the receptionist was not to leave her desk unattended.

"Ask her to have a seat, Karla. I'll be out front to collect her in a minute."

He released the intercom button and rubbed his palms together, dismayed to realize they were actually sweaty. He hadn't gotten sweaty palms over a woman since...he had to stop and think about it for a moment...since the time Janice Hawkins had agreed to leave the Harbor Club dance with him one hot summer night and go strolling down to the deserted boathouse in the dark. He'd been seventeen, she was nineteen, and by the time they'd finally left the boathouse—

barely making it back to the clubhouse for the last dance—he'd been head-over-heels in love, as only a seventeen-year-old boy who'd just lost his virginity to an older woman could be. Two months later she'd broken his heart by dumping him for a fraternity boy from Yale.

He wondered uneasily if Zoe Moon was going to break his heart, too, and then dismissed the thought as ridiculous. He'd been little more than a boy back then, too young and unsophisticated to realize that what he felt for the accommodating Miss Hawkins wasn't love but lust. He was all grown up now. Now he knew the difference.

What he felt for the luscious Miss Moon was very definitely lust. Primal, basic, uncomplicated lust the likes of which he couldn't remember feeling for any other woman before. He had no starry-eyed illusions about being in love with her, not the way he had with Janice Hawkins. He wasn't picturing her veiled in antique lace with ribbon-tied lilies in her hands. He wanted Zoe naked in his bed, every glorious inch of her exposed to his eyes and hands and mouth. White lace didn't enter into the picture at all, unless it was some scrap of nothing meant to hold up a pair of silk stockings.

And that, apparently—just the thought of *that*—was quite enough to make his hands clammy.

He opened a door to the right of his desk and stepped into his private bathroom to rinse his hands at the old-fashioned pedestal sink. He checked his hair while he was at it, leaning forward a bit to peer into the antique oval mirror as he skimmed his fingers over the top of his head. Was that a bit of gray there at the temple, mixed in with the brown? A few seconds of closer inspection assured him that it wasn't and, satisfied, he straightened, tweaked the knot on his silk tie into more perfect alignment, shot his cuffs so that the correct one-and-one-half inches of snowy Egyptian cotton showed below the sleeves of his suit coat, and tugged at the hem of his vest as if all those little adjustments were actually necessary.

They weren't. His suits and shirts were custom-made by one of the finest tailors on the Eastern seaboard, his housekeeper was scrupulous about keeping his wardrobe cleaned and pressed, and Reed himself was naturally fastidious about his grooming. He never left home less than perfectly turned out, and he never thought about how he looked or what he was wearing once he stepped away from the mirror in his bedroom.

Usually.

He met his own eyes in the mirror over the sink, smiling bemusedly as he realized that Zoe Moon had managed to make him nervous. Him! Nervous about seeing a woman. That hadn't happened since the Janice Hawkins debacle, either.

"Reed?" He heard a light tap on the outer door of his office. "You in there?"

He stepped out of the bathroom at the sound of his secretary's voice. "Right here, M.E. Come on in. I was just about to head down to reception and collect our guest."

"No need. I've got her," Mary Ellen said as she ushered Zoe into his office. "I came across her on my way back from the ladies' room. Karla said she'd already buzzed you to let you know she was here, so I brought her on back with me."

Something resembling a lightning bolt shot through him at the sight of his great-grandmother's gorgeous protégée, but he managed to smile graciously—as if every nerve ending in his body wasn't sizzling!—and stepped forward, offering his hand like the gentleman he'd been raised to be and the savvy businessman he instinctively was. Besides, he wanted to touch her. Desperately.

"Zoe. Welcome to Sullivan Enterprises," he murmured, hoping to hell his palms hadn't started to sweat again, laughing at himself for even worrying about it.

Lord, how could the woman tie him up in knots just by standing there?

She was wearing a dark, purplish suit that succeeded in looking prim and sexy at the same time. It had a long concealing skirt that ended well below her knees. The jacket was buttoned all the way up to the soft hollow at the base of her throat and had some kind of little flounce that covered the enticing swell of her hips, but it hugged her impossible waist and outlined the mouthwatering shape of her full breasts. She'd come up with yet another hairstyle, too, one that confined all but a few curling tendrils of her gorgeous red hair in an upswept do that made his fingertips itch to take it down.

"I'm sorry for the wait," he apologized, as cool and urbane as if he wasn't wondering just how many buttons he'd have to unbutton to get her out of that elegant little suit—and what would be under it when he did. Seamed stockings, he decided, and black lace garters. And one of those frilly Victoria's Secret corsets meant to fuel men's fantasies. "I was unavoidably delayed."

"Yes." She smiled her teasing gypsy smile and glanced toward the open bathroom door. "I can see that."

Unaccountably, Reed actually felt his cheeks warm.

He backed up a step, reaching behind him to pull the door closed. "Would you like coffee?" he offered, ignoring her comment, and what might or might not have been a blush. "Tea? A soft drink?"

Zoe could have kicked herself for making such a juvenile remark, nerves or no nerves. Apparently, proper Bostonians didn't allude to such earthy subjects as bathrooms in casual conversation, even teasingly. She didn't either, usually, but the words had popped out before she'd had a chance to censor them. Her words had an unfortunate habit of doing that.

"I'd love a cup of coffee," she said politely, trying to show him she really did know how to behave in public.

"M.E., would you see about getting us come coffee, please? And something to go with it." He looked at Zoe. "Croissant? Bagel? Danish?"

"I should say bagel, shouldn't I? But..." She shrugged and patted her hip lightly, disparagingly.

Reed's gaze automatically tracked the fluttering movement of her hand, his eyes all but glazing over as he imagined his own hand caressing that sweet swell of flesh below her waist. She had lovely, rounded, womanly hips, fashioned expressly for a man to hold on to in bed. He swallowed—hard—trying not to salivate at the thought of being that man.

"I'd...uh, really love a croissant," Zoe said haltingly, conscious of somehow having made yet another verbal gaffe. Apparently, judging by the carefully blank look on Reed's face, members of polite society didn't joke about their physical flaws, either. She probably ought to just keep her mouth shut unless he asked a direct question.

"Coffee and croissants, M.E." Reed swallowed

again, then lifted a loosely curled fist to his mouth and coughed softly to clear the slight huskiness from his voice. "And don't carry the tray yourself. Get someone else to do it."

His secretary rolled her eyes. "I'm pregnant, Reed, not crippled."

"Eight months and counting," he said, as if she needed reminding. "Get someone else to do it."

Mary Ellen smiled and shook her head. "Yes, boss." She executed a snappy salute that had him smiling in return, despite his preoccupation with his guest. "I'll get someone else to do it."

She closed the door behind her, leaving them alone.

Zoe looked around the office with feigned casualness, determined to be cool, determined to be professional and aloof despite the way her heart was fluttering against the wall of her chest. It was going to be harder than she thought to maintain the businesslike facade, because Gina was absolutely right.

The man was gorgeous.

And she most definitely, without a doubt, had the hots for him.

She'd never been much impressed by men in suits before, especially three-piece, pinstriped suits. They usually looked pompous or pretentious or just plain uncomfortable to her. Reed looked like Pierce Brosnan in *GoldenEye,* only better; like Cary Grant in every movie he'd ever made. He was sophisticated male elegance personified—at ease, in charge, elegant, devastatingly sexy. She wondered if it was merely coincidental, or if he knew the dark charcoal-gray material of his oh-so-proper suit made his brilliant blue eyes look even bluer in contrast.

"This is a lovely office," she said, casting about for

something safe to say. Even a proper Bostonian couldn't object to an innocuous comment about his taste in interior decoration, and the office *was* lovely. "And the view..." She moved away from him, toward the bank of tall windows behind his desk, and looked out over the strip of parkland that ran down the center of the street below. "It's fabulous. It must be very soothing to look out at grass and trees in the middle of a hectic business day."

"Yes, very soothing," Reed agreed, although he hardly ever paused long enough to notice the view. Besides, right now the only view that interested him was the one he had of her legs.

She had trim, elegant ankles and slim, rounded calves, both shown to advantage by the black heels she wore. There was a slit up the back of her narrow skirt, not deep, but it went high enough for him to see the tender back of her knee when she moved. She wasn't wearing seamed stockings, which was mildly disappointing, but he still had high hopes for the garters and the frilly corset. She looked like the kind of woman who would wear them...the kind of woman who *should* wear them. Otherwise, what were fantasies for?

"Don't you think we should get started?" she said, turning from the windows to face him as she spoke.

"Started?" In the second or two it took Reed to change gears, he had a full-blown fantasy of getting *started* on the desk. It produced an erection that was almost painful, and completely surprising. It had never happened in his office before. Never. He didn't know quite how to react. "Ah...yes, certainly," he said, falling back on protocol and good manners. "Let's get started. Why don't you sit here."

He pulled out a chair at the small oval dining-cum-conference table, standing behind it while she crossed the room. She reached out as she approached and set her purse on the table, then turned and seated herself. The scent of violets drifted up to him and he bent his head, eyes half-closed, breathing it in as he gently pushed the chair in behind her knees.

"Thank you," she murmured, turning her head slightly to smile up at him.

Her hair brushed the back of his hand, soft as a whisper. The tiny filigreed amethyst teardrops dangling from her earlobes swayed enticingly. Her scent beckoned him to come closer. It was all he could do not to give in to temptation—not to grasp her by the shoulders, haul her out of the chair and kiss her senseless.

But there were rules about that sort of thing, he reminded himself. This wasn't a Saturday afternoon in Bruno's Pub. This was his office. She was here on business. Even more to the point, she was here, in essence, to apply for a loan. Oh, yes, there were very definite rules. Rules that said he shouldn't even be thinking about what he was thinking about until business was settled, one way or the other. Under the circumstances, even what had happened at Bruno's on Saturday shouldn't have.

Reed took a deep breath, uncurled his fingers from the back of her chair and circled around the table. He seated himself at a ninety degree angle to her and pulled his chair in close, making very sure he was situated so the edge of the table concealed his condition.

"All right, let's get to it then, shall we?" he said, slipping into his businessman mode in an effort to hurry along the demise of his body's response to his guest.

The sooner they got *this* business settled and out of

the way, the sooner he could get on with the more important business of getting Zoe Moon into his bed.

He inserted his hand into an inside pocket of his suit coat and extracted his reading glasses. He slipped them on and flipped open the manila file folder on the table in front of him, his eyes intense and focused as he perused the first page.

Zoe watched the transformation from elegant man-about-town to no-nonsense financial guru, fascinated by this glimpse at yet another side of him. The man was a quick-change artist, slipping seamlessly from one persona to another. It was a bit disconcerting. And endlessly intriguing. It made her wonder just exactly how many sides there were to Reed Sullivan IV.

"Your credit report," he said, handing it to her. "It's excellent, by the way. No overdue accounts. No judgments or liens. Not much of anything beyond your monthly rent and a couple of credit cards, all paid on time and usually in full. That's an impressive feat in this age of runaway credit. And you paid your college loans off in record time." He tossed her a quick, approving glance. " *Very* impressive."

Zoe put the document aside without looking at it. She'd seen any number of variations on the theme in the past couple of months; bank officers loved credit reports.

"Not what you expected from a con artist, is it?" she said, giving him her slanting, sideways look.

He glanced at her over the tops of his glasses. "I've apologized for that," he said in a tone both patient and annoyed. "Is it going to be necessary for me to do it again?"

"No, that's all right," she said, chastened by his quiet words. "Once was enough. Really. Go on with what you were saying. What else have you got in that file?''

She wondered if he'd bring up the private investigator he'd sicced on her.

He didn't. Not directly, anyway.

''Your work history.'' He handed her another sheet of paper. ''Substantially less impressive. You've had—'' he counted silently, skimming a fingertip down his copy of the report ''—seventeen, no, eighteen jobs in the last six years.'' He glanced up briefly, his expression severe. ''My first question has to be why? This kind of job hopping doesn't give the impression of the kind of stability investors are looking for.''

As if she didn't already know that all too well!

''I get bored easily,'' she said, and then thought better of her answer. Financial types didn't appreciate levity, even when it held a grain of truth. More than a grain, in her case. ''I'm just not cut out for the traditional nine-to-five routine,'' she explained. ''I like variety, meeting new people, trying new things. Part-time work has that. It's given me the opportunity to try out a lot of different fields and meet a lot of people, as well as providing me with a more-or-less steady income while I got New Moon up and running. And if you'll look at the dates a little more closely,'' she advised him, ''you'll see that it's not quite as bad as it appears at first glance. I held a lot of those jobs concurrently, sometimes three at a time.''

He took another quick look at the list of jobs, checking the dates a bit more closely than he had the first time. '''A lot' does seem to be the operative phrase,'' he agreed after a moment, impressed in spite of himself. She had to be a real go-getter to work two jobs at once, let alone three. Maybe she wasn't quite as flighty as she appeared at first glance. "Salesclerk, telephone solicitation, a couple of clerical positions, several stints as a waitress, dog walker, makeup consultant, tour guide, personal shopper—" he looked at her over the tops of his glasses again, his expression amused this time "—clown?"

"I did children's parties, school fairs, that kind of thing. It was fun, but when New Moon finally began to take off, I just didn't have time for it anymore, even on a part-time basis."

"And New Moon finally started to take off when?" He ran his gaze down the list of figures again, rechecking the date of her last employment. "About six months ago?"

"Yes, about that." She gave a little nod that set her earrings swaying. "Yes, I'd say it's definitely been at least six months since I had to take a part time job to make ends meet."

"And you've worked exclusively on New Moon since then? It's been completely self-supporting?"

"Yes, completely," she said, and then paused, rethinking her answer, wondering if his definition of self-supporting and hers could possibly be the same. "I've been able to pay my bills without taking on extra work," she added, just so there'd be no question later of what *she'd* meant by the term.

He nodded absently, as if to himself, and reached for one of the sharpened # 2 pencils protruding from a leather pencil cup in the center of the table. After making a brief note in the margin of the report, he put the pencil down, took his glasses off and lifted his gaze to hers. His expression was serious as he regarded her across the table.

Zoe instinctively braced herself for some hard questions.

"Given your work history—" he tapped the report with one finger "—and your admitted penchant for variety in your work environment, what assurances can you offer that you won't get bored with New Moon in another couple of months and decide to go on to something else, leaving my great-grandmother with nothing to show for her investment aside from a possible tax write-off?"

Zoe pondered how to answer that for a moment, wondering what she could say to convince him that New Moon wasn't just another temporary, part-time job for her, that it was anything but.

"The only assurance I can offer is that it won't happen because New Moon is *mine*. It's my baby. I've been working toward it since my junior year in college, when I started making skin-care products for myself because I couldn't find what I wanted in the stores. I developed the formulas. I mix them. I bottle them. I market them. I show people how to use them. I'm involved in every aspect of New Moon—I *am* New Moon—and I've never found it boring, even for a second. No, that's not strictly true," she admitted, striving for absolute honesty. "I find the bookkeeping *extremely* boring." She pursed her lips in a little moue of distaste. "But I still do it."

He quirked an eyebrow at her, surprising her with the gleam of humor in his eyes. "I could argue that point. But I won't." He slipped his glasses back on and handed her another sheaf of papers. "These are the preliminary reports I've had compiled out of the raw data you so mistakenly refer to as bookkeeping."

"Raw data?" Zoe's forehead crinkled up for a moment. "Oh, you mean the stuff in my shoe boxes."

"The stuff that *was* in your shoe boxes. It's been organized and refiled into something a little more professional and efficient. I'll explain the system to you later. It's very simple and straightforward. Before we get into that, though, I want to go over these reports with you and see if we can fill in some of the blanks."

But Zoe wasn't quite ready to move on. "Does this mean you accept my assurances that I'm in this for the long haul? Because I am, you know. Whether Moira invests or not, whether anybody ever invests, I intend to build New Moon into a thriving business."

"It means that I can see you're sincere and I'm reserving judgment for the time being, until I get to know you and your business better."

"Or until you get Mr. Davies's full report," Zoe said shrewdly, letting him know she knew he'd hired a private investigator.

He didn't even have the grace to look guilty. "So you know about Leland Davies, do you? How did you find out?"

"The owner of the Ristorante Marcella isn't just my landlady, she's my surrogate grandmother. Her last name is Molinari," she said significantly.

"Ah," he said, his facility for names allowing him to put two and two together almost instantly. "She's related to your friend Gina."

"Yes. And she wasn't pleased to have some strange man asking questions about one of her *bambini*. She was sure it meant somebody was up to no good."

Reed felt a tiny spurt of guilt at that. He was definitely up to what he was sure any young woman's grandmother—surrogate or not—would consider no good, although it had nothing to do with the private investigator he'd hired. "I hope you assured her that it's just business. I'd investigate anyone or anything my great-grandmother was thinking of investing in."

"Yes, that's exactly what I told her. It's strictly business." Zoe looked down at the sheaf of papers he'd given her, deciding they'd better get back to it. "What kind of reports am I looking at here?" she asked.

The expression on her face made him think of a child who'd just been offered a new vegetable and was already sure she wasn't going to like it. "Cash flow. Assets and liabilities. P&L. That's profit and loss," he clarified when her forehead crinkled. "These are only preliminary figures, of course. Obviously, there wasn't enough information to come up with anything concrete at this point."

"Oh, obviously," Zoe said, nodding sagely as if she had any idea at all what he was talking about.

"The income and expense transactions report has a lot of holes in it, too. I'm going to need a lot more input on these—" he tapped his stack of papers with his forefinger "—before we can go any further. Most of your receipts were impossible to categorize without a more thorough knowledge of your business. We'll have to go over them together, item by item, and assign each one to a category before it's filed." He speared another look at her over the top of his glasses. "*After* we determine just what those categories should be," he said sternly, then paused, as if waiting for some kind of response.

Zoe nodded again. "Sounds reasonable to me," she said, wondering just how many categories he envisioned. As far as she was concerned, there were two; money came in and it went out, and the trick was to make sure the former amount was greater than the latter. Everything else was bean counting. That unenlightened attitude was undoubtedly why she'd had problems convincing bankers to give her the money she needed; they liked counting beans and had myriad ways of doing it that she didn't even begin to comprehend.

"That will be the easy part. The rest gets a bit more—" He broke off, frowning at the soft knock on his door. "Yes?"

The door opened to admit Mary Ellen, followed by a young woman holding a large silver tray. On it was a silver carafe, two gold-rimmed, white china cups and saucers with matching creamer and sugar bowl, a napkin-covered, silver filigree basket and three little crystal pots of what Zoe assumed were various jams. No wonder he hadn't wanted his pregnant secretary to carry it. The tray alone looked like it weighed a ton.

"You can put it right there," he said, gesturing at a spot on the conference table. "Thank you…it's Miss Fulton, isn't it?"

"Yes, sir." The young woman nodded, blushing a little as she set the tray down. "Cindy Fulton."

"Thank you, Cindy." He smiled, looking directly into her eyes as he spoke. "I appreciate your taking the time from your regular duties to help us out here."

Cindy bobbed her head. "Welcome, sir," she mumbled.

Zoe halfway expected her to drop a curtsy, as if he were royalty, but the young woman just stood there, staring at him with an adoring, awestruck look on her face. Reed didn't notice; the king of this particular castle had already turned his attention back to the open folder in front of him.

Mary Ellen noticed, though. "Come along, Cindy," she said dryly. "You've got filing to do."

With a last, lingering look at her oblivious employer, Cindy allowed herself to be herded out of the office.

"I'd watch that, if I were you," Zoe said, when they were alone again.

"Hmm?" Reed said absently, without even glancing up. He'd picked up the discarded pencil and was making check marks beside selected items on one of the reports. "Watch what?"

Zoe removed her purse from the table, setting it on the empty chair at her left, and reached for the silver carafe. "If you smile at her like that very often, she's going to fall in love with you," she said as she poured out two cups of coffee. "Cream and sugar?"

"Just sugar," he said, then looked up, startled, as he realized what else she'd said. "Who's going to fall in love with me?" he demanded, feeling a strange, unsettling leap in the region of his heart before he realized she couldn't possibly be talking about herself. "What are you talking about?"

Zoe couldn't help but smile at the befuddled look on his face. The man wasn't just gorgeous, he was adorable, too. There was nothing more appealing than a man who didn't know how appealing he was. And Reed Sullivan IV didn't appear to have a clue, at least in this instance.

"Cindy." Zoe gestured at the closed door. "Miss Fulton?" she added, when he just sat there, staring at her. "The woman who brought the coffee?"

"I know who Cindy Fulton is." He looked at Zoe over the top of his glasses, his expression both baffled and annoyed, silently demanding that she explain herself—and quickly. "What I don't know is what you're talking about."

Zoe might have gotten just the tiniest bit annoyed herself at his peremptory tone, if she hadn't been so amused by his obtuseness.

"It's a classic scenario." Remembering how he'd taken his tea, Zoe added a single cube of sugar to his coffee and pushed it toward him. "Practically a cliché," she said as she poured a heavy dollop of cream into her own cup of coffee. "Secretaries are always falling in love with their bosses."

It took a full five seconds for him to fully absorb her meaning. "That's ridiculous," he declared, as if issuing an edict. "Miss Fulton isn't my secretary. She's a file clerk."

Zoe shrugged, enjoying herself. It was kind of reassuring to realize the king of all he surveyed had a blind spot. "File clerks fall in love with their bosses, too."

"M.E. is her immediate superior, not me. Besides, our employee manual specifically forbids interoffice relationships."

"Oh, well, that should certainly take care of it, then." She reached out as she spoke, lifted a corner of the heavy damask napkin covering the filigree basket and chose a miniature croissant from the varied offerings. "But I'd watch where I smiled if I were you. Just a friendly warning," she said, and bit into the croissant, wondering if she ought to warn him about the possibility of clients falling in love with their financial advisors, too.

She almost choked on the flaky piece of pastry. Love? Where had that come from? There was absolutely no danger of her falling in *love* with him. It was lust she was falling into. Simple, uncomplicated lust, and she, womanlike, was trying to pretty it up and make it more acceptable. And that was stupid. Very stupid.

"Zoe? Is something wrong. Are you all right?"

"Yes, I'm fine," she lied. "I just realized there's something... That is, I think we should..." Very carefully, she placed the croissant on the rim of her saucer and pushed it away from her. "Kiss me," she said, surprising herself as much as she did him.

7

*her, she was falling...but somehow...somewhere...back
and then somehow...she managed to get...it up and
cradle it more...properly, her...other hand began very
slowly...*

"Zoe," he said, with almost a...child-quiet.

*"Um, I," in the...she said, "I just realized there's a
possibility." "Thinking I don't, we should..." very carefully she placed the crossbar...in the top of the saucer
and pushed it away from her. "Please..."*

"WHAT?!"

"Kiss me," she said calmly, as if it were a completely reasonable request. "The way you did at
Bruno's last Saturday."

"Zoe. Miss Moon," he amended in an automatic
effort to put some distance between them. Dammit,
they were in his office. There were *rules* about these
things. Didn't she know that? "I don't think that's such
a good idea."

"Probably not," she agreed. "But I want you to kiss
me, anyway. You want to, don't you?"

Surprise had him blurting out the truth before he
could think. *"God, yes!"*

"Well, then..." She reached out with both hands,
removed his glasses and set them carefully on the table
on top of his open file folder. "Kiss me," she repeated,
and leaned toward him, eyelids lowered, face lifted, her
luscious raspberry lips softly puckered.

Contrary to popular belief, Reed Sullivan IV was
only human. Despite the opinions of most of his business associates and the nasty rumor spread by a venge-
ful Boston socialite who'd failed to stir his interest, he
had a real live heart beating in his chest, with real
blood flowing through his veins. Right now, his very
human heart was laboring like a locomotive going up-
hill, sending warm red blood surging through his body.

Surging to one particular part of his body. And it wasn't his brain.

"Why?" he said, trying to cling to some final vestige of good sense.

She opened her eyes.

He thought he read exasperation in them but wasn't sure.

"*Must* there be a reason?" she asked impatiently, annoyed at having her motives questioned. Especially when she didn't know what they were herself.

"Yes." He nodded. "Yes, in this case, I think there most definitely must be a reason."

"Call it, ah...oh..." she pursed her lips in thought, mentally groping for just the right word "...an experiment," she decided.

"An experiment?" he murmured huskily, his gaze still on her mouth. Her luscious, utterly kissable mouth. He swallowed a groan. "What kind of experiment?"

Good question, she thought. Too bad she didn't have an answer. "Just an experiment." She drew back a little. "Are you going to kiss me or not?"

He reached out, quick as a striking snake, and curled his hand around the back of her neck to keep her where she was. "Oh, yes," he declared. "I'm definitely going to kiss you."

"Well, then..." she invited again.

"Just like I did at Bruno's?" he murmured, wanting to be absolutely sure he understood what she wanted—on one level, at least.

"Yes." She closed her eyes. "Just exactly like that, please," she said, all the while hoping for...more.

He tightened his hand on the back of her neck and eased her toward him over the edge of the table, leaning forward to meet her halfway. He had just enough presence of mind to stay seated, realizing in some tiny rational part of his brain that if he touched her in any other way, if he actually stood up and took her in his arms and pressed her luscious body to his, he'd end up breaking every rule in the book instead of just bending them a little. And that's all he was going to do, he assured himself, just bend them a little. What could one insignificant little kiss hurt?

But the kiss, despite his best intentions, wasn't exactly like the one he'd given her at Bruno's. And it wasn't little. Or insignificant.

His lips were already parted when they touched hers, hungry to taste her fully this time. His breath was warm and moist against her mouth. His tongue came seeking, delicately tracing the seam of her lips until she opened to him.

He changed the angle of the kiss then, tilting his head, using the hand curled around the back of her neck to alter her position as he slipped his tongue between her lips and took the kiss deeper. His fingertips caressed her tender nape, exerting gentle pressure to keep her exactly where she was. His palm cradled the side of her neck, supporting it and holding her steady. His thumb traced the delicate whorls of her ear, then moved lower, brushing along the edge of her jaw, slowly, hypnotically, soothingly, back and forth...back and forth...while he feasted on her open mouth.

The position was awkward, both of them leaning across the edge of the table, straining toward each other. Zoe murmured softly, the sound a low humming noise mingling appreciation and impatience. She hitched herself closer and lifted one hand, curling her slender, beringed fingers around his wrist to anchor herself more firmly to him. Reed rose half out of his chair, wanting to get closer, wanting to pull her into his arms and *really* kiss her. He was desperate to feel her breasts pressed against his chest. To thrust his hips against the cradle of hers. To—

It was the backs of his knees pressing against the edge of the chair that made him realize what he was about to do. He almost—*almost*—ignored the warning screaming in his brain in favor of answering the more insistent clamor in his loins. But some things were just too deeply ingrained, and he'd been born and bred a gentleman, with all that implied. To give in to his baser instincts would be to violate a trust—to himself if no one else. He sank back down onto his chair seat and lifted his mouth from hers, just far enough so he could speak.

"So," he murmured, his lips brushing hers as he spoke, "was the experiment a success?"

Zoe sighed audibly, a soft, stuttering sound like a baby startled awake. Her lashes fluttered once, then lifted slowly. She stared at him, the expression in her eyes clouded and confused. "Experiment?" she whispered, as if she had no idea what he was talking about.

Reed grinned. He couldn't help it. It had been a while since he'd reduced a woman to dazed confusion. And never with just a kiss. It was better than his fantasies. Almost.

"You said this was an experiment." Still smiling, he brushed her lips with his lightly, to remind her what *this* was. "Was it a success?"

"Oh. Oh, the experiment. Yes, I guess it was. I..." She uncurled her fingers from his wrist and drew back, straightening away from him, putting some distance between them so she could figure out how to breathe again. "Yes, it was." She picked up her cup and took a fortifying sip of the heavily creamed coffee. It didn't even begin to erase the taste of him. "I think."

He cocked an eyebrow at her. "You think? You don't know?"

"All right, it was a failure, okay?" she flared, glaring at him as if the fault had been entirely his. She set the china cup back in its saucer with a sharp little click. "A dismal failure."

His eyebrow rose a bit higher. "A failure?" he said, his tone disbelieving, his expression steady and unblinking as he regarded her from across the table.

Her creamy skin was delicately flushed. A long tendril of hair, pulled loose when he withdrew his hand from her nape, drifted down the side of her face to lay curled over her shoulder. Her eyes weren't simply clouded now, but stormy, roiling with emotions that bubbled very close to the surface. She looked like a woman who'd been thoroughly kissed—and had enjoyed it. Thoroughly.

"Are you saying you didn't enjoy it?" he asked, finally. "Because if you are, I don't believe you."

"Oh, I enjoyed it." Too much. Way too much. So much so that if there had been room in the pointed toes of her black suede pumps, all ten, tiny painted digits at the ends of her feet would have been permanently curled. "It isn't that. It's just..."

She jumped up from her chair and began pacing, too agitated and aroused and just plain mad at herself to sit still for another moment.

Reed watched her with the deep, instinctive appreciation of a sorely smitten man. He had no idea what the problem was, what combination of emotions compelled her to agitated motion. He simply enjoyed the view: the quick, impatient way she moved her head;

the straight, almost militant line of her shoulders; the restless, ground-eating stride that tightened her skirt against the long, lovely line of her thighs as she ranged from the table, to his desk, to the windows and back again.

She'd been fooling herself with all that nonsense about an experiment, Zoe fumed, furious at the self-deception. There was no experiment. There were just hormones run amok. The simple, unadorned truth was he was gorgeous and sexy and adorable and she'd *wanted* to kiss him, even though she knew it wasn't a good idea, even though she knew mixing business and pleasure was a mistake, especially in this case.

God, it was her mother all over again! Falling in lust with a man and calling it love, when it was just her hormones in an uproar.

But Zoe was made of sterner stuff. She'd seen what self-delusion did to a person's life, not to mention the life of that person's child. She believed in facing the truth straight on, no matter how unflattering a light it cast on her. And the truth was she was in the throes of a serious case of lust for a man with whom she had absolutely nothing in common. A man who'd called her a con artist…which he'd apologized for, true, and she'd accepted his apology. But still, he was having her investigated—all in the name of business, true, and she'd probably have him investigated under the same circumstances, but still…

It was *galling* to realize that none of that seemed to make one iota of difference in her desire to swap spit with him. Apparently, she could find a mitigating excuse for every objection if the man was a good kisser. *And, oh Lord, Reed Sullivan was one great kisser!* Which made her not as unlike her mother as she wanted to think she was, and just as shallow as she'd accused Reed of being.

The first was something she was always on guard against.

The second was something she'd never in a million years admit to.

Not to him, anyway.

She sat back down, determined to set a few things straight. "Look," she said, starting off in tones of extreme reasonableness. "*Experiment* was the wrong word to use here. Totally wrong. There was no experiment. No success and no failure involved."

"Then what was it?"

"It was, uh..." She reached for her coffee cup again and sipped, stalling for time while she came up with the right words. Usually, she was much better at this kind of let's-lay-all-our-cards-on-the-table-and-tell-it-like-it-is conversation, but telling it like it was, without telling the *entire* truth—which was none of his business and not pertinent to the conversation, anyway—was proving to be a bit more complicated than she would have thought. She took a quick breath and plunged ahead.

"I think it's fair to say that we...that we're... attracted—" it was as good a word as any; pitifully inadequate, but basically accurate "—to each other. Would you agree with that?"

Reed nodded. "Yes, I'd say that's a fair assessment." Wholly inadequate for the surprisingly violent feelings she aroused in him, but fair, so far as it went. "So?" he asked, wondering where she was going with this.

"Well, I just thought that if we, um..." She shrugged and sipped again, then squared her shoulders, set the coffee cup in the saucer and pushed them away from her again. "I thought we should just go ahead and deal with it, up front."

"Deal with *it?*"

"Yes. We were both wondering what it would be like if we really kissed each other. For real, I mean, not like that little peck at Bruno's."

She paused, as if waiting for a reply. Reed nodded, not quite trusting his voice at this point. So she'd been wondering, too, he thought, elated by the information.

"I thought it would be best if we got it out of the way. If we just went ahead and satisfied our curiosity so we could forget it and get on with the business at hand. That's what I meant when I called it an experiment."

"And did it?"

"Did it what?"

"Satisfy your curiosity?"

"Oh, yes. Uh-huh. It did. Absolutely," she vowed, as sincere and earnest as a child who'd been asked if writing "I will not call my brother names" one hundred dred times had cured her of the desire to do so.

Reed wondered if he should call her on it. It was obvious she was lying through her pearly white teeth. He decided to tell her a few truths of his own, instead. To keep her from jumping up again, he reached out, covering her hand where it lay on the table. "You didn't ask if it satisfied my curiosity, Zoe."

She started, but didn't jerk away. "Didn't it?" she asked, looking at him with a wary expression in her big brown eyes.

He shook his head. "No, it didn't. Not by a long shot."

She did try to pull away then, but he tightened his

fingers on her hand, pressing down, and she decided it was beneath her dignity to struggle.

"Do you want to know what it did do for me, Zoe?"

She shook her head, wary of the gleam in his eyes. "I don't think so."

"Well, I'm going to tell you, anyway, because I think you're absolutely right. I think we *should* get everything out in the open."

He was looking at her with that heat in his eyes again. That primal, predatory male heat that made her want to run for her life, and throw herself at his feet in abject surrender at the same time. The last time he had looked at her that way he'd been sweaty and bleeding, wearing grass-stained rugby shorts and a torn jersey. They'd been surrounded by scores of people, with half the width of a rugby field between the two of them.

It was inexplicably more thrilling, more exciting, more…menacing, somehow, to be the object of that ravening gaze when it was leveled at you by a man wearing an elegant three-piece suit, sitting at his ease less than two feet away. Maybe because such a man would have to break through several more layers of civilization to tear your clothes off and carry you to his lair than one who had already released some of his aggression on a rugby field. Maybe it was because she was already in his lair and he wouldn't have far to drag her once he'd given in to his desires and stripped her naked. And maybe it was just because they were alone and there was no one around to keep him—or her—from acting out each primitive impulse should those layers of civilization be breached.

Zoe swallowed convulsively and tried to tamp down the excitement that look engendered in her. It was just hormones. Or pheromones. Or something. Whatever it was, she knew that if she showed the least bit of weakness, he'd pounce. If she ran, he'd chase her down. With the finely honed instincts of any female animal being run to ground by a male of the species, she turned and launched a counterattack.

"Openness is a vastly overrated commodity," she said airily, lifting one shoulder in a nonchalant little shrug. "Some things are better kept to yourself."

"Oh, no. I want to be completely open about this, just the way you were. Deal with it right up front so we can get on with the business at hand."

She cocked an eyebrow at him, head tilted, chin up. "Fine, then. Let's get it all out in the open," she said, managing to sound just the slightest bit bored with the subject. "What did that kiss do for you, Mr. Sullivan?"

Damn, she's a gorgeous piece of work, he thought admiringly, wondering how he could ever, even for a second, have made the mistake of thinking she was ordinary. In velvet pants, faded jeans or sexy schoolmarm suits, she was the most exciting woman he'd ever encountered. She might look like a frivolous sex kitten, but she stood her ground with the arrogance of a duchess—or a swaggering, streetwise kid.

He could feel the tension in the hand that lay deceptively passive beneath his; he could see the blush tinting her cheeks; he could almost smell the heat rising off of her violet-scented skin. But she lifted her chin and looked down her nose, challenging him with an expression of haughty indifference, as if she couldn't care less what his answer was.

He could no more have resisted the challenge in her eyes than he had the invitation to kiss her.

"That kiss piqued my curiosity, Miss Moon," he

said, his voice low and silky and lethal. "It made me wonder how it's going to be the next time I kiss you."

"I sincerely doubt there's ever going to be a next time. My curiosity has been satisfied, remember?"

"Oh, there'll be a next time, all right. And the next time, I don't intend to stop until *my* curiosity has been satisfied. Completely satisfied." He smiled wolfishly and brushed his thumb across the back of her hand, trying to make her jump or pull away. "And that won't be until I've got you flat on your back and stark naked, lying spread-eagle under me in blissful exhaustion."

"Oh, really?" It took every bit of willpower she possessed to keep her gaze steady on his, to keep her voice even, to keep her hand perfectly still. "I think I might have something to say about that, don't you?"

He smiled a marauder's smile, the kind of smile that made her wonder how she could have ever thought he was a stuffed shirt. "You'll be saying yes," he promised. "You'll be screaming the word before I'm through."

She laughed lightly, as if the very thought was just too absurd to take seriously. "In your dreams," she said coolly, but her voice was less insouciant than it had been only a moment before.

"It's already happened in my dreams, Zoe. Dozens of times." The look in his eyes as he stared into hers was that of a shameless voluptuary, hell-bent on conquest and seduction. "Do you want to hear about them?"

Zoe abandoned all pretense of coolness and leveled a killing look at him. "No, I do not," she said through her teeth, trying—unsuccessfully—to ignore the wanton thrill of excitement that shuddered down her spine. "I have no interest in your prurient imaginings."

"Even when you have a starring role in them?"

"Especially not then."

"Liar." The word was a caress. An endearment. A goad. "You're dying to know. I can see it in your eyes," he said, doing his level best to rattle her into doing more than just spearing him with her hot gypsy gaze. "The heat. The attraction. The fascination."

"Then you're seeing things that aren't there."

"You, Zoe. I'm seeing you."

"If that's what you think, I suggest you put your glasses back on and take another look."

He gave a short bark of laughter and gave it up. It was going to take more than words to make Zoe Moon cut and run. And words were all he had at the moment. All he would allow himself.

"All right. You win this round, sweetheart. I surrender." He released her hand and reached for his glasses, turning his attention back to the open folder as if the kiss and all that came after it hadn't happened. "We've got a lot of work to do here to if we're going to turn this data into anything useful."

It was then that Zoe almost lost it. Work? He thought she was going to sit there in his office with him and work on a bunch of computer-generated reports, as if nothing had happened? As if he hadn't kissed her nearly breathless? As if he hadn't said those...those scandalous, thrilling, *arousing* things to her?

Apparently, he did.

He was.

"I don't believe you," she said in exasperation, staring at his bent head.

"Don't believe what?" He glanced up briefly, all innocence and strictly business, barely making eye contact before he turned his attention to the open folder. "That we have a lot of work to do here?"

"No. I can see there's a lot of work to do. What I don't believe is how you can just turn it on and off like that. How you can just pick up your pencil as if nothing happened. Just what am I supposed to think now that—" She broke off, aghast at what she was saying.

She should be happy that he was just going to drop it. Thrilled. Instead she seemed to be doing her darnedest to prolong the situation, to provoke him into shedding the mild-mannered Clark Kent business persona he slipped on with his glasses, and unleashing the stalking wolf again. Gina was always telling her she should learn to keep her mouth shut and leave well enough alone. This seemed like a good time to start practicing the skill.

"Never mind," she said.

But she'd pricked his conscience. What was she supposed to think, indeed? There were rules and he had broken them. Not bent. Broken. Under the circumstances, it was an unconscionable thing to have done.

He put his pencil down and took off his glasses. "It looks like I owe you another apology." He stared straight at her, manfully holding her gaze, the fingers of one hand playing with the stems of his glasses. "My behavior just now was entirely inappropriate. I had no business saying what I did to you. I don't know what made me do it."

Well, he did know, of course, but frustrated desire and male ego were no excuse for what he'd said to her. Not that he regretted saying it, exactly. He fully intended to have her lying under him naked and spread-eagle at some not-too-distant point in the future. What he regretted was the time and place he'd imparted that particular bit of information to her. He should have kept everything proper and aboveboard, and waited until their business together was concluded. "I'm sorry if I made you uncomfortable, or frightened you in any way."

"You didn't frighten me," Zoe said, a bit insulted that he would think she was so easily cowed.

"But I did make you uncomfortable, and I'm sorry for that." He was feeling just the tiniest bit satisfied about it, too. More than a bit, actually, but he was far too intelligent, and far too interested in smoothing things over, to acknowledge the feeling out loud. He could pound his chest later, in private. "I hope you can forgive me for that, and I want you to know it won't happen again."

"There's nothing to forgive. Really," Zoe assured him, feeling a prick to her own conscience in the face of his sincerity. There was nothing perfunctory about this apology. He wasn't just mouthing the words to appease his great-grandmother; he meant every one of them. "I'm as much to blame as you are," she confessed contritely. "More to blame, actually." She looked down, fiddling with the rings on her hands, unable to hold his gaze while she made her confession. "I shouldn't have asked you to kiss me. It was unprofessional and stupid."

"Yes, it was," he agreed promptly.

She lifted her gaze to his face again, surprised by his ready agreement with her culpability. She'd have thought he'd be more...well, more gentlemanly and insist on taking the blame entirely upon himself.

"But it was even more stupid for me to have complied with your request," he continued. "This is my office. I know the rules."

"Rules?" Her surprise showed in her voice. And in her eyes. "You have rules about kissing women in your office?"

"It depends on the woman and why she's *in* my office. You came to see me today, in essence, to secure my approval for a loan," he explained, sounding just a bit pompous, even to his own ears. "To treat you with anything less than respect, or to suggest in any way that the withholding or granting of sexual favors might influence my decision, is not only inappropriate and immoral, it's also illegal."

"You didn't suggest any such thing!" Zoe protested, as shocked as if a third party had made the accusation. Her eyes narrowed. "Did you?"

"No, I didn't," he assured her. "What happened here a moment ago was an aberration. An unfortunate lapse of judgment on both our parts. Mine, especially." He leaned forward, as earnest and sincere as a Boy Scout. "I want to be absolutely sure you understand that you will or will not get your investment money *strictly* on the basis of whether I think you're a good risk with a viable business opportunity to offer."

Zoe nodded. "Yes, I understand that. The thought that it would be based on anything else never even crossed my mind. Not for a second," she insisted. "And as long as we're making a clean breast of it here…" She took a quick breath and steeled herself to say what had to be said. "I want *you* to understand that I wasn't trying to influence your decision in my favor by, uh…by seeming to offer you a sexual relationship in exchange for you okaying your great-grandmother's investment in New Moon. I know it might have looked that way because I asked you to kiss me but, believe me, it wasn't.'' She smiled sheepishly. ''The words just kind of—'' she shrugged and made a little fluttery motion with one hand ''—popped out before I knew what I was saying.''

Reed nodded understandingly. ''We're agreed then.'' He slipped his glasses on and picked up his pencil, ready to get back to work. ''Our sexual relationship has absolutely nothing to do with the business at hand.''

Zoe blinked. ''We don't have a sexual relationship,'' she reminded him.

He looked up at her over the top of his glasses, his eyes blazing with a sudden, intense heat. For the split second before he managed to snap the leash on it, she saw the wolf that lay in wait just beneath the surface.

''We will,'' he said.

8

"CAN'T YOU STICK AROUND for just a little while?" Zoe pleaded shamelessly as she followed Gina into the hall between their apartments. "Thirty minutes. Twenty, even. Surely you can spare twenty minutes to help out your best friend since the seventh grade?"

"Nope. Sorry. Not even five," Gina said cheerfully, unmoved by the blatant attempt at manipulation. "I've got a really full schedule today and if I don't get moving in the next two minutes, I'll be running to catch up with myself all day long." She paused at the top of the stairs, the handle of her massage table in one hand, her equipment bag slung over her opposite shoulder, her lips turned up in a sly grin. "If you're so afraid to be alone with him, why don't you ask Mama Marcella to come up while he's here? She'd love to play chaperon for you."

Zoe scowled at her friend. "Very funny. And totally off base," she lied, wondering why she even bothered. Gina had had the really annoying knack of seeing right through her since that first day in the seventh grade. "I'm not looking for a chaperon," she declared, pride demanding that she make the effort to save face, even if Gina wouldn't believe a word of it. "I'm not afraid to be alone with him, either. There's nothing to be afraid *of*."

"Except yourself," Gina said.

Zoe chose to ignore that remark as beneath her. "Reed is coming here on business, so he can see my operation in action," she said primly. "And that's all there is to it."

"Uh-huh." Gina remained unconvinced. "So why do you want me to hang around then?"

"So you can talk me up. Tell him how long you've used New Moon products and how good they are. How you use my different aromatherapy massage oils on all your clients and how much they like them."

"You can tell him that yourself."

"But it would sound so much better coming from you," Zoe wheedled. "He's already heard me say how good my products are at least a dozen times. He needs to hear it from someone else. You know, a real live customer."

"Mama uses New Moon products, too," Gina reminded her. "And old Mrs. Umberto next door, and Michele Soleri at the pizzeria on the corner, and Carleen Purchio at the butcher shop across the street. I'm sure any one of them would be glad to come over here and talk you up." Her grin widened. "Any one of them could make sure you both behave yourselves, too."

Zoe gave it up as a lost cause. "Aren't you late for an appointment?" she snapped, as if she hadn't just been practically begging Gina to stay.

"Not if I leave now," Gina said with a laugh as she turned and headed down the stairs. "Have fun today," she added heartlessly.

Zoe heard the massage table bang against the wall of the stairwell, followed by a colorful Italian curse and the protesting screech of the wrought-iron gate as Gina opened it. Zoe was just about to step into her apartment and check one last time to make sure everything was ready and in order—as if she hadn't checked a hundred times already!—when, unexpectedly, Gina's voice came floating back up the stairs.

"Oh, sure, go right on up," Zoe heard her say, loud enough so that Zoe would be sure to hear. "It's the apartment on the left."

Oh, God, he's here! Zoe felt her stomach clench and her heart leap into her throat, making it difficult to breathe. She swallowed convulsively, trying to clear the obstruction, fighting the instinctive urge to turn and run to the safety of her apartment. She closed her eyes instead, pressing a hand against her chest as if to quiet the wild beating of her heart and took a deep breath, trying to center herself the way she did before her morning yoga sessions. She let the air out of her lungs slowly, all the while telling herself to just calm down and act like a responsible, rational, reasonable businesswoman instead of a silly schoolgirl with a wild crush on the coolest, cutest guy in school.

Reed Sullivan's visit to her apartment this morning was all part of the evaluation process. He wanted to see, firsthand, how she made her skin care products. Wanted to go over the revised business reports—the P&L, the itemized categories and whatever else he deemed it important she have before he made any kind of decision. Wanted to show her how to use the new filing system he'd had set up for her.

Strictly business.

And that was exactly the way she wanted it.

Of course it was.

She couldn't afford to let it be any other way, financially or emotionally. What she had at stake, businesswise, was much more important than what she might have if she let it get personal with him. Especially when she knew that all she'd really have with him was hot sex and the very real possibility of a broken heart and shattered dreams. She was pretty sure that no matter how hot the sex was, it wasn't worth the risk to her heart. She was positive it wasn't worth the risk to her dream of expanding New Moon.

She squared her shoulders and dropped her hand from her chest, smoothing it down the embroidered front of her blouse as if to make sure the soft linen fabric was still neatly tucked into the waistband of her paisley skirt. Not exactly business attire, true, but the eggplant suit was the only item of clothing she owned that fit that description, anyway. Besides, she'd been wearing the very same skirt and blouse when she made her first big sale to The Body Beautiful over on Newbury Street. If the outfit was good enough for her biggest customer, it was certainly good enough for Reed Sullivan.

Plastering a cool, confident, businesslike smile on her face—the one she'd practiced earlier that morning in her bathroom mirror—she stepped forward to greet the man who held her future in his hands. And stopped stock-still as she saw who was ascending the stairs.

"My goodness. Don't move another step until I get there." Zoe hurried down the stairs, her long paisley skirt swirling around her ankles, her bare feet silent on the polished wood, to meet Reed Sullivan's very pregnant secretary halfway. "Let me help you," she said, reaching out to cup the other woman's elbow in one hand as she gathered up a fistful of her skirt with the other to avoid stepping on it as she turned and re-mounted the stairs.

Mary Ellen laughed softly. "Why does everyone insist on treating a pregnant woman as if she were either aged or infirm, or both?'' she asked, tacitly accepting the offered support by leaning into the hand under her elbow.

''Probably because you look like you're about to burst open like that guy in *Aliens,*'' Zoe said, and then slanted her a teasing glance, mixed equally with concern. ''Not to mention the way you're puffing like a steam engine. Are you okay?''

''I'm fine,'' Mary Ellen assured her. ''Just a little out of breath. I haven't climbed many stairs lately.'' She smiled fleetingly and blew a puff of air upward, ruffling the smooth blond bangs that covered her forehead. ''It takes a bit more effort than I thought it would. And if you tell Reed I said that, I'll deny it,'' she warned, only half-humorously. ''He already fusses enough as it is. Almost worse than my husband does.'' She shook her head. ''Drives me crazy.''

''I won't say a word,'' Zoe promised, wondering where Reed was and why he'd sent his secretary in his stead without advising her of the change ahead of time.

It was a bit disappointing. Zoe was proud of what he'd termed her operation, and despite the risks of prolonged contact, she wanted to show it off to him. Somehow it just wouldn't be the same showing it off to his secretary. And besides, secondhand information was never as good as seeing a thing for yourself. How could he be impressed enough to okay Moira Sullivan's investment in New Moon if he didn't see what Zoe had already accomplished without it?

''Reed's parking the car,'' Mary Ellen said, anticipating Zoe's unasked question with the uncanny sixth sense of a really top-notch executive secretary. ''The closest lot he could find was a good five blocks away. He dropped me off out front so I wouldn't have to walk

it. He should be here any minute. In the meantime..."
she paused at the top of the stairs, pressing a hand to
the small of her back as she arched "...I could really
use a bathroom. The baby seems to be sitting right on
top of my bladder this morning."

REED HOOFED IT DOWN Salem Street, briefcase in hand,
his gait easy but purposeful, congratulating himself on
the brilliantly simple strategy of bringing M.E. along
to his meeting with Zoe. It wasn't that he was actually
worried about being alone with Zoe in her apartment,
but with M.E. along to chaperon, he wouldn't even
have to think about the possibility—remote though it
was, he assured himself—of giving in to temptation
again.

And anyway, M.E. would be of real use. She could
certainly explain the filing system to Zoe better than
he could, since she had actually been the one to set it
up. She could take any notes that might be necessary
about Zoe's existing methods of operation, and she'd
have a chance to sit down for more than fifteen minutes
at a time. Besides, if providing M.E. the opportunity to
sit down meant she'd also be available to provide that
little extra impetus he needed to keep things on a completely business-like basis with him and Zoe Moon, so
much the better. He was a great proponent of killing
two birds with one stone.

Which was exactly what he was doing, he told himself, when he let the smell of fresh baked goods lure
him into the open door of a bakery half a block down
from Zoe's apartment. M.E. had a fondness for pineapple Danish. Zoe had evidenced a weakness for croissants. And he hadn't had breakfast. Which made *three*
birds with one stone.

A propitious start to the day, he thought with satisfaction, despite the fact that the reason he hadn't had
breakfast was because he'd been too distracted by the
upcoming meeting with Zoe to take more than a bite
or two of the fluffy egg white omelet his housekeeper
had prepared that morning. A sorry state of affairs, but
there it was. Just thinking about the delectable Miss
Moon put him off his feed. And that had *never* happened before, not even when he was breaking his adolescent heart over the perfidy of Janice Hawkins. He
didn't even want to venture a guess as to what it might
mean.

The bakery was crowded with customers, the air inside fragrant with the yeasty smell of warm bread and
sugary, cream-filled cakes and pastries. Reed took his
place in line at the counter alongside two women conversing in an animated mix of English and Italian about
the merits of the ricotta-filled tubes of *cannoli* versus
the chocolate covered *cassata*. By the time his turn
came he was debating the wisdom of adding a couple
of rich, calorie laden delicacies to his own order.

"Zoe is very fond of almond *biscotti* with her morning coffee," one of the women said as he hesitated over
his selection.

Reed broke off his perusal of the pastries to look at
her. She was plump and grandmotherly, with iron gray
hair peeking out from beneath the edge of a flowered
scarf tied under her double chin, and the most beautiful
dark eyes he'd ever seen looking at him out of a face
networked with hundreds of tiny wrinkles. The top of
her head barely reached his breastbone.

"Beg pardon, ma'am." he said. "Were you speaking to me?"

"Yes, certainly, I am speaking to you," she said in

heavily accented English. "You are the same man who brought Zoe home last Saturday, yes?"

"Yes, I am," he said, wondering if this might be Zoe's surrogate grandmother. The one who was none too pleased about his having hired a private investigator. "Are you Mrs. Molinari?"

The old woman chuckled, as if she sensed his trepidation. "No. I am Signora Umberto, from the dry cleaners next door to the *ristorante*." She flicked a hand in the direction of the woman standing beside her. "This is my granddaughter, Claudia."

Claudia glanced over her shoulder, acknowledging the introduction with a smile and a nod. "Pleasure," she murmured before turning back to the teenager behind the pastry counter.

"And your name is?" Signora Umberto demanded, tapping Reed on the arm to regain his full attention.

Reed reached out and took her hand in his. "Reed Sullivan, ma'am," he said. "It's a pleasure to meet you."

A wide, delighted smile split her face, deepening the web of wrinkles she wore. "Oh, such a nice boy. Such lovely manners." She lifted her other hand to capture his between her palms, patting it approvingly as she spoke. "I knew you would be a nice boy from the first time I saw you."

"When you saw me?" Reed questioned, wondering where all this was leading.

"When you brought our Zoe home," she reminded him. "By chance only, I happened to glance out the window—" she hunched a shoulder, pointedly ignoring the derisive snort that came from her granddaughter, who was now counting out dollar bills on top of the counter to pay for their purchases. "By chance only," Signora Umberto repeated. "I happened to glance out my window when you brought the girls home last Saturday, so I remember you. You drive a very fancy car. Very expensive." She slid one hand up his forearm and grasped the sleeve of his suit jacket, rubbing the material between her thumb and forefinger. "Nice suit. Good wool. Very expensive. That is very good." She patted his hand again. "You can afford to give Zoe the money for her company—" she jerked her chin for emphasis "—yes?"

"Nonna!" Claudia turned from the counter to glare at her grandmother. "You can't go around asking strangers questions about money. It's not polite."

"Pah! Polite! When you are my age you don't worry so much about polite. If you are polite no one tells you nothing." She waved a dismissive hand. "Mind your own business, Claudia," she ordered, and looked back up at Reed, her beautiful black eyes bright, inquisitive and amused.

He couldn't help but smile. He had a definite soft spot for spunky old ladies, and this one was a pistol.

"So." She poked him in the arm with a stubby finger. "Are you going to give our Zoe the money for her company?"

"Well, actually," Reed hedged, unconsciously using the same gentle but evasive tone he used with Moira when she was demanding answers to questions he didn't want to answer, "nothing's been decided yet."

"What is to decide?" Signora Umberto demanded. "Zoe makes good beauty creams and lotions. The best. I know this for a fact. I have been using the cream in the little glass jar for three years now." She lifted the hand she still held to her face. "Feel," she ordered, flattening his fingers to her cheek. "As soft as a young girl, yes?"

"Yes, it's very soft," he said, wondering if it was the result of Zoe's cream or just the way a woman's skin felt, no matter what her age or the number of wrinkles she wore.

"It is settled then, yes?" She gave his hand another approving pat before releasing it. "You will give Zoe the money?"

"Perhaps," he said, unwilling to commit himself further. "Things are still in the investigative stages."

"Ah, pah!" Signora Umberto snorted derisively, than narrowed her eyes, glaring at him for a long moment before turning to follow her granddaughter out of the bakery.

ZOE'S APARTMENT WAS VERY like her—exotic, colorful, sensual, and inviting—Reed decided ten minutes later. The floor was pale bleached wood, bare except for the fringed square of faded jade green carpet that defined the living area. The walls were palest lavender, so light as to be a mere wash of color over a white base coat. The furnishings were eclectic: a white, wood-framed, futon-style sofa meant to be turned into a bed with minimum effort, piled high with plump pillows; an intricately carved Chinese chest used as a coffee table; a distressed Country French armoire; an art deco floor lamp in the shape of an elongated dolphin with a frosted while globe balanced on its nose; a pair of Regency-style chairs with curved wooden arms and yellow floral upholstery on the seats and backs. A modern, free-form glass bowl with swirling ribbons of color that echoed and reflected those in the room sat atop the

Chinese chest, sharing space with an elegant, un-matched pair of old silver candlesticks.

It shouldn't have worked, but it did, all the disparate parts coming together in a pleasing, intriguing whole, like Zoe herself.

Reed stood silently just inside the open door of the apartment, admiring the room and the women in it, wondering how long it would be, exactly, before the two of them realized they weren't alone. They sat perched atop a pair of white wrought-iron stools placed in front of the counter that separated the tiny kitchen area from the rest of the apartment. Their backs were to the door, heads together over the various small jars and bottles spread out in front of them, totally oblivious to his presence.

They were quite a study in contrasts. M.E. in her classic navy suit and practical, low-heeled pumps, her gold button earrings and smooth blond bob, looked sleek, polished and professional, despite her advanced pregnancy. Zoe looked more like a gypsy than ever, slim and colorful and exotic—but somehow bewitch-ingly wholesome, too—in a soft white blouse tucked into a flowing skirt, the heels of her bare feet braced on the bottom rung of her stool and her flame-colored curls tumbling freely down her back.

He wondered briefly if he should teach the two a small lesson concerning the importance of keeping doors closed and locked, but decided that a fright prob-ably wouldn't be good for a woman so far along with child. He rapped gently on the doorframe instead.

"Hello, ladies," he said pleasantly when they both started and glanced around. "Waiting for someone?"

Zoe jumped down from her stool and hurried across the room, trying hard not to appear any happier to see him than she had Mary Ellen. "Reed," she said, ignoring her sudden breathlessness and the funny way her heart was beating, wondering when and how a man in a double-breasted suit had managed to become her yardstick for measuring masculine attractiveness. "I didn't hear you buzz. How did you get in?"

"The gate at the bottom of the stairs was propped open with a brick," he said pointedly, letting his disapproval of such lax security show. "*Anyone* could have gotten in."

"Your neighbor did that," Mary Ellen said to Zoe as she carefully shifted around on her stool to face the door and her employer. "So you could get in as soon as you got here," she explained, looking at Reed. "I told her you'd only be a few minutes." Her glance flickered down to the white paper bag in his hand. "Is that a bakery sack?" she asked hopefully.

"It is," he said, advancing across the room as he spoke. After a quick, comprehensive glance at the cheerful clutter of bottles and jars that littered the counter, he set his briefcase on the stool Zoe had vacated and rested the bakery sack on top of it. "I thought we could have coffee and a little something to fortify us before we got on to the business at hand." He looked at Zoe as he spoke, the rising note of the last word making it a polite question, guest to hostess. "I know it's been at least a couple of hours since M.E. had breakfast, and she's eating for two, you know—" his glance flickered teasingly to his secretary for a moment, but his attention never really left Zoe "—so she's always hungry."

"Sounds good. I can always eat, too. Unfortunately." Zoe started to pat her hip, then checked in midmotion, curling her fingers into her palm as his eyes followed the fluttering gesture. Something in his expression—a sudden avid interest, an instant, all-too-gratifying heat—had her hurriedly slipping around the end of the counter into the tiny kitchen.

She turned her back to him, reaching up to open the cupboard that housed her motley collection of cups and saucers. It took a good thirty seconds of rattling china for the heat in her cheeks to cool.

"The coffee's already made," she said finally, glancing over her shoulder at Mary Ellen as if she were the only other person in the room. "It's full octane, I'm afraid." She arranged the cups and saucers on a lacquered wooden tray as she spoke. "I don't have any decaf. But there's skim milk or orange juice. I'd offer to make some herbal tea but I've only got two burners and, well..." She gestured toward the small stove where two large, shiny, stainless steel pots sat simmering over very low flames. A cloud of fragrant steam rose off the surface of each, perfuming the air with the fresh clean scent of wildflowers and herbs. "I'm making hand lotion and it's kind of at a critical stage right now."

"Skim milk will be fine, thank you," Mary Ellen assured her, her eyes focused on the pastry bag on Reed's briefcase. "What goodies did you bring?" she demanded of her boss.

Reed opened the bag, holding it up to her nose so she could sniff. "Pineapple Danish," he said, pulling the bag away as she reached for it. "Blueberry muffins and—" He craned his neck to look at Zoe, who'd hunkered behind the counter to rummage around in a low cupboard "—almond *biscotti*," he announced, so pleased with himself that she could almost hear the "ta da" in his voice.

Zoe looked up from her crouched position, not quite meeting his gaze over the edge of the counter. "How did you know I like almond *biscotti*?"

"I ran into a friend of yours at the bakery."

Zoe cocked her head, sending a stray corkscrew curl tumbling into her face. She brushed it back with a careless flick of her hand and returned to burrowing through the contents of the lower cupboard. "A friend of mine?"

"Signora Umberto." He managed to roll the name off his tongue in a close approximation of the Signora's thick Italian accent. "I'm not sure, but I think she gave me the evil eye."

Zoe rose to her feet and set a lacquered wooden tray on the counter, carefully edging the clutter of small glass jars and bottles out of the way. "Signora Umberto gave you the evil eye?" she asked, still not looking directly at him as she stretched across the counter to reach the nested stack of baskets sitting on the other side.

Reed manfully averted his gaze, trying not to notice how the gauzy white fabric of her blouse dipped away from her body as she leaned across the counter. "She wasn't thrilled to hear that I'm not quite ready to hand you a blank check to finance the expansion of New Moon," he said, deliberately refocusing his gaze on her hands as she lined a small basket with a pale yellow napkin.

Her hands stilled. "Oh, dear," she murmured.

He lifted his gaze to her face to find her looking at him, head tilted, eyebrows raised, bottom lip captured between her teeth, an expression of half-amused consternation in her big brown eyes.

"I hope she wasn't too terribly rude to you."

"Not at all," Reed said, wishing he could lean over and salve that plump bitten lip with his tongue. "Merely, uh..." he hesitated deliberately, drawing it out, ridiculously delighted to finally have her full, undivided attention "...opinionated."

Zoe felt the tension flow out of her as the laughter bubbled up. "Something tells me you're being diplomatic," she said approvingly and leaned over the counter again, accidentally affording him another peek at her pale peach-colored bra and generous cleavage as she plucked the white bakery sack out of his hand. "Signora Umberto has been known to terrorize the neighborhood with her *opinions*."

This time he didn't even try to avert his eyes. After all, her cleavage *was* spectacular and he was only looking. Looking couldn't hurt—as long as he didn't get caught.

"She's a tough old dame, all right," he said, deliberately shifting his gaze from her cleavage to watch the graceful flutter of her hands as she shifted the pastries from the bag to the napkin-lined basket and arranged the charmingly mismatched cups and saucers on the wooden tray. "I liked her." His lips quirked up in a smile. "She reminded me of another tough old dame I know."

Zoe looked up from under her lashes, her eyes twinkling. "Is that any way to talk about a lovely, refined woman like your great-granny?" she asked, shaking her head in mock reprimand. "And behind her back, too."

"Not behind her back," Reed objected, his own eyes alight with an answering gleam as he sparred with her. "I've told her that straight to her face. On more than one occasion, I might add. She was flattered."

Zoe snorted. ''I'll bet,'' she scoffed, and turned away to get the skim milk out of the refrigerator. ''More than likely, she was just humoring you.''

''I'll have you know, Miss Moon, that Moira Sullivan never humors anyone. She's a—''

''Tough old dame. I know.'' Zoe poured the milk into a footed amethyst glass and added it to the tray along with a flowered cream pitcher and sugar bowl.

''Grab the pot, will you, please, Reed?'' she asked, nodding toward the coffeemaker as she lifted the tray. ''I'll take this over to the living room so we can all sit down and eat where it's more comfortable and less crowded.''

The coffeemaker was next to the tiny sink, behind her. Reed came around the dividing counter to get the pot just as Zoe moved forward with the tray. There was a minor traffic jam as they met in the narrow bottleneck between the minuscule kitchen and the rest of the apartment. Zoe smiled and turned sideways, her back to him, the tray held high, her hips pressed lightly to the counter in front of her to let him squeeze past.

He had plenty of room, more than enough to pass without touching her, but he just couldn't let the opportunity go by. It was, quite simply, beyond his ability to resist when giving in to temptation offered so few risks. He reached out and put his hands on her hips, very lightly, bracketing them between his palms as he slid around behind and then past her. The contact lasted only a few seconds and was, on the surface, entirely innocent.

Still, Reed's palms felt seared by the all-too-brief encounter.

Zoe would have sworn the imprint of his hands was burned into her skin.

Both of them stubbornly ignored the sensation of heat, pretending nothing had happened. Because nothing, they each assured themselves, *had* happened. Nothing they were prepared to do anything about, anyway.

Not yet.

Zoe moved across the room and set the tray down on the Chinese chest. Reed picked up the coffeepot, grabbed a brass trivet from a hook by the stove and followed her. Mary Ellen sat perched on her stool, stock-still, her eyes wide and round as she looked back and forth between the two of them.

Reed set the trivet on the Chinese chest and placed the coffeepot on top of it, lowering himself to the futon sofa beside Zoe as he did so.

Mary Ellen cleared her throat. Loudly.

Reed glanced toward the sound. It seemed to take him a moment to remember who she was. "Oh. Sorry, M.E." He jumped up from the sofa and crossed back to the counter, his hand graciously extended. "Are you all right? Do you need some help getting down from there?"

"I'm fine. Just a little backache is all. It's nothing." She put her hand in his, letting him steady her as she slid from the stool, and then held him there for a moment, looking up at him with a half-amused, half-concerned expression on her face. "Are *you* okay?" she asked, her voice hushed and low.

"Yes, of course. I'm fine," Reed said, automatically lowering his voice in response. "Why do you ask?"

"Because I've worked for you for eight years and I've never seen this side of you before."

"What side is that?" he asked, his attention already

wandering back to the sofa where Zoe sat pouring out two cups of coffee.

"You're always such a perfect gentleman."

"Yes," he said, watching as Zoe stirred one spoonful of sugar into his cup. "So?"

"So, with her you aren't."

That got his full attention. His gaze snapped back to his secretary's upturned face. "I beg your pardon?"

"You looked down her blouse, Reed. Twice."

He opened his mouth to deny it, found he couldn't and closed it again, hoping to hell he wasn't blushing.

"Don't worry. She didn't notice," she assured him. "I wouldn't have noticed, either, except that I know you so well and you've been acting so strangely lately."

"Strangely how?"

"Let's just say, if you'd ever once looked at your fiancée the way you look at her—" she tilted her head toward their hostess "—you wouldn't still be Boston's most eligible bachelor." She grinned when he scowled at her. "Face it, boss. You're smitten. Big time." She reached up, giving his cheek a motherly little pat, much the way Signora Umberto had done in the bakery. "I think it's sweet," she said, and stepped around him, leaving him standing there, feeling like a fumbling schoolboy and wondering where all his *savoir-faire* had gone.

Smitten, was he? Well, okay, that was as good a word as any. Better than some. She could have said besotted. Or obsessed. Smitten wasn't so bad. He could live with smitten. *But business first,* he reminded himself sternly, reaching up to smooth his tie with the flat of his hand. Smitten or not, there would be no more lapses. No more sneaking peeks down the front of her blouse. No more letting himself get distracted by her smile, or the graceful way she used her hands, or the way the sunlight coming in through the window turned her hair to fire or—

"Reed, would you please pull that chair a little closer to the table so M.E. doesn't have to reach so far?" Zoe asked as he approached the table.

"Yes. Certainly." He put his hands on the back of the graceful Regency chair and shifted it closer to the Chinese chest. "M.E.?" he said, holding it steady for her.

Mary Ellen leaned back, putting both hands on the arms of the chair, sending a pointed little smile at him over her shoulder as she lowered herself into the seat.

Reed just as pointedly ignored it.

"Tell me about your operation," he said to Zoe, as he seated himself on the futon sofa beside their hostess, absently reaching out to accept the cup of coffee she offered. "I want to know everything about how you make your cosmetics. Walk me through each step from beginning to— Marbles?" he said, his attention suddenly caught by the contents of the free-form glass bowl sitting on one end of the large chest. He set the cup and saucer back on the lacquered wooden tray with an audible click. "May I?" he asked, his hand already hovering over the bowl.

"Be my guest," Zoe invited, glad to have a few extra moments to gather her scattered thoughts before she tried to answer his questions about New Moon. "Everything" was pretty all-encompassing. She stirred cream into her coffee and then sat with the cup forgotten, cradled in her hands, as she watched Reed sift through the contents of the glass bowl like a man on a mission.

He'd scooted to the edge of the futon sofa and leaned forward, forefinger extended to explore through the jumbled marbles. The eclectic assortment was a small boy's dream and a collector's nightmare. Mixed in with the mostly machine-made clearies, slags and various swirls and cat's-eyes were some fine handmade examples of the marble-making art. A cursory inspection yielded a Joseph's Coat swirl, an End of Day onionskin and a banded lutz, any one of which could be worth two hundred dollars or more in mint condition, which was highly unlikely given the way they were jumbled together. He plucked one of the tiny glass spheres from the bowl to examine it more closely. It was about an inch in diameter, opaque white with two wide, swirling bands of blue and six narrow pink bands, grouped by threes.

"Did you know this is a very rare peppermint swirl?" he asked, holding it up to the bright sunlight shining in through the window.

"Rare how?" Zoe asked, her gaze on his face rather than the marble, intrigued by the look in his eyes. She'd seen the same avid expression on the faces of the neighborhood boys when they hunkered down after a cutthroat game of potsies to count up the marbles they'd won from each other.

"See the glittery bits of mica in the blue bands?" He slid her a sideways glance to make sure she was paying attention.

She hurriedly shifted her gaze to the object in question. "Yes, I see them." She lifted her coffee cup to her lips as she spoke. "Very pretty," she said, and sipped.

"If it were in mint condition this little beauty would

be worth somewhere between seven-fifty and fifteen hundred dollars.''

Zoe nearly choked on her coffee. ''Fifteen hundred dollars? For a *marble*?''

''In mint condition,'' he clarified. ''Which means it's never been used. This one would be graded good at best because of all the hit marks and tiny chips. It's probably worth, oh, somewhere around three hundred, maybe a little more or less depending on the collector and how badly he wants it.'' He flashed her a wolfish grin. ''I'll give you three-fifty for it.''

Zoe shook her head; he couldn't be serious. ''I got most of those marbles at a flea market up in New Hampshire a couple of years ago.'' She leaned forward and set her coffee cup back in its saucer. ''I think I paid three dollars for a jar this big.'' She held her hands about eight inches apart to illustrate.

''You got yourself a bargain, then. There are several marbles in there—'' he gestured at the bowl ''—worth three times that, at least.''

Zoe quickly did the math in her head. ''Okay, nine dollars for a marble I can believe. Barely.'' She shook her head again. ''But you can't seriously expect me to believe you'd pay three hundred and fifty dollars for one, no matter what condition it's in.''

''A few years ago a collector at the Philadelphia MarbleFest Auction paid nearly seven thousand dollars for a peppermint swirl. It was larger than this one,'' he hastened to assure her. ''Nearly two inches in diameter, which is extremely rare. And it was in near mint condition, with an odd number of pink bands—five instead of the more usual four or six. But it didn't have mica.''

He held the marble up to the light again, rolling it between his thumb and forefinger to examine it from all sides, watching as the sunlight glittered off the flecks of mica.

"I've got a weakness for the glittery ones," he admitted, thinking of the Indian lutz he carried in his pocket. "I'll give you three-seventy-five."

"Well, gee, I don't know," Zoe drawled, as if she actually believed he was serious. "Maybe I ought to have it appraised first to make sure I'm not being taken to the cleaners."

"Okay, four hundred, but that's as high as I'll go."

Zoe laughed. "Really, Reed, I'm not trying to drive the price up. I was only teasing. If you want it, take it. My gift."

Reed put the marble back in the bowl. "That's a very kind offer, but no, thank you. I couldn't accept a gift from you."

"I don't see why not. After all you're doing for...ahh," she said, as comprehension dawned. "It's those pesky rules again, isn't it?"

"Rules?" Mary Ellen said, looking back and forth between them.

"The unwritten ones governing what can and can't go on between a man and a woman who are doing business together," Zoe explained without taking her eyes off Reed. "He's afraid if he takes the marble it will look like he accepted a bribe or something in exchange for recommending that Moira make an investment in New Moon."

"A man and a woman who are *contemplating* doing business together," Reed reminded her, ignoring the second half of her statement. His gaze held Zoe's as he spoke. "What happens after we do or do not strike a deal is another matter entirely."

"Yes, well...we'll see," she said with a shrug, trying to sound unaffected by what they both knew he meant.

"We don't have a sexual relationship."

"Yet."

She shifted, turning sideways, trying to put a little more space between them without looking as if she were backing away. She bent her right knee, bringing it up on the sofa as she resettled, turning so that her bare foot dangled over the edge. She waggled it nervously.

"How about if we lag for it?" she suggested brightly, eyes downcast as she busily smoothed the bright paisley fabric of her skirt over her lap.

"Lag?" His gaze drifted down to her bobbing foot. It was small and slim and very white, with a high, elegant arch. Her toenails were painted the same coppery color as her fingertips. She was wearing a delicate gold bracelet around her ankle, and a narrow gold ring on her second toe. He didn't know any other woman who wore an ankle bracelet, let alone a toe ring. Not one that he'd ever seen, anyway. His imagination suddenly shifted into overdrive as he wondered where else she might wear body jewelry. His eyes glazed over as he considered all the intriguing possibilities.

"You know. Lag," Zoe said, still industriously smoothing her skirt to avoid having to look at him. "The way you do to determine who goes first in a game." Her hand stilled in her lap. "You have *played* with marbles, haven't you? You don't just collect them?" She lifted her gaze to his face. "Reed?"

He gave himself a mental shake and replayed the words she'd just said, damping down the image of her nude but for the rings on her fingers and toes and...other places.

"Yes, I've played with marbles," he said, with an attempt at dignity. "That's how I got started collecting them."

"Okay, then, we'll lag for it. If I win, you take the peppermint swirl as a gift. If you win, I let you buy it from me for three hundred dollars." She was already gathering her skirt up, bunching the excess fabric in one hand as she slid to the floor. "Deal?"

"Four hundred," he countered recklessly, his eyes on her bare, rounded knees and the narrow sliver of thigh she'd inadvertently revealed, "and you've got yourself a deal."

"You're on," Zoe crowed, already envisioning herself the winner.

Mary Ellen watched in openmouthed amazement as her boss hitched up the legs of his impeccably tailored, navy worsted slacks and got down on his knees beside their hostess to lag marbles. She would have liked to see the outcome of the contest, but the nagging ache in her lower back suddenly moved front and center with a surprising amount of force.

"Uh...excuse me," she said softly, too low to be heard over their squabbling about where the lag line should be and just exactly what distance they should each shoot from. Reed was all for allowing a handicap on account of gender. Zoe was insulted by the implication that she was a less accomplished player just because she was a girl.

"Excuse me," Mary Ellen said again, a bit louder. They still didn't hear her.

Zoe was insisting that, as her guest, Reed should shoot first.

Reed was determined to be a gentleman and let her precede him.

"Hey, you two!"

That got their attention. They turned their heads in perfect unison, cheek-to-cheek, both of them on their knees, looking over their shoulders at her with nearly the same expression of irritation, astonishment and inquiry.

"I hate to interrupt your contest," Mary Ellen said contritely, "but I think I'm about to start my maternity leave."

9

"MATERNITY LEAVE?" Reed said politely, hoping he'd heard wrong.

"I'm sorry, boss," Mary Ellen offered the apology with a sheepish shrug and a wry smile, "but I'm pretty sure I'm in labor." She pressed her hands against her distended abdomen. "Make that I'm *positive* I'm in labor."

"But you aren't due for three weeks yet," he objected.

She almost managed another insouciant shrug, but stopped midmotion and gasped softly, hunching over a little.

"Oh my God. She's in labor." Zoe surged to her feet. "I'll call 911. No, a taxi. I'll get a taxi. A taxi would probably get us there quicker. But an ambulance would have medical personnel in case she needs it." She ricocheted around the tiny apartment like a loose marble shot across a hardwood floor, her skirt swirling around her ankles as she ran from the phone to the door and back to the phone again, unable to decide the best course of action. "I'd better call 911."

Telling himself not to give in to panic, Reed rose to his feet and calmly took control of the situation. "Can you stand?" he asked solicitously, bending over his secretary as he spoke.

Mary Ellen nodded gamely.

"Then let's get you and that baby to the hospital."
He cupped his hand under her elbow. "Just take it
slow," he instructed as he helped her to her feet. "Nice
and easy. No need to hurry. There's plenty of time,"
he said soothingly, as much to reassure himself as her.
"Plenty of time."

He almost lost his grip on Mary Ellen when she doubled over and wrapped her arms around her stomach.
"I think it's coming *now*."

Reed could feel himself starting to sweat. "It can't
be coming now, M.E.." His voice was still soothing,
still calmly reassuring, still I'm-in-complete-control-of-
the-situation, despite his inner agitation. "First babies
take a long time to get born, remember? You told me
that yourself."

"*Now*," she repeated, and started panting like an
over-heated pug.

"Nine-one-one isn't answering." Zoe slammed the
telephone receiver into its cradle and whirled back toward the door. "I'll get a taxi."

"Forget the taxi," Reed said, the authority in his
voice halting her in midmotion. He dug into the pocket
of his slacks with his free hand. "Take my keys." He
tossed them to her. "I'm parked in the lot next to a
florist about five blocks down the street. Marie Something with a blue striped awning. I'll get M.E. down
the stairs while you get the car."

"Marie's Flower Shoppe." Zoe was already heading
for the door as she spoke. "I know the one you mean."

"Shoes," he said, halting her again.

She made an abrupt about-face, skittered across the
floor in her bare feet, yanked open the armoire and
grabbed the first footwear that came to hand.

"And don't forget your purse," he added as she

stomped into a pair of lipstick-red cowboy boots. "You'll need your driver's license and cash to get the car out of the lot."

Zoe grabbed her purse from the coat stand by the door and raced down the stairs and up the street to the parking lot. By the time she'd paid for the car, maneuvered it out of the lot and circled back around the five blocks to the front of her building, her hands were shaking and sweaty—both from nervousness about driving the hideously expensive Jaguar and worry that Mary Ellen would have the baby before they could get her to the hospital.

But Reed and Mary Ellen were both upright, standing on the curb, waiting for her. True, Mary Ellen looked a little flushed and frazzled, but Reed...well, even as preoccupied as she was with the crisis at hand, Zoe couldn't help but notice that Reed still looked like an ad in the glossy pages of *GQ*. It really shouldn't have set her heart to fluttering—especially under the circumstances—but it did.

It took both of them to lower Mary Ellen into the back seat of the car and then, just as they got her settled—half sitting, half lying down on the supple, pale gray leather—her water broke, flooding the upholstery and carpet with pink-tinged fluid.

Zoe began to dither again. "I'll get some towels. Should I go back upstairs and get some towels?"

"Forget the towels," Reed ordered in a voice that permitted no argument, even if she was inclined to make one. Which she wasn't. "You get in back and hold her hand. I'll drive."

And drive he did. He somehow managed to avoid attracting the attention of Boston's finest, despite his flagrant disregard of the speed limit and the two red lights he ran, and got them to the emergency room entrance of Massachusetts General Hospital in record time. He managed to call the hospital on the way, too—he'd had the number stored in the memory banks of his cell phone for months—to alert them to the imminent arrival of the incoming patient. A nurse met them at the curb with a wheelchair.

"It's going to be all right now, M.E.," Reed said, leaning into the back seat to help her out of the car. "These people know what to do. They'll take good care of you."

Mary Ellen grabbed his elegant, striped silk tie and yanked his face down to hers. "Call John," she growled, sounding like a cross between a wounded lioness and a frightened kitten. "I want John."

Without missing a beat or wasting precious time trying to disengage his tie from her clutching fingers, Reed retrieved his cell phone from an inside pocket of his suit jacket, hit a single button—he'd had the man's office number programmed in memory for months, too—and called her husband. It was only after Reed had made the connection and handed the phone to her that Mary Ellen let go of his tie.

She had the phone pressed to her ear as the nurse wheeled her down the hall toward the elevators that would take her upstairs to the maternity ward. As the doors slid closed she could be heard alternately declaring her undying love for her husband, cussing him out for getting her into her current predicament, and exhorting him to hurry to the hospital before his son was born.

Reed and Zoe were left standing in the hospital corridor, feeling rather superfluous—and glad of it.

"Well." Zoe expelled a huge, heartfelt sigh. "I'm

glad that's over. I didn't think we were going to make it in time.''

"Neither did I," Reed admitted.

Zoe shifted her gaze from the elevator doors to his face. "Really? But you were so cool about the whole thing. So confident. You knew exactly what to do, while I was running around like a chicken with my head cut off.''

"Self-preservation," he said. "I've been scared to death she'd go into labor in the office so I read up on it, just in case." The corners of his mouth quirked in a wry, self-deprecating smile. "When she doubled over like that, believe me, all I wanted to do was turn tail and run. And when her water broke..." He shuddered. "Neither I nor my car will ever be the same."

"Scared to death, huh?" Zoe tilted her head, giving him a long, considering look from under her lashes. "You don't look as if you were scared to death. You don't even look as if you were very much worried. You *do* look a little rumpled, though." She reached up as she spoke, adjusting the knot of his tie with one hand, smoothing down the length of the silky fabric with the other. "There, all better now." She smiled teasingly and gave his chest a friendly little pat. "You're restored to perfection. No one will ever know—"

He reached up and captured her hands, trapping them against his shirtfront with his, trapping her voice in her throat. She forgot whatever it was she'd been going to say and just stood there, transfixed, staring up at him in the middle of the busy hospital corridor. It was, suddenly, as if they were alone. As if there was no one else in the world. In the universe. She could feel his heart beating under her palms, steady and strong. She could feel his fingers, warm and hard, against the backs of her hands. She could feel the heat of his gaze caressing every curling tendril of her hair, every curve and angle of her face as if he had never seen a woman before and wanted to memorize every nuance of her appearance in case he never saw one again.

Fantasies were running rampant through his mind, as they seemed to do when she was near. Fantasies of her soft, slender hands with their painted nails and flashing rings, caressing the bare skin of his chest. Her wild corkscrew curls fanned out across his pillow. Her eyes half-closed in ecstasy as she gazed up at him. Her luscious, bee-stung mouth, moist and ready for his kisses. It seemed as if all he had to do was be near her...look at her...breathe in that heady combination of old-fashioned violets and heated sensuality that was so uniquely her, and everything he'd ever learned about good manners and civilized behavior vanished in a maelstrom of rampaging hormones. It didn't seem to matter where they were, or with whom; one look and he wanted to reach out and touch...taste...take.

Known for his cool self-possession and sangfroid, Reed found his reaction decidedly disconcerting. And wildly exciting. No other woman—ever—had made him so hot.

"You're driving me crazy, do you know that?" he whispered, his voice low and throaty and intimate. "You are the most—"

"Well, for goodness sake, if it isn't Reed Sullivan. Look who's here, Aunt Katherine. It's Reed."

Reed blinked once, slowly, as if he were coming out of a trance, and turned his head toward the speaker.

Oh, no. No, wait, Zoe thought a bit frantically. *Wait. I'm the most what?*

"My eyesight is still as good as it ever was," snapped the woman addressed as Aunt Katherine.

Aunt Katherine was obviously a contemporary of Moira's, both in age and status. She was wearing an elegant wool suit with a large cameo broach adorning the lapel, and from the crook of her arm dangled a classic Chanel handbag that matched to her suit and shoes exactly. She leaned lightly on a gold-headed cane.

"I can see very well for myself who it is." She inclined her head very slightly in greeting, her manner as supercilious as a dowager queen who'd just caught one of her courtiers dallying in the hall with a chambermaid. "Good morning, Reed."

Reed released Zoe's hands and stepped back from her. "Aunt Katherine." There was a slight stutter, a tiny hesitation in his usual suavity as he uttered the name. "What a surprise to see you here."

"Yes." Something that might have been humor flashed in her eyes for a moment as she glanced back and forth between him and Zoe. "I imagine it is."

"I trust you're not here to see one of the doctors in a professional capacity," Reed said solicitously, hoping to avoid an interrogation, knowing it was impossible. There was nothing Katherine Hightower liked better than interrogating people.

"Certainly not," she said, insulted. "You know very well I am never ill."

"We've been talking to the hospital administrator about the final arrangements for this year's charity fund-raiser. It's in two weeks, you know," said Katherine's companion. She was a younger, far less vivid version of her autocratic aunt, more aging East Coast preppie than Boston aristocrat. "We're holding it at the

Isabella Stewart Gardner Museum. It's going to be quite grand this year. A lovely dinner in the Tapestry Room, with musicians from the Boston Symphony for dancing and a silent auction running throughout the ev—''

"Oh, do stop blathering, Margaret." Katherine rapped her cane against the floor. Margaret jumped. "He knows all about it. He's on the board of directors of the hospital and I'm sure the event has been marked on his calendar for months. If it hasn't, it certainly should have been." She pinned Reed with a sharp look. "We'll be expecting you early to stand in the receiving line with the other directors. Now—" she transferred her gaze to Zoe "—introduce this young woman to me."

"I'm sorry, I should have done that immediately," Reed apologized.

"You certainly should have," Katherine snapped.

"Aunt Katherine, Margaret—" he smiled charmingly at each woman as he spoke her name "—may I present Miss Zoe Moon. Zoe, Katherine and Margaret Hightower."

Margaret offered a toothy smile.

Katherine nodded her head imperiously. "Which one of you is ill?" she said.

"Ill?" Zoe echoed.

"We're standing in the hall outside the emergency room, are we not? And it looks as if Reed was attending to some small…" Katherine hesitated slightly, a grand master of the fine art of social interrogation "…hurt." She glanced down at Zoe's hands, which were still clasped together in front of her. "Have you injured your hand, Miss Moon?"

Manfully, Reed stepped into the breach, putting himself in the line of fire. "No one is ill or hurt, Aunt Katherine," he said, saving Zoe from having to find an answer for the nosy old gorgon. "We were in the middle of a meeting when my secretary went into labor. Miss Moon and I drove her to the hospital, and now we're waiting until her husband arrives before we leave."

"Business meeting?" Katherine's eyes widened slightly, the better to take in Zoe's wild mass of hair, her gauzy embroidered blouse, her long paisley skirt in shades of purple and gold, her bright-red cowboy boots. She didn't have to say a word to express her skepticism; it was there in every aristocratic line of her body.

Zoe lifted her chin and stared back blandly, stifling the urge to drop her head and shuffle her feet like a kid who'd been sent to the principal's office. What business was it of this imperious old woman how she dressed? she thought rebelliously.

"Yes, a business meeting," Reed said firmly. "Miss Moon is a client. She's the president and CEO of a very successful new cosmetics firm here in Boston. We've been discussing the possibility of expanding her business to the national level. Uh..." He glanced toward the doors of the emergency room as they whooshed open. "It looks as if the father-to-be has finally arrived. If you'll excuse us?" He put an arm behind Zoe's back, preparatory to escorting her toward the exit. "I need to have a quick word with him before we head back to the office."

"It was a pleasure to meet you both," Zoe said over her shoulder as Reed shepherded her toward safety. She heard the thump of Katherine Hightower's cane against the linoleum floor as they made their getaway.

The aforementioned quick word with the anxious father-to-be was indeed very quick, exchanged on the move, with the panting voice of his laboring wife coming in loud and clear over his cell phone. And then they were out the door, on their way to the Jaguar, which was still, miraculously, parked unmolested in the yellow zone in front of the emergency room entrance. They hurried down the concrete walk to the car at a fast but measured pace, two truant children intent on making their escape from school without calling any unwanted attention to themselves in the process. Nearly breathless with giddiness at their successful escape, Zoe all but tumbled into the front seat when Reed opened the door for her.

"President and CEO of a very successful cosmetics firm?" she said, sending him a laughing glance as he slid behind the wheel. "Wasn't that laying it on a bit thick?"

"I don't think so." Reed turned the key in the ignition. The Jag came to life with a low, throaty purr of pure power. He eased it away from the curb. "That's what you are, aren't you? President and chief executive officer of New Moon?"

Zoe snorted inelegantly. "I'm the *only* officer of New Moon."

"Like I said—" he shrugged "—president and CEO. It's all in how you look at it."

"Well...maybe. But I don't think Katherine Hightower will look at it in quite the same way."

"No, probably not." He slanted Zoe a brief glance from under a lifted eyebrow as the car merged into the flow of traffic on Charles Street. "Isn't it fortunate the old harridan doesn't have anything to say about it?"

"Then you don't think her opinion will carry any weight with Moira?"

"No. Why should it?"

"Well, since they're sisters and all, I just naturally assumed they'd discuss it. There is a great deal of money involved." Zoe shot him a glance out of the corner of her eye. "If Moira decides to invest, that is," she added, not wanting to sound presumptuous, as if she thought a decision had already been made in her favor. She'd already made that mistake once and wasn't looking to do it again.

"Where'd you get the idea my great-grandmother and Katherine Hightower are sisters?"

"Sisters-in-law?"

Reed shook his head. "They're not related in any way at all."

"But you called her Aunt Katherine."

"Oh. That." He shrugged. "The title is strictly honorary. The Sullivans and the Hightowers have known each other for generations, and when Kate—Kate is her great-niece," he explained, his eyes on the road as he maneuvered into the left turn lane. "When Kate and I finally announced our engagement, *she* announced that I was henceforth to call her Aunt Katherine. I didn't have the backbone to say I'd rather not, so now I'm stuck with it."

Something inside Zoe tightened painfully. "You're engaged?"

He'd looked at her like that…kissed her like that…and he was *engaged?!* Zoe felt the rage boiling up. He was a pig. Pond scum. Lower than pond scum. *Cazzone cafone,* as Gina would say.

He glanced over at her, alerted by her sudden still-ness and the tense, simmering silence that filled the air.

Her face was slightly flushed; her delicate jaw was clenched. Her long-fingered hands had curled into fists in her lap.

"*Was* engaged," he said, finding her unwitting show of jealousy surprisingly satisfying. "The bride-to-be ran off three days before the wedding and married someone else."

"Oh." Zoe's nascent anger deflated like a burst balloon, the tight, painful feeling in her chest dissolving before she had a chance to analyze or examine it. "Oh. I'm…I'm so sorry," she lied, trying not to show how relieved she was.

He glanced over at her again, the leashed wolf peering out of his eyes. "I'm not," he said.

MIRACULOUSLY, THEY FOUND an empty parking space just half a block from her building. Reed maneuvered the Jag into it just seconds ahead of a driver in a white SUV who'd seen it at the same time, commandeering the prized space without a flicker of guilt or remorse. He was out of the car and around the hood, opening Zoe's door, before she'd had a chance to unhook her seat belt. She put her hand in his when he offered it, letting him help her out of the passenger seat as if she were some delicate society debutante at a ball.

He drew her out and shoved the door closed with a careless push. Setting his hand on the small of her back, he steered her across the street toward the red-brick building that housed the Ristorante Marcella. An unnatural silence enveloped them as they made their way down the alley and around to the back of the building. A tense, tingling silence, ripe with expectation and the guilty excitement of knowing they were heading for her apartment. Her *empty* apartment. Zoe began to babble.

"The hand lotion should be just about ready for the next step in processing," she said as she unlocked the wrought-iron gate and led the way up the stairs. "I strain it through a stainless steel mesh sieve for extra creaminess and then let it cool and thicken before I bottle it. It has to cool slowly, at room temperature, and that takes a while. It probably won't be ready for bottling until late this afternoon. So you probably don't want to hang around here for that. But I can show you the infusion process for my various body oils and...well, uh..." She darted a quick glance over her shoulder at him and hurried her pace, putting some distance between them, like a skittish doe fleeing a buck in rut. "I've been working on a new formula for eye cream. It has to be thicker and more emollient than regular moisturizer, as well as hypoallergenic. Not that all my lotions aren't hypoallergenic, but an eye cream has to be especially gentle because the skin around most people's eyes is very sensitive and..."

He watched her hurry up the stairs ahead of him, just out of reach, her luscious hips swaying seductively at eye level, her corkscrew curls bouncing gently against her back, her sweet, old-fashioned scent teasing his nostrils. Her chattering voice was a pleasant buzzing in his ears, betraying her nervousness with every syllable, feeding the wild, erotic fantasies that were, once again, running rampant through his brain.

He imagined her hips, bare and dimpled, between his hands as he held her still for his possession...her hair drifting down across his naked chest...her scent surrounding him as he buried his nose between her lush, naked breasts...her voice breathless, hot and pleading, whispering a lover's demands in his ear as he thrust into her. He could see himself kissing his way up her leg, from the gleaming toe ring, to the ankle bracelet, to the soft white skin of her inner thigh. He imagined himself reaching up under her bright flowing skirt and tearing off her panties...imagined taking her against the wall of the stairwell, her long legs wrapped around his waist as he pounded—

Good Lord, what was happening to him? He'd never felt the urge to take a woman up against a wall before. Never been tempted to tear her clothes off to get at bare flesh. The longer he was around Zoe Moon, the more basic and primal his fantasies became.

At the moment, it was all he could do not to reach out and drag her backward into his arms, stopping the rapid-fire flow of words with his lips, making all his most prurient fantasies come true.

"...could show you how I make my astringents," she said as they reached the door to her apartment. Her key ring clinked against the brass plate surrounding the dead bolt, loud as a shot in the dark, as she unlocked it, "Or at least I could talk you through the process, since I'm not actually going to make any more until this weekend. I use a nonalcohol base so my astringents are extremely gentle and—"

"I'm not coming in, Zoe."

She turned her head, her hand on the doorknob, the keys still dangling in the lock, and looked at him over her shoulder. "I thought you wanted to see my operation," she said, disappointment warring with relief in her voice.

"We both know that's not a good idea. Not right now."

"Why not right now?" she asked, as if she didn't

know, all too well, why not right now. "You're here. I'm here. We've both scheduled the whole day for it. I've got a batch of hand lotion brewing on the stove. I'd say right now is just about perfect."

He shook his head at her. "Zoe," he said warningly, the look in his eyes hot enough to melt steel.

She knew she should just let it go. It would have been the smart thing to do. The safe thing. It was what she would have done with any other man. She was normally a very cautious woman when it came to men and relationships, men and sex. She didn't play at love or treat sex like a teasing game, never offered what she had no intention of giving. Sex was too dangerous to be taken lightly, or indulged in on a whim. It had a way of getting tangled up in a woman's mind, a way of confusing her and making her think it was something it wasn't. Rampaging hormones had probably gotten more women into situations they regretted than any other ten things combined. She'd seen it happen over and over again, and she'd determined, early on, that it wasn't going to happen to her; *she* wasn't going to lose her head just because some man sent her libido into overdrive. There were thousands of things more important than sex. Unfortunately, at the moment she couldn't think of a single one.

She turned around to face him, head-on, leaning back again the door with both hands behind her. "What's the matter, Reed?" There was a hint of the gypsy in her eyes, tempestuous and challenging, an instinctive response to the predatory look in his. *You are the most—* She could still hear the echo of that unfinished sentence in her mind. The need to know how he might have finished it drove her just a little crazy, pushing her past all caution and good sense. "Are you afraid I'll jump you now that your secretary's not here to protect you?''

It was all he could do not to reach for her, to answer that challenge then and there. To hell with the rules.

"No," he said tightly, as the wolf lunged wildly against its leash. "I'm afraid *I'll* jump *you*." He leaned forward, bracing his hands against the doorjamb on either side of her head, trapping her against her own front door. "I'm afraid that if I got you alone in your apartment, I'd forget I was there on business and do exactly what my instincts have been urging me to do since I laid eyes on you. And I'm afraid you wouldn't stop me if I did."

Zoe's eyes widened and her tongue snaked out, licking at suddenly dry lips. But she didn't back down. It wasn't in her nature. And she was—God help her—enjoying the chase. How far could she push him before he cracked and took what they both wanted?

"You're taking an awful lot for granted, aren't you?" she taunted softly. "Just because I asked you to kiss me the other day in your office doesn't mean I—"

"That kiss is the least of it, and you know it. It's the look in your eyes, right now. It's the heat that zings back and forth between us whenever we get within ten feet of each other." He leaned in just a bit closer, almost but not quite brushing his body against hers. "You feel the heat, don't you, Zoe? The fire. You feel it."

Oh, yes, she felt it, all right. She was enveloped in heat. Encompassed by it. Surrounded by it. His heat. Her heat. Their heat. It scorched her nerve endings, setting her whole body ablaze with desire. She bit back a moan.

"I know," he murmured soothingly. "It burns,

doesn't it? It makes you ache inside, as if your whole body were going to burst into flames." The words were spoken a hairsbreadth away from her lips, so close she could feel the warmth of his breath against her skin. "But we have to wait to put the fire out. You don't want to wait, I know. Neither do I. But it will be better that way. There won't be any questions about why. No suspicions about motives. No second-guessing the reasons. When we finally give in to it and come together, we'll both know why."

"Why?" she breathed. The word was little more than a whimper.

"Lust," he growled, low; the wolf was breathing down her neck. "Pure, unadulterated lust. We're going to burn each other up and it's going to be glorious. But until that time comes—" with superhuman effort, he pushed away from the door frame, releasing her from the spell he'd woven with his words and his body and the hot, dangerous look in his eyes "—we aren't going to take any chances."

"Chan—" She had to lick her lips again before she could form the complete word. "Chances?"

"Until this deal is settled, we're not going to be alone together. It's too dangerous. Too tempting." He reached around behind her and opened the door. "Go inside and get my briefcase," he said gently, giving her a little nudge. "I'll wait out here."

Trancelike, she obeyed him, using the few moments it took to complete the task in a frantic effort to marshal her thoughts into some kind of coherent order. "What about New Moon?" she said as she very carefully— making sure their fingers didn't touch—handed the briefcase across the threshold. "How are you going to assess my business if you don't see it in operation?"

"Are you free tomorrow at one o'clock?"

She nodded.

"I'll bring a staffer from the office with me. We'll get this thing wrapped up, one way or the other, before the week is out. And once it's wrapped up—" his eyes burned into hers like blue lasers, making both a threat and a promise "—I'm coming back. Alone. And we're going to throw away the rule book and see just how hot it can get between us. And, Zoe..."

"Yes?" she said breathlessly when he paused.

"I'm predicting a meltdown."

10

BECAUSE REED RAN A TIGHT ship, because he was thorough and fair and scrupulously honest, because he didn't want anyone to be able to say—no matter what the final outcome—that the New Moon deal hadn't been handled in exactly the same way, with exactly the same care and attention to detail, as any other deal ever considered by Sullivan Enterprises, it took more than one week to get all the loose ends tied up.

It took twelve days, to be exact.

Twelve days of watching Zoe mix formulas for body lotions and massage oils. Twelve days of compiling, organizing and interpreting her methods and records. Twelve days of interviewing her vendors, her suppliers, her creditors and her clients. Twelve days of intensive, extensive due diligence, and never, ever, not once, being alone with her. In short, it was twelve days of the most hellish frustration Reed had ever experienced.

And at the end of those twelve days, he had to admit that his great-grandmother had been absolutely right. New Moon was a stellar investment opportunity: an up-and-coming company, well run despite the eccentric bookkeeping system, with excellent prospects and a beautiful, brilliant and admittedly unorthodox CEO who'd discovered an unfulfilled need in the marketplace and exploited it to the best of her ability. Which, he'd belatedly come to realize, was considerable. The sex kitten not only had an attitude, she had a brain.

It was a formidable combination—the bohemian facade, the sassy in-your-face attitude, a first-class brain, and a work ethic any investor would wholeheartedly approve of, all wrapped up in a package that could make a man throb with the need to throw his head back and howl. In frustration, if nothing else.

Reed felt as if he might be reduced to doing exactly that before the interminable afternoon was over. They'd been discussing the fine points of the deal over tea in Moira's front parlor, all very civilized and businesslike, with Zoe seated on the settee beside his great-grandmother and him in the wing chair across the piecrust table, the same as before. She was wearing a loose chenille sweater in old gold that she probably thought was demure, but which made him think about how easy it would be to slip it off of her when the time came, and the long paisley skirt she'd had on when they'd rushed Mary Ellen to the hospital. This time, Zoe wore purple boots instead of the red ones that had raised Katherine Hightower's eyebrows. Her hair was drawn softly back from her face, the wild red curls loosely caught and held in a gold-velvet scrunchie, the style exposing the shiny gold rings in her ears, making him think of the one she wore on her toe...and the one he imagined she wore elsewhere.

Manfully, trying desperately not to let himself get distracted from the business at hand by thoughts that more appropriately belonged in the bedroom, Reed carefully, thoroughly, exhaustively, leaving no stone unturned, explained every term and clause in the contract and the accompanying paperwork, determined that Zoe should understand it completely, especially in light of her blithe refusal to hire an attorney to evaluate it for her.

"I trust you," she'd said the first time he'd suggested she retain her own lawyer. And then those dark gypsy eyes of hers had turned teasing, flirting with him from under the extravagant sweep of her auburn lashes. "With my business, anyway," she'd added, her voice gone all silky and smooth and seductive, just the way he imagined it would when she finally invited him into her bed. Into her body.

It had been all he could do not to shove the tidy pile of folders and paperwork to the floor and drag her up onto his conference table, then and there, and to hell with the bean counter from accounting who was acting as unwitting chaperon. It had taken every ounce of self-control Reed possessed, but he'd managed to rein himself in with the promise of later.

And now, thank God, it was later. Almost. Just thirty minutes more, he told himself. Thirty minutes more, and the deal would be done, every i dotted, every t crossed, all the legalities satisfied, all the rules carefully preserved. Thirty minutes more and all his most carnal, hedonistic fantasies would be well on their way to coming true.

"You'll need to sign all four copies," he said, showing no hint of his simmering impatience as he placed a thick stack of documents on the piecrust table in front of his great-grandmother. "Sign and date each one at the bottom, above the line where you name is typed in, please, Gran. And then, Zoe—" he glanced at her as he said her name, and the wolf tugged at the leash, peering out at her over the top of his black-framed reading glasses "—it will be your turn."

Zoe felt a quick, answering tug and she flushed

slightly, hastily averting her gaze to avoid the heated anticipation in his. His voice had gone all throaty and deep. His blue eyes gleamed with blatant sensuality— unadulterated lust, he'd called it—and an echo of the promise—or was it a threat?—he'd made twelve days ago, standing in the hall outside her apartment. "I'm predicting a meltdown," he'd said, in exactly the same smoky, seductive tone, with exactly the same ravening, rapacious, predatory look in his eyes.

She glanced uneasily at Moira, wondering if the elegant old lady had picked up on any of the sexual subtext in her great-grandson's last remark. It seemed not. Although how that could possibly be, Zoe had no idea, when Reed was sitting not four feet away, his laser blue eyes radiating heat like a nuclear reactor. Meltdown, indeed! She'd be lucky if there wasn't a nuclear explosion involved, she thought fancifully, then shivered in helpless anticipation, and instinctive feminine fear.

What on earth was she getting herself into?

And why was she sitting here, on the cusp of having all her dreams for New Moon become a reality, letting herself get sidetracked by the possibility...okay, the probability...oh, hell, the *certainty* that she was going to end up in bed with the man who was most responsible for making those dreams come true? Oh, not because he was helping to make her dreams real. Never that. If she was honest with herself—and she always tried to be honest with herself—she'd have to admit she'd be just as willing to climb into bed with him even if he advised his great-grandmother against investing in New Moon.

She wanted him that much. Pitiful, but there it was. That's what raging hormones could do to a woman, she reminded herself sternly, just as she had, over and over again, during the last interminable twelve days. Sex wasn't a game. It wasn't something to be taken lightly or indulged in indiscriminately just because two people had the hots for each other. Unfortunately, the reminders hadn't—and weren't—doing any good.

She still wanted him.

She meant to have him.

So now the trick was to keep things in perspective. To remember that, as dangerous as sex was, it was still, well...just sex. If a woman kept her head, if she kept a firm lock on her emotions and her imagination, indulging her libido didn't have to mean messing up the rest of her life, or anyone else's. Compartmentalization, that was the ticket, she'd decided. Men did it all the time and it seemed to work well enough for them.

After all, that's the way *he* was handling it, wasn't it? He made no bones about it, either. Business first. Pleasure later. No mixing the two. Very sensible of him. And if he could do it, she could do it, too.

"There, now. That's done." Moira looked up when she finished signing her name to the final document and smiled at her new business partner. "A brand-new company. New beginnings. New experiences. I've never invested in a cosmetics company before." She placed the pen on top of the contracts and pushed the whole pile over in front of Zoe. "It's all so exciting, isn't it, dear? I find that I'm quite beside myself."

"Yes, it is. Very exciting." Zoe smiled at her benefactress with real warmth and affection, then turned her head slightly, shifting her gaze to include Reed. "I'm so excited I can hardly stand it," she said, and the look in her eyes was pure female provocation mixed with undisguised sensual speculation, wrapped up in a wordless invitation no man with blood in his veins could miss...or resist.

Reed felt the heat from the top of his head to the soles of his feet, and all points in between. His eyes all but glazed over and he nearly dropped his copy of the contract.

Satisfied with his reaction, Zoe shifted her gaze back to her hostess. "So..." She picked up the pen Moira had offered and bent her head over the contracts. "I guess I'd better sign these before anyone changes their mind."

"Oh, no one's going to change their mind," Reed assured her, his voice as smooth as silk, as dangerous as the growl of a crouching wolf. "Not now."

"No, indeed," Moira agreed happily, still seemingly oblivious to the byplay between her great-grandson and her new business partner. She retrieved each copy of the contract as Zoe signed it, slipping it off of the top of the stack to reveal the next one. "There, now." She took all four copies of the document between her hands, rapped the edges against the tabletop to align them and handed them to Reed, who was already opening his briefcase to stow them away. "It's official. Almost." She gestured toward the frosted silver ice bucket sitting on the tea cart. "Reed, dear, would you do the honors?"

"I thought you intended to have some kind of party to celebrate your new business venture." He lifted the bottle of champagne from the ice bucket as he spoke, catching the icy droplets of water with the linen napkin, and went to work on the wire muzzle guarding the cork. "I seem to recall the mention of a dinner party." He laid the tangled bit of wire on the tray and began to ease the cork out of the tight embrace of the smooth green glass. "Black tie, I think you said."

"Oh, I still intend to have a dinner party," Moira said. "This Saturday, I think, would be perfect. Would that work for you, Zoe, or do you need more notice?"

"Uh…" It took a conscious effort for Zoe to shift her gaze from Reed's hands to her hostess's face. She'd never paid all that much attention to any man's hands before, but the combination of brute strength, expertise and gentleness necessary to ease the cork from the bottle was suddenly quite…fascinating. "Saturday would be fi—"

There was a soft pop, a quiet hiss, as the cork slipped free.

Zoe gasped softly and bit her bottom lip, feeling as if the release had been coaxed from her own body. Unable to stop herself, she flicked a quick, furtive glance at Reed.

He smiled wolfishly, as if he knew exactly what that soft gasp had meant.

She quickly shifted her attention back to Moira. "Saturday would be fine," she said, only just a tiny bit breathless…not nearly enough for anyone to notice, she assured herself. "I'm not doing anything Saturday."

"Wonderful," Moira said. "Then Saturday it is."

But Reed was shaking his head. "Saturday is the charity shindig for Mass General," he reminded his great-grandmother.

"Oh, yes. I'd forgotten about that." Moira's face fell for a moment, then brightened. "Well, that will work, too. We'll have cocktails here first," she said, planning as she went. "Mrs. Wheaton can make some of those wonderful crab puffs of hers and those delicious smoked salmon canapés everyone always raves about. Much easier than putting on an entire dinner on such short notice, and we ladies will still get to get gussied up, because the benefit is always black tie. Oh, thank you, dear.'' She accepted the glass of champagne from Reed, her mind obviously on other, more important matters. "Afterward, we can all go to the Isabella Stewart Gardner together from here. How does that sound to you, Zoe?''

"The cocktail party sounds lovely. I certainly wouldn't want to pass up a chance to sample more of Mrs. Wheaton's cooking.'' She smiled at Moira to show she was only teasing about her reasons for finding the idea lovely, while, out of the corner of her eye, she watched Reed filling the other two champagne glasses. Cary Grant couldn't have done it better. "But I'm afraid I haven't been invited to Mrs. Hightower's charity benefit.''

Moira's eyebrows rose expressively. "Mrs. Hightower's benefit?'' she said, with a significant look at her great-grandson.

"We ran into Katherine in the emergency room when we took M.E. in to have her baby,'' Reed explained easily, his smile conspiratorial and somehow intimate as he handed Zoe a glass of champagne.

She countered with a deliberately bland gaze over the rim of the glass, refusing to give him the satisfaction of looking away again.

He sent her a long, smoldering glance before turning back to his great-grandmother, a glance that said *you just wait until I get you alone* and sent shivers down her spine.

"She'd just come out of a meeting with the hospital administrator about the benefit,'' he said to Moira.

"And she very kindly reminded me that I had to be early to stand in the receiving line." His left eyebrow lifted. "Or else."

Moira gave a dignified little snort. "Did she, indeed? Interfering old busybody. Loves to tell everyone what to do. Puts people's backs up. It's no wonder young Kate ran off to New Orleans instead of mar— Well, that's neither here nor there, is it? And it isn't Katherine Hightower's benefit, in any case." Moira reached out with her free hand and patted Zoe's arm. "You are most definitely invited, my dear girl. Reed always buys an entire table, so there's always an extra place or two. Now, let's have that toast, shall we?" Moira lifted her glass, waiting until Reed and Zoe did likewise before she made her toast. "To New Moon," she said, turning her head to include both of them in her beaming smile. "And new friends. May this relationship be a warm and lasting one."

"To New Moon," Zoe echoed, as she lifted the glass to her lips.

"And new relationships," Reed said, and drained his glass in one long gulp without ever taking his eyes off of Zoe's.

FIVE MINUTES LATER, they were buckled into the front seat of the Jaguar as it headed due west on Beacon Street. Both of them were nervous and excited and more than a little scared by what they knew was about to happen.

"Are we going to the bank?" Zoe asked, just to be absolutely sure they were on the same wavelength.

"No, we aren't going to the bank."

"Are you going to drop me off at my apartment so you can go to rugby practice?"

"No, I'm not going to drop you off at your apartment so I can go to rugby practice."

"Then what *are* you going to do?"

He glanced at her out of the corner of his eye as if he couldn't quite believe what he'd just heard. "Do you really need me to spell it out for you?" There was a spot of color high on his chiseled cheekbone, and his large, well-kept hands were tight on the steering wheel.

He was, she realized with amazement, just as tense and uncertain as she was. She didn't know if that made her less—or more—nervous. While it was nice to know they were on an even footing...shouldn't one of them be sure about this?

"Yes," she said, suddenly realizing she wanted to have it spelled out. *Needed* to have it spelled out. There'd be less room for error or misunderstanding that way. "Yes, I think I do need to have it spelled out. Tell me."

Reed waited until he'd braked for the red light at the intersection at Embankment Road before he turned his head to look at her.

"I'm going take you to my place," he said deliberately, his voice low and husky and unbearably intimate in the close confines of the idling car. "I'm going to make sure my housekeeper has done as I said and taken the day off, and then I'm going to carry you straight upstairs to my bedroom and peel off every stitch of your clothes, one piece at a time." He held her gaze with his while he spoke, but he kept his hands firmly on the steering wheel. He didn't quite trust himself to touch her. Not now. Not yet. Not until he could keep on touching her until they were both completely, utterly satisfied. "I'm going to kiss every inch of your skin. And I'm going to touch you all over, everywhere, so that there's no part of your body I don't know. And then I'm going to lay you down on my bed and take you, over and over again, until this heat between us burns itself out or we reduce the bed to cinders, whichever comes first." He paused a moment for that to sink in. For both of them. "If that's all right with you?"

Zoe swallowed, her slender throat working as she tried to get her heart to settle back where it belonged. That was quite a plan. Specific. Explicit. Exciting. With no room for error or misinterpretation on either side. They were going to have sex. Hot, erotic, mind-blowing sex. Well, that was exactly what she'd had in mind herself. Wasn't it?

"Yes," she said, and paused to swallow again. "Yes, that's all right with me. Except..." She hesitated, unsure how to say what she knew needed to be said, now, before he put his plan into action and the heat they generated burned away all her good sense.

"Except what?" he prompted.

"Well...I didn't hear any mention of, um..." Why was it so hard to say? They were going to have sex. They were going to get naked together and roll around on his bed and he was going to know every inch of her. As she was going to know him. And if they were going to do it, they should be able to talk about...about the things the women's magazines said they should talk about before it actually happened. Besides, not talking about it was just plain irresponsible. Not to mention stupid. "The light's changed," she said, and gestured toward the traffic signal.

Reed lifted his foot off of the brake and eased it down on the gas pedal. "You didn't hear any mention of what?" he asked, refusing to let it go.

She stared at the burled wood of the dashboard as if

she found the pattern fascinating, and hoped she wasn't about to insult him. "Condoms," she blurted, determined to get it said, despite the blush she could feel heating her cheeks...and her chest...and her breasts. It was the curse of having red hair; when she was really embarrassed, she blushed with her whole body. "I didn't hear any mention of condoms while you were telling me what you're going to do. You'll have to wear one."

"Naturally."

"It's not any reflection on you. On your morals or anything. It's just—" She turned her head to look at him. "Naturally?"

"I insist on it. Always."

"Oh. Well. Good. No problem, then."

"It's not any reflection on you, either. On your morals or anything," he said, mocking her gently, just to see if she could turn any pinker than she already was. Her obvious embarrassment was so unexpected. And so unexpectedly charming. "I'm sure you've been as choosy about your lovers as I have. It's just that you can't ever be sure unless—"

"I haven't."

"Haven't what?" He felt a sliver of disappointment snake through him. Not enough to make him change his mind about what he wanted to do to her...with her...but enough to spoil some of the pleasure. "Been choosy?"

She shook her head. "Had lovers."

"Excuse me?" he said politely, positive he couldn't possibly have heard her right.

"I haven't had any lovers," she said, blushing so

furiously that the sprinkling of freckles across her nose and cheekbones stood out like tiny gold coins. "You'll be my first."

11

To Reed's credit, he didn't doubt her for a second. Another man, one less astute, less perceptive, less willing to change an opinion when confronted with new information, might have failed utterly to see beyond her spectacularly sexy exterior and breezy, bohemian attitude. Might have insisted that the bold, flirtatious way she used her eyes, the sensual banter she parried with such apparent ease, precluded the kind of innocence she'd just laid claim to. But one look at her blushing face, at the earnest, aching embarrassment in her big brown eyes, and he knew she was telling the truth.

He'd seen the shy, uncertain schoolgirl once before, on the sidelines of the rugby field at Magazine Beach. He'd wondered about her then—that fresh-faced ingenue who'd suddenly replaced the bold-eyed gypsy—but he didn't wonder now. He could see, quite clearly, that the innocent and the seductress were part and parcel of the same woman.

He wished, fleetingly, that it wasn't true, that he'd misunderstood what she'd said and that she wasn't a virgin, but in the very next instant, he found himself experiencing a fiercely primitive thrill, a kind of joy, almost, at knowing she was untouched. It was the kind of feeling he could never admit to, not if he wanted to retain his image of himself as a civilized, sensitive, enlightened, modern male.

Modern men weren't supposed to care about anything so medieval as a woman's chastity. Only her fidelity was supposed to matter. He certainly hadn't cared before, or even given it much thought. As long as a woman was faithful while they were together, any previous lovers she might have had didn't concern him, except insofar as they may have affected her health. Or unless she'd stepped over that undefined and nebulous line into promiscuity, in which case he fastidiously declined to join the ranks of her lovers. He didn't care to be one in a long line of previous paramours in a woman's life; on the other hand, he'd never cared about being first, either.

He found it disconcerting to realize that he cared now, to be forced to acknowledge some deep, dark, primitive, heretofore unknown corner of his male psyche. It mattered to him to know that the luscious Miss Zoe Moon was a virgin, and he found that unnerving. He also found it unbearably exciting.

He would be her first.

It changed everything, of course. Oh, not his intention to take her to bed—nothing could change that, especially not now! But the way he'd been planning to go about it had undergone a swift revision. A civilized man didn't ravage a virgin. Even when the virgin in question was so obviously willing to participate in the process.

"We might as well go into the den," Reed said as he escorted her through the front door of his silent Back Bay town house. "I'm going to need a drink in my hand while we discuss this."

Zoe hitched the strap of her tapestry bag higher onto

her shoulder and followed him across the marble floor of the elegant foyer, through a short hallway to the back of the house. She hovered uncertainly in the middle of the cozy, masculine room he'd led her to, watching silently as he crossed the wide square of colorful Turkish carpet that covered the center of the room to the elegant cherry-wood sideboard. Without pausing, or turning around, he picked up one of the heavy crystal decanters that decorated its polished surface. It was a measure of how much she'd rattled him that he didn't think to inquire as to whether she might like a drink, too.

"I don't see what we need to discuss," she said, as he unstoppered the decanter and poured two fingers of dark amber liquid into a matching crystal highball glass. "Unless you've changed your mind about wanting to have sex with me?"

"No, I haven't changed my mind."

"Well, then...?"

Reed tossed back half his drink before he answered. "Zoe, you're a virgin," he said, as if that explained it all.

"Yes, I know." She stood with her head up, her chin lifted, her back ramrod straight...but the fingers of her right hand were sliding up and down the strap of her shoulder bag in a quick, nervous gesture. "What I don't know is why it seems to have turned you off."

"Turned me off?" He tossed back the rest of his drink with a quick, almost savage gesture, then carefully set the empty glass on the sideboard before turning around to face her. "Not hardly. I'm more turned on now than I've ever been in my entire life."

She could see, quite clearly, that he was telling the truth. The knowledge settled her nerves. A little.

''Well, then...?'' She dropped her purse onto the seat of a burgundy club chair and took a step toward him.

''No.'' He held his hand up, palm out. ''Stay right there. Give me a minute to think this through.''

''To think *what* through?''

''Do you have any idea—any idea at all?—how I've imagined taking you? What I've imagined doing to you? Hell, what I've imagined you doing to me?''

''Oh, I think I have a pretty good idea. You told me in the car on the way over here, remember? And a couple of times before that, too, if you'll recall. You were very—'' she shivered slightly, remembering ''—explicit.''

''I apologize for offending you.''

''Oh, please.'' She all but rolled her eyes. ''Do I look offended?''

''Well, if you're not,'' he said, stung by the raillery in her voice, ''you certainly should be. It was inexcusably crude of me to say those things to you.''

''Why? Because I'm a virgin?'' Amused exasperation had replaced any lingering trace of embarrassment. Who would have thought the urbane, oh-so-sophisticated Mr. Reed Sullivan IV had such antiquated ideas about women? ''Would it make you feel better if I blushed and stammered? Or how about if I fainted? Would that fit in better with your idea of how a virgin should act?''

''You did blush,'' he reminded her. ''And you were stammering so much you could barely say 'condom.'''

''That didn't have anything to do with me being a virgin,'' she informed him. ''Lots of experienced women have trouble getting that word out.'' At least, according to the women's magazines she'd read, they did. "Mostly because they know men don't want to hear it."

"So you're saying you're not the least bit nervous? Not the least bit scared or unsure about facing something you have no experience with?"

"Well, of course I'm nervous. But I'm not scared." She paused for a moment, trying to gather her thoughts so she could say what she wanted to in exactly the right way. "Being a virgin doesn't mean I'm some terrified, ignorant little girl. I know what sex is and how it's done. I've been to R-rated movies. I've even been to a few X-rated ones. I've heard all the words before, too, including the four-letter ones you're too much of a gentleman to use. I've read the *Joy of Sex* and the *Kamasutra* and I even—now brace yourself," she warned, "because this might come as a shock to you— I know what an orgasm feels like. I can give myself one whenever I want. What I don't know is how it feels to have one with a man inside me."

Reed groaned audibly and took a half step toward her. "Zoe—"

"No." She held up the restraining hand this time. "Let me finish. I want to make sure we're perfectly clear on this before it goes any further."

He halted in midstep and waited, his eyes riveted to her face, like a wolf who'd scented prey. Or a mate.

She hesitated a moment, startled by the sheer, sensual force of his unwavering gaze. She'd never been the focus of so much sexual heat before, so much concentrated masculine energy, so much honest, unabashed, blatantly carnal hunger. It was a bit intimidating...and unbearably arousing...and strangely empowering.

She moistened her lips with the tip of her tongue and

lowered her chin, returning his stare from under a provocative, protective veil of auburn lashes. "That very first day we met in Moira's parlor I felt this incredible spark of instant attraction that was stronger than anything I'd ever felt before. I told myself it was just basic biology and that I should ignore it. I could tell you didn't approve of me and I was pretty sure I didn't approve of you, either. Which didn't really matter one way or the other, since it didn't look like we were going to do business together. And then we did do business and I told myself it was even more important to resist the feeling I had for you, no matter how strong it was, at least until we got things settled, one way or another. Well, things are settled, and I don't have to resist it anymore." She lifted her lashes and met his gaze head-on. "I don't *want* to resist it anymore."

She began to move toward him, gait slow and measured, chin up, eyes steady and unflinching, her usual sassy bravado replaced by something both more honest and more artful. She was a woman dead set on seduction. His. And her own.

"I've finally come to a place in my life where I want the entire sexual experience. I want to know what it feels like to be touched by a man. Everywhere. I want to know what it feels like to have a man on top of me. Inside me." She was standing right in front of him now, her head tilted back to keep her gaze locked on his, her breasts almost, but not quite, brushing his chest. The look in her eyes was soft and sweet and as hot as the flames of a gypsy campfire. "I want the man who shows me what it feels like to be you."

He stood stock-still for a long breathless moment, his fists clenched at his sides, the muscle in his jaw twitching, his heart hammering frantically against the wall of his chest. The wolf inside snapped and lunged against the tight leash of Reed's rapidly waning control. She was every man's fantasy as she stood there gazing up at him: a wanton innocent, a passionate virgin, an eager, inexperienced voluptuary.

And she wanted *him*.

She'd just said so in perfectly clear words that had him as hard as the wrought-iron poker by the fireplace. He'd never felt so ready before. So turned on. So incredibly needy. He wanted to reach out and ravage...devour...*possess*. And he wanted to do it over and over again with innumerable inventive variations, fueled by two weeks of lurid fantasies

Which was all the more reason for him to take it slow, to proceed with the care and caution she didn't seem to realize she needed. By her own admission, what she was feeling now was something she'd never felt before. One of them had to treat her innocence with the respect and reverence it deserved.

Even if it killed him.

"Would you like to go out for something to eat?" he asked, desperate to find a way to slow things down before his grip on gentility slipped any further and he committed an unforgivable, ungentlemanly outrage on her untried body. "There's a charming little French bistro less than three blocks from here. We could walk it, if you'd like." A walk would cool him off. Maybe. "You barely ate anything at Gran's."

"No, thank you." Zoe smiled, enthralled by the look in his eyes. No one had ever looked at her in quite that way before. All heat and longing, mixed with a sort of befuddled consternation and a fierce, dogged determination that was somehow very sexy. "I'm not hungry."

"Would you like a glass of champagne? You only sipped at the one—"

"Let's save it for later," she said, and lifted a hand to touch her fingertips to the hard curve of his jaw. *"After."*

Reed bit back a ragged groan and shoved his balled fists into the pockets of his trousers to keep from dragging her down onto the patterned Turkish carpet beneath their feet. The knuckles of his right hand brushed the smooth round globe of the Indian lutz he kept in his pocket. Inspiration struck.

"Are you still willing to play for the peppermint swirl?"

Zoe blinked. "Am I what?"

"The peppermint swirl with the six pink bands." He pulled his lucky marble out of his pocket and held it up between them. "I'll play you for it."

"Play me for it...?" She blinked again, forcing her eyes to focus on the shiny black-and-gold sphere he held an inch in front of her nose. "That's a marble."

"Yes." He nodded. "An Indian lutz."

"Are you telling me you want to play marbles? Now?" Her eyes widened in confusion. And doubt. Had he changed his mind? Had something about her— her virginity? her unconventionality? her boldness?— made him decide he didn't want her, after all? She dropped her hand and took a hesitant half step back, shifting her gaze from his, looking down and away. If he didn't want her, then he didn't want her, and she had to get out of there. Now. Fast. She had to—

There, before her eyes, bulging against the front of his tailored charcoal gray trousers, was unmistakable proof that he did, indeed, want her.

Startled, uncertain, confused, she lifted her gaze to his face again.

Reed Sullivan IV blushed like a schoolboy.

And she was suddenly, absolutely certain that whatever his reasons for backing off, it wasn't because he didn't want her.

"All right," she said. "If you want to play marbles, we'll play marbles."

She turned away from him and moved across the room to the purse she'd dropped in the leather club chair. "I've been carrying this around with me since that day in my apartment when your secretary went into labor." She drew out a tiny blue velvet drawstring bag and opened it, dumping the glittering peppermint swirl out into her palm. "I meant to give it to you as a gift as soon as we finished the business with New Moon, whether we struck a deal or not. But I guess we can still play for it, if that's what you'd rather do." She gestured at the tilted, glass-topped cases displayed in one section of the floor-to-ceiling bookcases on either side of the fireplace. "Do you have any marbles besides those? Ones we can actually play with without worrying about a chip reducing their value?"

Suppressing a rueful sigh at the success of his strategy, he turned and lifted a colorful tin box off one of the shelves, flipped open the lid and presented it to her. "I played with these when I was a boy. Take your pick. We can use the edge of the rug as a lag line.'

Zoe shook her head. "If we're going to play, let's play."

He arched an eyebrow at her.

"Ringer," she said, the glint of challenge in her eyes.

Ringer was a tournament game, *the* tournament

game, played every year at the National Marbles Tournament in Wildwood, New Jersey. It was a cutthroat, winner-take-all game that demanded a great deal of skill and concentration. As good as batting averages for taking a man's mind off of...other things. Especially when it had been fifteen or twenty years since he'd played the game.

"Same terms as last time," he said. "If you win, I take the peppermint swirl as a gift. If I win, I buy it from you for four hundred dollars. Agreed?"

Zoe nodded. "Agreed."

Hitching up the pant legs of his elegant charcoal-gray suit, Reed dropped to one knee and rolled back the Turkish carpet. He carefully laid out target marbles in the regulation cross pattern and surrounded them with a six-foot circle made of string. Officially, the rules called for the circle to be ten feet in diameter, but a smaller one was allowed if space was limited.

Zoe waited until he'd won the lag and was down on both knees, the knuckles of his shooting hand to the floor, preparing to take his first shot, before she elaborated on the rules of their particular game.

"Strip Ringer," she said, just as he sent his shooter into the circle.

It slammed into the target marbles, sending them rolling and bouncing across the hardwood floor. When everything stopped moving, he lifted his head and eyed her across the playing circle. "Strip Ringer?"

"Don't worry. It's easy. There are only two additional rules," she informed him, making them up as she went along. "Every time you lose a turn, you have to take off an item of clothing."

The position of his shooter—outside the ring—had cost him a turn.

Reed made no move to take off any of his clothing. "And the second rule?"

"For every target marble you manage to get outside the ring, your opponent takes off an item of clothing."

There were four target marbles outside the ring. Reed eyed them longingly, practically licking his lips as he imagined exactly which items of clothing she might remove in forfeit, trying very hard to remember why it was so important that they take things slow. He recalled, vaguely, that he meant to be a gentleman about this. Meant to pay the proper homage to her innocence. Meant to—

One of her boots landed on the floor by his knee.

His stupefied gaze shifted from the marbles, to the discarded boot, to her face.

She flashed him a glance from under her lashes, half cheeky-street-urchin, half hot-eyed-gypsy, all seductive-feminine-challenge. "One."

"Ah...Zoe, wait a minute now. I really don't think—"

She tugged off the second boot and tossed it across the circle to collide with the first. "Two."

"This isn't..." He cleared this throat and tried again. "This isn't a good idea, Zoe."

She hitched up one side of her long paisley skirt and rolled her lace-topped, thigh-high stocking down her leg. Black gossamer drifted slowly to the floor. "Three."

"I'm trying to be a gentleman here," he pleaded desperately, his veneer of civilization starting to crack.

He knew he should stop her from going any further. There were really good reasons why he should stop her. And he would. In a minute. Just as soon as she took off that other stocking so he could see if she was wearing her gold toe ring.

But instead of rolling down the other stocking, she reached up and behind her, pulled the velvet scrunchie out of her hair and shook her mass of curls free. They cascaded over her shoulders and down across the front of her gold sweater, as bright as fire, as soft as a cloud. "Four."

Reed sighed like a lovesick schoolboy, half in crushing disappointment that she still wore the one stocking, half in heartfelt relief that she hadn't tested his wavering resolve by taking it off. Yet.

Zoe sent him a slow, bewitching smile. "Your turn," she murmured, putting everything she had into it, hoping it would be enough. If it wasn't, if he still put her off, she would die of acute and total embarrassment.

There followed five long seconds of tortured, tense, expectant silence while both of them wondered what was going to happen next.

And then Reed groaned and yanked his tie off so fast he nearly choked himself.

On her first shot, he lost his shoes and one sock.

She gave up her second stocking, revealing both the toe ring and a delicate gold ankle bracelet adorned with a trio of dangling crescent moons.

He discarded his remaining sock, his suit jacket and his trim-fitting vest.

She shimmied out of a silky, black, lace-edged half-slip, sliding it off from under her skirt without revealing more than a teasing flash of slender, well-toned thigh.

He whipped his belt out of the loops of his slacks and tossed it over his shoulder as if it were a live snake.

She surrendered both of the golden hoops in her ears, and the trio of glittery rings on her right hand.

He added a pair of discreet gold-and-ebony cuff links to the pot.

She removed her bra, reaching up under the cover of her loose chenille sweater to unclasp it, wriggling a bit as she maneuvered the straps off her shoulders, smiling a secret, female smile as she slid it, magician-like, through the length of her sleeve and dropped it on the floor.

Reed stared, transfixed, at the scrap of purple satin and black lace lying on the hardwood floor among the scattered marbles and other bits of clothing, fantasizing about the twin mounds of magnificent female flesh still hidden, but gloriously unrestrained now, beneath the nubby fabric of her sweater. He wondered if her underpants matched her bra…imagined her wearing them and nothing else…imagined her *not* wearing them…and missed his next shot by a mile. He gave up his custom-made, white cotton dress shirt as forfeit.

Like Clark Gable in the movie that sent T-shirt sales plummeting back in the mid-thirties, he wore nothing beneath it but skin. And muscles. Smooth, rounded deltoids, swelling, apple-hard biceps, well-developed pectorals covered with dark crinkling hair; a washboard abdomen.

Zoe caught her breath and lost her grip on her shooter. It clinked noisily as it hit the hardwood floor and then rolled backward, toward her knees and away from the circle. It didn't even occur to her to call a do-over. Instead, she sank down on her bottom, leaned back on her hands and extended her right leg—the one still adorned with both the toe ring and the ankle bracelet—across the shooting circle. "Take whatever you want," she invited huskily.

Reed automatically reached out and took her bare foot in his left hand. He grasped the toe ring with the thumb and index finger of his right, as if he meant to slip it off, and then sat there motionless, staring at her elegant, arched instep, her painted toenails, the fantasy-inspiring body jewelry—and wondered what in the hell kind of game they were playing here.

"Reed?"

He looked up at her then, slowly, his gaze moving from her slender ankle and long, bare leg to the pool of bright paisley fabric tangled around her smooth thighs and luscious hips. To her firm, braless breasts beneath the baggy gold sweater, her tangle of wildfire hair, her lush, seductive mouth, her expressive gypsy eyes.

She was looking at him with a sort of helpless fascination—part wide-eyed wonder, part breathless anticipation, part trembling excitement. He could see a bit of wariness and trepidation in her gaze, too, no matter what she said to the contrary. But mostly there was heat. Fierce, smoldering, female heat. And need. And desire, for him.

His hand tightened on her foot as he waged one last hopeless battle with his baser instincts. She was innocent, he reminded himself, clamping down on the snarling, snapping wolf inside by sheer force of will. She didn't know what she was inviting by looking at him that way. Not really. No matter what she thought, she deserved careful handling, sensitivity and consideration—and all he wanted to do was ravage her.

"Reed?" she said again. Her voice was breathy and trembling, ripe with invitation. Her eyelids drifted down. Her head fell back. Her tongue darted out to lick at those luscious raspberry lips. Her foot flexed in his hand. "Reed, please..."

The leash snapped and the wolf sprang free. "To hell with being a gentleman," he growled, relinquishing what was left of his good intentions as he dragged her across the playing circle on her back. He'd take her as carefully as he could but, dammit, he'd take her!

It was what they both wanted.

Zoe uttered one high-pitched squeak of surprise and delicious excitement as her hands skittered out from under her and she fell backward on to the floor. She felt her skirt slide up under her, felt his hands slide up her legs. And then she was under him, pinioned to the smooth hardwood floor by his greater weight, her bare thighs spread wide to cradle his hips, her breasts flattened by his hard, hairy chest. His fingers tangled in her fiery corkscrew curls as he tenderly lifted her face to his kiss.

He claimed her mouth with almost brutal force, ravishing it with a long, deep, devouring kiss. His mouth was wet and rapacious, greedy and giving. Ruthlessly demanding and exquisitely, savagely tender by turns. When he plunged his tongue between her lips, blatantly miming the sexual act they both desired so desperately, she whimpered and squirmed against him.

"I'm sorry," he murmured, drawing back to look down at her. Her lips were shiny and swollen, as red as bitten cherries; her cheeks were flushed, her eyes closed as if in pain. "I've hurt you already. I'm sorry." He pressed his hands flat to the floor on either side of her head and started to push himself up. "I didn't mean to hurt you."

Zoe grabbed his shoulders, desperate to hold him

where he was, now that she had him where she wanted him. "No. Don't go. Don't stop. You didn't hurt me. I'm not hurt." She slid her hands up under his arms, hooked them over his shoulders from behind and raised herself against him. Head back, chin lifted, she tried to reach his lips with hers. "Kiss me again," she pleaded.

"Zoe, sweetheart—"

She nipped at his chin. *"Kiss me again!"*

He kissed her again.

And again.

And kept on kissing her. Her open, avid lips. Her flushed cheeks. Her closed eyelids. The soft, sweet skin on the underside of her chin. The tender place behind her ear. The tempting hollow at the base of her throat. He used his lips and teeth and tongue, nipping, nibbling, licking, sucking. Deep soul kisses meant to arouse and inflame. Quick, fleeting kisses meant to tease and tantalize. Moist baby kisses meant to cosset and coddle. And while he kissed her...tasted her...breathed her in with every deep, shaky inhalation, his hands wandered, touching her everywhere, the way she'd said she wanted them to...the way he'd fantasized about touching her.

He stroked the length of her bare thigh with his fingertips, slid the flat of his hand over the curve of her satin-clad hip, slipped it up under her sweater to tease the flat, quivering skin of her belly, and farther up, to cup her breast in his palm.

She writhed and whimpered beneath him, making little mewling noises in her throat, her lush, supple body responding to his lightest caress as if it had been made for him and him alone. Her kisses were as avid, as hungry, as his. Her hands moved restlessly over his bare back and shoulders, stroking and kneading, her smooth copper-colored nails leaving little indentations in his skin.

He forgot about hurting her, or frightening her. Even through the red haze of passion that clouded his mind, it was obvious to him, now, that she was neither hurt nor frightened. No woman could respond the way she was responding if she was in any way uncertain about what she was doing.

Abandoning all thoughts of stopping, all thoughts of slowing down, he wrapped his arms around her and rolled over onto his back, reversing their positions. She shifted with him, her mouth still pressed to his, her slender arms still coiled around his neck as if she would never let him go. He reached up behind his head and grasped her hands, loosening her grip easily enough, then slid his palms along her arms to her shoulders, pushing her upright, so that her knees parted and draped bonelessly on either side of his hips.

She looked down at him, her expression simmering, expectant, compliant...waiting.

"Take your sweater off," he ordered.

Without a word, she crossed her arms over her waist and grasped the hem of her sweater in both hands.

"Slowly," he added as she started to pull it off. "Very slowly."

She hesitated briefly and then started again, slowly, as ordered, drawing her crossed arms up, revealing her torso inch by agonizing inch. The first tantalizing slice of skin appeared above the waistband of her paisley skirt, then the delicate bones of her narrow rib cage came into view... The lush underside of her breasts...her nipples, pebbled and pointed, and the same deep raspberry-pink as her lips...the fragile upper chest and elegant line of her collarbone... The vulnerable hollow of her underarms, her sleek, smooth shoulders—all revealed and then partially concealed again by the fiery cascade of curls that tumbled down around her as she drew the sweater over her head and dropped it on the floor.

Reed rumbled a low growl and just barely managed to keep himself from grabbing at her as if he were a hormone-ridden sixteen-year-old faced with his first real live, naked female. Lord, she was magnificent. Her arms were slim and well toned. Her waist was impossibly slender. Her breasts were…oh, Lord, her breasts were perfect. Lush and round and firm. And all that wild hair, curling down around her torso, playing peekaboo with perfection. She was a *Sports Illustrated* swimsuit model, a *Playboy* centerfold and Botticelli's *Venus,* all rolled into one. Sleek, sensual, delicate. In a word, magnificent. She was everything he'd ever imagined.

And she was, at this moment, his.

All his.

Only his.

He clamped his hands around her waist and drew her infinitesimally closer. "Arch your back," he whispered raggedly, exerting subtle pressure against her spine to exaggerate the position he wanted her to assume. "That's it. Now, lift your arms and brush your hair back behind your shoulders so I can see all of you. Don't go shy on me now, sweetheart," he coaxed when she hesitated. "You have a beautiful body. Beautiful breasts. More beautiful than I could possibly have imagined. You should be proud to show them off. To me," he added, in case she misunderstood. "Only to me." His hands tightened on her waist. "Say it."

"Only to you," she murmured obediently, thrilled by the demand in his voice. In his eyes. In his hands.

"I want to touch them. You." He slid his palms up along her sides, over her rib cage, until his thumbs just brushed the underside of her breasts, lightly, back and forth.

She sucked in her breath and held it.

"Do you like that, Zoe?"

She nodded. "Yes."

He moved his hands higher, so that his thumbs brushed her nipples "And this?" He strummed them lightly—once, twice—his eyes on her face while he caressed her. "Do you like this?"

"Yes."

"Do you want more?"

"Oh, yes. Please."

"Please what?"

"More."

"More what?"

"Touch me."

"Touch you where? How?" His fingertips danced over the lush swell at the side of her breast. "Like this?"

"No...my...my nipples. Like you did before."

He strummed her nipples again, very lightly. "Like that?"

"Yes. No." It wasn't enough, what he was doing. She needed—wanted—something more. She arched her back again, of her own accord this time, trying to press her throbbing nipples more firmly against his thumbs. "Harder."

He grasped the raspberry-pink tips between the thumb and forefinger of each hand and pinched lightly. And then again, not so lightly.

She moaned and her head fell back as hot, searing pleasure shot through her. She'd never felt anything like it before. Not an orgasm, exactly. But close, tantalizingly close, as if the nerve endings in her nipples were directly connected to the throbbing button of flesh between her legs. The not-quite orgasm made her achy and itchy, and demanding.

"More." She grasped his wrists, trying to move his hands so that they more fully covered her breasts. "Oh, please. More."

Reed reared up and over, supporting her with a hand splayed against her bare back, rolling her beneath him, dipping his head to her breast in one smooth movement. He took her tightly pebbled nipple into his mouth, sucking strongly, so that she moaned and arched helplessly against him. He slid his free hand along her leg under her skirt, skimming up her thigh, cupping his palm over the narrow strip of damp purple satin between her legs. He pressed the heel of his hand against the swollen mound of her pubis. Just that, just a fleeting downward pressure, and she came.

It was a white-hot burst of feeling, like nothing she'd ever experienced or produced on her own. Her whole body tensed with it, straining, holding on to the feeling as long as she could. And then she moaned again, deep in her throat, and her hips rolled, undulating against his hand, instinctively seeking more of the same. Reed slipped his fingers under the elastic leg of the panties to stroke her still-vibrating flesh. She came again, the second peak building upon the first, and the feeling was higher, sharper, more focused, more intense than before, but still not enough. Not nearly enough. She reached down blindly, grabbing at his hand, pressing it more firmly to her, desperate to feel the pressure where she need it most.

"Inside," she demanded, tilting her pelvis up to meet the hard thrust of his fingers. "I need you insi—"

Her third climax left her breathless and shaking and frantic for the ultimate joining. Her whole body strained upward. Reaching. Yearning. She was painfully, passionately aroused, wild with the desire to be filled, to be taken, to be his.

"Now." She grabbed at his hip, trying to pull him more fully on top of her, twined her leg over his, bit at his shoulder like a female animal in heat, blind to everything except the burning need for his complete and utter possession. "Now, now, *now!*"

He didn't make her wait. Couldn't. His need was as desperate as her own, as mindless, as frantic. As much as she needed to be filled, he needed to fill her.

Still holding her in the cradle of one arm, he rolled slightly away, just enough to yank at the fly of his trousers and free himself. With worsted wool and silk boxer shorts shoved down around his thighs, he reached back under her skirt, shoving it up around her waist, and tore her satin panties off with one sharp, savage tug. And then he was on top of her again, between her thighs, his throbbing, rock-hard cock poised at the entrance to her body.

It was then, with the feel of naked flesh against naked flesh, and her open and quivering beneath him, that he realized he'd forgotten the condom. Forgotten the damned condom! He'd never made love to a woman without protection. Not even the first time, when Janice Hawkins, experienced woman of the world that she was, had produced one out of her little beaded evening bag and put it on him before she'd let him do the deed she'd lured him to the boathouse to do. Ever since then, gentleman that he was, he'd taken care of supplying the protection. And he'd forgotten! Well, no, he hadn't actually forgotten, he assured himself, remembering the two foil packets he'd slipped into his pants pocket before he'd left his bedroom that morning in anticipation of doing just what he was doing.

"Reed. Reed, please," she moaned, and lifted her body to his. She was panting lightly, her body still vibrating with the aftershocks of her first three orgasms, her eyes wide-open and glazed with passion as she stared up at him.

Sweat broke out across his upper lip as the need to take, to ravage, tore through him. Oh, Lord, it was tempting. So tempting to take what was offered, to sink into that sweet female flesh without protection and worry about the consequences later. She wouldn't stop him. She wouldn't even realize until later that they'd made love without that little latex barrier. She wouldn't blame him, either. They'd both been lost in the moment…both forgotten…both…

"Oh, hell." He pulled back and reached down again, scrambling for his pants.

"Reed?"

"It's all right, sweetheart. Just give me a minute here." His voice was nearly as shaky as his hands. "Just a second. There, that's got it." He took her into his arms again, settling her back under him, pressing soft, soothing baby kisses over her face as he positioned himself for entry.

She was still at fever pitch, as ready for the next step as she would ever be. And he was more ready than he had ever been. He pressed forward, telling himself to go slow, to be gentle. No matter how aroused she was, how ready, this first time was bound to be uncomfortable, if not downright painful. He eased into her a little way, then a little more, quaking with eagerness, barely controlling the urge to bury himself to the hilt.

Zoe was less cautious. "Do it," she demanded. "Do it now. Please!"

She arched eagerly, wildly, impatient for his full possession, just as he drove his hips downward. There was a sharp, burning pain as he broke through the barrier of her virginity, more intense than she'd expected, but not unbearable. She sucked in a short, hard breath—more in surprise than anything else—and went rigid for a second.

He went stock-still.

But he didn't pull out. He couldn't. Not now. Maybe not ever. She was so tight! Hot and wet and incredibly tight. He wanted to stay right where he was for the rest of his natural life. Well, maybe not *right* where he was. He had a powerful urge to thrust himself into her, as hard and as fast as possible. The effort it took to restrain the urge had him shaking again, every muscle in his body rock hard and trembling with the effort to hold back. His breathing was labored, his heart pounded, his engorged penis twitched with the need to *move,* but he held himself immobile and waited until she was ready to take more of him.

"Okay now, sweetheart?" he said when he felt the rigidity seep out of her.

"Yes. I'm fine." Her voice was a little reedy, but the tone was firm and sure. "It just took me by surprise, is all."

He lifted a shaking hand and brushed a long, curling tendril of hair back from her face. "Are you in any pain?"

"No." The pain had faded into a kind of dull, throbbing ache and a feeling of fullness that was more unfamiliar than uncomfortable. "I just feel kind of…stretched." She smiled up into his eyes. "I like it."

He withdrew slowly and entered her again, just as slowly. "How about that?" He held her gaze with his as he moved above her, watching intently for any sign of pain or discomfort, gauging her reaction, measuring her response. "Do you like that?"

"Oh, yes. I like that. A lot."

"And that?" He thrust again, a bit harder, adding a little grinding motion on the downstroke that caused her breath to catch in her throat, her eyes to widen in pleasure and surprise.

"Yes, that, too. Oh…" Her eyes glazed over. "Oh, yes. Just like that."

It took several more slow, grinding thrusts to raise her level of arousal to the point it had been at before the pain of her deflowering had surprised them both. But he was a notoriously thorough man, obsessed, some said, with doing things in just exactly the right way. In less than ten minutes he'd increased his pace and was thrusting into her like a pile driver, and she was taking it greedily, thrusting back. Five minutes after that, she was rigid in his arms again, her nails digging into the hard muscles of his back, her eyes glazed with mindless passion, her body shattering into white-hot sparks of pure, incandescent pleasure as she experienced her first orgasm with a man inside her. Ten seconds later, he followed her into the fiery bliss with a groan that sounded as if it had been dredged up from the bottoms of his feet.

"Meltdown," he murmured, his voice rich with satisfaction and pleasure.

He collapsed against her, his body drained, his mind dazed, his arms still hard around her as if he would never let her go. He lay with his face burrowed into the damp hollow of her neck, panting like a long-distance runner who'd just set a new record at the Boston Marathon. Zoe held him, her breath still shuddering in and out of her lungs, her body still throbbing in the afterglow, her hands stroking the long smooth muscles of his back in an effort to soothe them both. It took a few minutes for the world to right itself around them, for their hearts to stop pounding, for their chests to stop heaving, for their eyes to clear and refocus.

And, as the world slowly reformed around them, Zoe became aware of a slight discomfort. She sighed and shifted beneath him in an attempt to ease it.

Reed pressed a tender, openmouthed kiss to the soft, sweet place where her neck curved into her shoulder. "I'll move in a minute," he promised, the words muffled against her throat. "Just as soon as I can."

"I'd like to stay just like this all day but—"

She squirmed again, moving in a way that made him think it might not take him as long to recover as he'd thought.

"—it feels like there's a marble under my rear end."

"Which side?"

"Left."

He rolled to her right, holding her to him with one hand against her bare back while he reached down with the other, blindly searching through the rumpled fabric of her paisley skirt to find the offending marble.

"Well, well. Would you look at this." He chuckled

softly and held the peppermint swirl where she could see it. "Looks like I win."

Her lips curved upward in an answering smile. "How do you figure that?"

"Possession is nine-tenths of the law," he said, casually tossing the marble over his shoulder. "And I've got you—" his eyebrow quirked upward, making him look, she thought, like a very elegant, very satisfied pirate; his hand curved around the swell of her buttock, pulling her flush against him "—don't I?"

12

ZOE SLIPPED INSIDE the gate at the bottom of the stairs and closed it oh-so-carefully behind her. Then she took off her boots and, skirt fisted in her hand, tiptoed upstairs in her bare feet, very quietly, hardly breathing, refusing to glance at Gina's door, as if doing so would somehow rouse her sleeping friend.

She had no desire to answer Gina's questions about where she'd been and what she'd been doing. Not yet, anyway. She needed to think about it by herself for a while and sort things out in her own mind before she'd be ready to talk about it.

Unfortunately, one of her boots slipped out from under her arm as she was unlocking her apartment door. The stacked heel struck the bare wooden floor with a sharp, clattering sound that seemed to bounce off the walls of the narrow hallway, loud enough, Zoe was sure, to wake the dead and alert the entire building to her predawn return. With a sinking feeling of inevitability, Zoe heard the creaking of the door behind her.

"So," Gina said. "How was it?"

Zoe sighed, slumping for a moment, thinking briefly of just going into her apartment and shutting the door behind her, pretending she hadn't heard the question. The only thing that stopped her was the knowledge that Gina would follow her inside and keep asking until she got an answer. Diversion was the only thing that had a chance of working. For a while, anyway. Zoe pursed her mouth into an annoyed pout and turned around to face the music.

"Jeez, Gina, what were you doing? Lurking at the door, waiting to pounce on me the minute I got home?"

"Yep. I had my door open a crack so I'd be sure to hear you when you came in." Gina shuffled across the narrow hallway in her fuzzy bunny slippers and bent down to retrieve the fallen boot. "I wanted to be sure to get all the juicy details while they were still fresh in your mind. So..." She offered the boot to Zoe. "How was it?"

Zoe snatched the boot out of her grinning friend's hand and pushed open the door to her apartment. "How was what?"

"Oh, please." Gina entered the apartment behind her, just as Zoe had known she would. "You left here yesterday afternoon in that sexy black car of his, all gaga and excited—"

"About signing the contract." Zoe flipped on the light, set her boots on the floor and slipped the strap of her tapestry bag over one of the curving hooks on the coat rack next to the front door, just as if it were any other homecoming on any other day. "I was excited about finally signing the contract for New Moon," she said as she headed purposefully toward the tiny kitchen.

Gina snorted inelegantly. "Uh-huh."

"Okay, maybe not completely about the contract." She turned on the water faucet with one hand, at the same time reaching for the glass coffeepot on the Mr. Coffee with the other. "But mostly."

"Uh-huh," Gina said again.

Zoe set the filled pot on the heating element with a sharp little click. "*Mostly* about the contract," she insisted stubbornly.

"Oh, please." Gina rolled her eyes again. "No woman in the entire history of the world has ever been that excited about signing a contract." She hoisted herself up onto one of the stools at the kitchen counter to watch as Zoe measured coffee grounds into the cone-shaped filter. "No, indeed. The only thing that puts *that* look in a woman's eyes is the prospect of finally getting hot and heavy with a new guy. Or in your case, getting hot and heavy with *a* guy. Period. And besides, signing a contract doesn't take all night, anyway. So—" She leaned across the counter and curled her fingers around Zoe's forearm, claiming her full attention before she repeated her original question. "How was it? As wonderful as you thought it would be?"

"It was better," Zoe said, and surprised them both by bursting into tears.

Gina was immediately all solicitude and concern. "Oh, my goodness. Zoe. Honey. What's the matter? What happened?" She let go of Zoe's arm and slipped off of the stool, coming around the counter to gather her weeping friend into her arms. "What did that pervert do to you?"

"N-n-nothing." Zoe sniffled the words into Gina's flannel-covered shoulder, even though she had to stoop a little to do it. "He's not a pervert. He just…he just…"

"Come on, sweetie. He just what?" She made small, soothing circles against Zoe's back with the flat of her hand. "You'll feel better if you talk about it. And I'll feel better if I know what I'm cussing him out for."

"He j-just made me…he made me…"

"He *made* you do something?" Gina's hand stilled on Zoe's back. Her arms tightened protectively. "As in *forced?*" she said, her voice rising in outrage. "Are you saying he forced you to do something you didn't want to do? Forced you sexually?"

"No. Of course not!" Aghast, Zoe drew back out of her friend's embrace and wiped at her eyes, struggling to pull herself together before Gina's very active imagination took her any further down the wrong road. "He didn't force me to do anything. He wouldn't. He couldn't. Reed's far too much of a gentleman to make a woman do anything she didn't want to do."

"Well, then...I don't get it. Why are you crying? What did he *make* you do?"

"Nothing. He didn't make me do anything." She turned away, wiping surreptitiously at her eyes again, and opened the cupboard where she kept her collection of mismatched china. "Far from it." She got down cups and saucers, fussily placing them just so on the counter, focused intently on her task in an effort to avoid Gina's probing gaze. "He was a perfect gentleman." Until he'd lost control and wasn't, anymore. And then he'd been perfect in another way entirely. She shifted one of the cups a millimeter to the left and refused to think about it. "He's always a perfect gentleman."

"Then why the waterworks?" Gina demanded.

"Oh, I don't know. I guess..." Zoe shrugged helplessly. "It's just that there's been so much going on lately, with the worry over whether I was going to get the money to expand New Moon. And then the legal mumbo jumbo I had to go through, and Reed and all his minions looking into every aspect of my life, and having to deal with the new bookkeeping and filing systems and…just everything. I've been on edge for months, really, when you think about it, and…oh, hell!'' She smacked her hands down on top of the counter, making the fragile coffee cups rattle in their saucers. ''The truth is, I'm an idiot. I knew this might happen if I went to bed with him. I knew it, and I did it anyway, because I wanted—want,'' she corrected herself, determined to be scrupulously honest ''—because I *want* him so much. I told myself I could handle it. That it was no big deal. I mean, it's just sex, right?'' She glared at Gina as if daring to her to deny it.

''Uh…yeah, right,'' Gina mumbled. ''Just sex.''

''Everybody has sex sooner or later.'' Zoe yanked opened another cupboard and began rummaging through it. ''Almost everybody, anyway.'' She set a blue soup bowl on the counter and continued rummaging. ''I know it was later rather than sooner for me, but I figured that would work in my favor. I mean, I wasn't an impressionable teenager with romantic dreams like so many women are the first time. And that has to be a good thing, right?'' She turned from the open cupboard and gestured at Gina with the empty creamer she'd just taken from the shelf. ''Right?''

''Right.'' Nudging Zoe aside, Gina picked up the soup bowl and returned it to the cupboard. ''Not being a teenager your first time is a very good thing,'' she said as she lifted the sugar bowl off of the shelf and set it on the counter.

''I've been out in the world and on my own for years now,'' Zoe continued, totally unaware of the gently mocking tone of her best friend's voice. ''I've seen what sex can do to a woman's emotions. How it can mess up her mind and her life if she lets it. God, I've seen my mother go off the deep end enough times! I've

seen you go off the deep end, too." She pointed the
creamer at Gina. "Twice. And both times it was because of sex."

"Well, not entirely because of sex," Gina objected.
"I was really in love with Keith. For a while, anyway.
And with Bruce, well..." She shrugged. "He was just
so gorgeous. And such a great kisser. I got a little carried away."

"Because of sex," Zoe said, feeling Gina had just
made her point for her. "You got carried away because
of all those raging female hormones running amok,
making you think you were in love and going to live
happily ever after behind a white picket fence. Just like
my mother's done—" she waved the hand that held
the creamer in a vague dismissive gesture "—I don't
know how many times."

"So?"

"So you'd think I'd know better, wouldn't you?"
she said in disgust. "But, nooo, it turns out I'm just as
susceptible as the next woman when it comes to ro-
manticizing what's really just a basic biological func-
tion."

"Susceptible how?" Gina murmured encouragingly.

"I was so *sure* I wouldn't get all starry-eyed and
stupid just because I'd gone to bed with some guy.
Only..." she sighed wistfully and ran a fingertip over
the curved lip of the creamer "...he's not just some
guy. I think, maybe, he's *the* guy."

Gina reached out and took the creamer from her.
"*The* guy?" she said casually as she set it on the
counter next to the sugar bowl.

"Oh, no. Not *the* guy. Jeez, I can't believe I actually
said that. It's so stupid and...and...just forget I even
said it. I didn't mean it. It's just the sex talking." She

turned away from the knowing look in Gina's eyes and opened the refrigerator, pulling out a half-full carton of cream. She lifted it to her nose, absently sniffing at it before she poured it into the creamer. "We both know no rational woman can make a decision about whether or not a man is *the* guy based on one night of sex, no matter how wonderful it was. *Especially* if it was wonderful." She sighed again. "And it was wonderful...." Her busy hands stilled, her voice trailing off as she got lost in the memories.

Gina picked up the little cream jug, sniffed delicately and poured the contents into the sink. "Wonderful how?" she prompted, still casually.

Zoe shook her head as if trying to banish the mind-drugging memories. "That's not important." She returned the now empty carton of cream to the refrigerator and closed the door. "What's important is that if I don't pull myself together and start acting like a mature, rational adult, I'm going to ruin everything."

Gina opened the refrigerator, took out the empty carton and tossed it into the trash. "Ruin everything how?"

"By acting like an idiot, that's how. Do you know I snuck out of his house this morning before he woke up because I was afraid I'd say something that would have embarrassed both of us?" She shuddered at the very thought. "I actually snuck out, like some kind of thief. I tiptoed downstairs in his bathrobe and then scrambled around on the floor of his den in the dark to find my clothes so I could get dressed." She glanced down at her hands. "I couldn't find all my rings. Or my gold hoop earrings." Her cheeks turned pink as she thought of what else she hadn't been able to find in the dark. "His housekeeper will probably find them," she said in a horrified whisper, thinking of the torn, purple-satin panties.

"Your clothes were all over the floor?" Gina said enviously, diverted by that bit of news. "Wow. That must have been some—"

"I couldn't take the time to find them. I had to get out of there before he woke up or I would have made a complete fool of myself. I know I would have. And he would have thought I was nuts. He'd be right, too. I *am* nuts."

"Nuts about the stuffed shirt," Gina said.

"No. Oh, no." Zoe shook her head. "I'm not. Definitely not. Not really. It's just...it's..." She spread her hands in front of her, palms up, in a gesture unconsciously copied from Mama. "What I'm feeling right now is a combination of plain old-fashioned lust," she said, remembering what Reed had called it, "and... and..." she groped for a word "...gratitude? Does that make any sense?"

"I don't know," Gina said. "Does it?"

"He made it very special," Zoe said. "He was such a gentleman. So sweet and concerned and considerate. He was worried about hurting me or scaring me because it was my first time. And then, after a while, he wasn't anymore—worried, I mean—and it was—" she couldn't stop the small, dreamy, utterly satisfied smile that curved her lips at the memory "—wonderful. Completely, absolutely wonderful. The most wonderful experience of my life."

"Ohmygod," Gina muttered. "You're in love with him."

"No." Zoe shook her head again. "It's *not* love," she said firmly, horrified at the very thought. "If I know anything, I know that. It's definitely not love. It's gratitude and chemistry and…and—''

"It's love," Gina insisted. "You're head-over-heels, crazy in love with the stuffed shirt."

"No," Zoe insisted, desperately trying to make herself believe what she was saying. "It's the afterglow of good sex, is what it is. Infatuation. And if I keep my head and don't do or say anything stupid, I'll get through it and over it without embarrassing him or making a fool or myself." She took a deep, fortifying breath. "I hope."

REED AWOKE WITH the morning sun shining on his face. Aroused and wanting, he reached for Zoe before he even opened his eyes, and realized, much to his dismay, that he was all alone in his king-size bed. His first thought was that she'd simply gotten up to use the bathroom, or get a drink of water, or had even wandered downstairs for a cup of the coffee he knew his housekeeper would be brewing about then, but after a moment's reflection, he knew she hadn't. The bedroom was too silent, too empty for her to be in the connecting bathroom. And despite her in-your-face sassiness, he couldn't quite picture her sashaying into the kitchen to beg a cup of coffee from his housekeeper while dressed in his bathrobe, which was what she'd been wearing late last night when they'd crept down to the kitchen for some scrambled eggs and toast to keep their strength up. They'd left her clothes—and his—scattered all over the floor in the den when they'd moved upstairs to his bedroom after that first frenzied encounter, and somehow they hadn't found a moment to go back down and get them.

No, Zoe had left. Gone. She'd sneaked out while he

was sleeping, without even bothering to wake him up and say goodbye. The only thing she'd left behind in her mad dash to be gone before he woke up was the memory of the hottest sex he'd ever experienced and the delicate gold ankle bracelet that had been transferred from her leg to his wrist at some point during the heated activities of the night.

He lay there for another few moments in the big bed, his eyes still closed, his arm outstretched across the cold, empty space where she'd been, breathing in the faint scent of violets and sex that lingered in the sheets, and told himself it was ridiculous to feel as if he'd been deserted.

But that was *exactly* how he felt.

Deserted.

Abandoned.

Used, dammit!

The previous twelve hours had encompassed some of the most exciting, most frightening, most satisfying experiences of his life. He'd lost track of how many times they'd made love. Four times? Five? Six? He had never been so insatiable before; never felt such a driving need to possess; never experienced such a whirlwind of emotions, one after the other, and all tumbled together. Towering, intemperate, unstoppable passion. Bone-melting tenderness. An uncharacteristic playfulness that was halfway embarrassing and wholly delightful. Each incredible encounter had blended seamlessly into the next, and each time had been better than the time before. More intense. More shattering. More perfect. More satisfying.

He'd thought she felt the same.

How could she not?

And then she'd gotten up and tiptoed out in the wee,

small hours in the middle of the night as if he were some guy she'd picked up in a bar and didn't want to face in the bright light of the morning after. It left him feeling...what, exactly? Insulted? Well, yes, definitely insulted—Reed Sullivan IV was *not* some cheap one-night stand!—but it was more than that. Much more. There were hurt feelings underneath that injured male pride. And not far underneath, at that.

Amazing.

He'd never had his feelings hurt over a woman, not since his aborted adolescent romance with Janice Hawkins, anyway. Not even when Kate Hightower had left him standing more or less at the altar in front of their families and friends. A few months later, when she'd married her laid-back Southern charmer, Reed had kissed the bride's cheek and shaken the groom's hand without a glimmer of regret or jealousy.

And yet now, incredibly, just the mere *thought* of Zoe with another man made him feel...murderous.

She was *his*. He'd claimed her, branded her—she wore the crescent shaped mark of his teeth on her luscious fanny, dammit!—made her his own in the most basic way possible between a man and a woman. If *she'd* bolted at the altar, he'd have chased her down and dragged her back in front of the priest by that glorious red hair, and not turned her loose until she said "I do." And then he'd have hauled her off to bed and loved her so thoroughly that she'd never think about leaving him again.

He was already up, the covers thrown back, his feet on the floor, about to put thought into action, when he pulled up short and sank back down to sit on the edge of the bed. What in the hell was the matter with him? Where was his legendary savoir faire? His self-control?

His well-honed ability to stand back and look at things coolly, rationally and logically? He was thinking like a hormone-obsessed adolescent.

It was just sex, for crying out loud.

Spectacular, mind-blowing, heart-stopping sex, to be sure. But still, just sex. And she was just another woman. An incredibly exciting, phenomenally sexy woman, who just happened to be incredibly smart, too...and outrageously sassy...and unbelievably sweet...and passionate...and hardworking...and ambitious...and opinionated...and funny...and honest...and giving...and—

Reed braced his elbows on his knees and dropped his head into his hands, making the trio of tiny crescent moons on the ankle bracelet around his wrist tinkle merrily. "Oh, good Lord," he muttered, aghast and amused and amazed all at once. "I'm in love with her."

A DELIVERY BOY from a very exclusive Back Bay florist arrived at Zoe's apartment shortly after nine that morning bearing two frilly lavender orchids in a pale yellow porcelain pot. The delicate arching stems of the flowers were tied to natural bamboo stakes with wispy, sea-green raffia bows. The accompanying envelope was made of heavy cream-colored stock with the name of the florist discreetly embossed in gold in the upper righthand corner.

The delivery boy had already been very generously tipped. "Dude slipped me a twenty to make sure you got them first thing this morning," he said cheerfully, waving away Zoe's crumpled greenbacks before he thumped on back down the stairs.

Zoe turned from the door with the pot of orchids in

her hands, her expression somewhere between pleased and annoyed as she stared at Gina over the delicate blossoms. "He sent orchids! Ruffled lavender orchids in a yellow pot," she wailed. "Why couldn't it have been something mundane and ordinary, like roses? I would have expected roses. I could have *sneered* at roses. But *no,* he has to go and do something like this." She tenderly placed Reed's gift on the Chinese chest next to the bowl of marbles. "What kind of man sends a woman lavender orchids in a yellow pot?"

"Oh, I don't know." Gina lifted her shoulders in an exaggerated shrug. "The considerate, thoughtful, imaginative kind?"

Zoe glared at her.

"Obviously, only an insensitive jerk would do such a dastardly thing," Gina amended. "Imagine." She tsked like a disapproving maiden aunt and shook her head. "Sending orchids in one of your favorite colors. How *could* he?"

Zoe had to struggle not to be amused. "Very funny," she said reprovingly.

"Thank you. I thought so, too." She glanced down at the little square envelope Zoe held clutched in her fingers. "Open it, and let's see what an insensitive jerk who sends orchids has to say."

Zoe glanced down at the envelope, but made no move to open it. "I'm afraid to," she admitted. "What if it's a brush-off? What if it's one of those last-night-was-great-and-I'll-call-you-sometime notes?" Her eyes widened as another thought, equally unsettling, occurred to her. "What if it isn't?"

"Only one way to find out," Gina said.

Zoe hesitated another moment, then took a deep, steadying breath and slid one long, copper-colored fingernail under the flap of the envelope. "Oh." She lifted one hand to her chest, as if to still the sudden fluttering of her heart. "Oh, my."

"What?" Gina demanded. "What does it say?"

Wordlessly, Zoe handed the card to her.

Gina's eyebrows practically disappeared under the spiky fringe of her bangs as she read the bold masculine scrawl. "Well." She blew out a breath. "It's definitely not a brush-off."

REED SAT AT HIS DESK, pretending to read through the mail M.E.'s temporary replacement had left on his black leather blotter, and wondered if maybe he should have gone with his first instinct and sent roses. There was a good reason, after all, why roses were the flower of choice for Valentine's Day, wedding anniversaries and other special occasions having to do with matters of the heart. Women *liked* roses. They were elegant, traditional and classic, and the message they conveyed was unequivocally, unabashedly, unmistakably romantic.

Exactly the message he wanted to send.

But as he'd stood there at the florist's cash register, with his gold card out and his mouth open to place his order for a dozen long-stemmed American Beauty roses, he'd realized that was what he'd always sent to every other woman he'd ever been involved with, and suddenly roses were too ordinary. Too predictable. Too calculated and shallow and insincere. Too cliché.

And that wasn't nearly good enough for Zoe.

She deserved something better. Something different. Something special and beautiful, as unusual and unique and exotic as she was. Something that conveyed sincerity as well as romance, love as well as lust. Something that would tell her exactly how he felt about her and the incredible night they'd spent together.

Which was a lot to ask of any flower.

Even exotic hothouse orchids.

Maybe *especially* exotic hothouse orchids. In the unspoken language of flowers, who knew what message orchids conveyed?

He sat there a moment, wishing now that he'd gone with his first instinct and sent roses, wondering just how much damage he'd done with the orchids. And that note. That note hadn't been the least bit romantic, either. ''I woke up wanting you. Again.'' All that would accomplish was to make her think he wanted to take her to bed again. Which he did, of course. Desperately. But that wasn't *all* he wanted. Not by a long shot. No, he wanted...he wanted—

Everything, he realized. Everything she was. Everything she would be. He wanted to go to sleep with her beside him every night. To wake up with her every morning. He wanted to know what made her laugh, what made her cry, what she yearned for, what she dreamed of, what she feared. He wanted to...my God, he wanted to make babies with her! Little brown-eyed, red-haired babies. In all the time he'd been engaged to Kate Hightower he'd never once considered what any of their prospective offspring might have looked like, only that they would have the requisite two children at some time in the future. Now, just thinking of the beautiful curly headed babies he wanted to make with Zoe brought a funny kind of tickle to his throat.

But she was wary, he knew. Skittish. Probably not even thinking of happily ever after or making babies with him. And who could blame her? He'd insulted her at their first meeting, calling her a con artist and a hustler, all the while lusting after that luscious body. Then he'd hustled her into his bed without so much as a whispered endearment or a candlelight dinner to suggest his intentions were anything other than strictly carnal.

Was it any wonder she thought he was only interested in her body? Or that she was only interested in his?

Well, that was about to change. He was going to start over. He was going to woo her, slowly, the way he should have from the beginning, that's what he was going to do. He was going to buy her flowers and take her to dinner and...

"HE SENDS YOU so many flowers just for doing business?" Mama cast a suspicious eye over the vase of yellow roses decorating Zoe's kitchen counter before turning the same gaze on Zoe herself. "Monkey business, I am thinking."

"Not monkey business, Mama." Zoe tweaked the purple satin bow around the neck of the vase to avoid looking at Mama while she told the lie. "We signed the contracts for New Moon yesterday afternoon. The flowers are a sort of, um, congratulations."

"A man sends a nice potted plant for congratulations. Roses are for seduction."

"Mama!" Zoe pretended indignation at the very suggestion. "Reed is not trying to seduce me."

"Because he already has, maybe? Hmm?"

Zoe shrugged and looked down at the flowers, refusing to answer that.

"I know you did not come home from signing that contract until this morning. Signora Umberto saw you get out of the taxi at the crack of dawn," Mama told her. "You were with him last night, yes? With this Reed Sullivan?"

Zoe lifted one shoulder in a sheepish little shrug. "Yes," she admitted.

"Ah, *bambina.*" Mama reached out and cupped Zoe's cheek in her hand, turning her head so they were eye-to-eye. "You already know how I stand on such things so I will not waste my breath to tell you it is wrong, but I will say it is, perhaps, not wise, yes? He is a man of much experience, I think. And you have none at all. Or did not, before last night," she amended with a soft little smile. "You are like one of my own, my Zoe, as dear as my own blood, and I would not like to see you left sad and weeping over a broken heart."

"You don't have to worry, Mama. There's absolutely no chance of that." Zoe reached up and pressed the older woman's hand to her cheek for a moment, relishing the tenderness of the motherly touch. "My heart is completely safe from Mr. Sullivan," she added, willing it to be true.

And terribly afraid it wasn't.

13

AS SHE RELAXED AGAINST the sumptuous leather upholstery in the back of Reed's black Jaguar, the sound of a meltingly romantic violin concerto drifting through the speakers behind her head, Zoe came to the realization that it was more than just sex that turned a woman's mind to mush. It was everything that went with it. At least, everything that went with it the way Reed Sullivan IV did it.

The lavender orchids and yellow roses had only been the first salvo. Violets had come next, a miniature nosegay of velvety purple flowers, done up with a ruff of delicate white lace. He'd pinned them to the lapel of her eggplant suit with a whimsical antique hat pin just before they entered the lobby of Le Meridien on their way to what she assumed was going to be a business lunch in the hotel's very popular restaurant.

They'd actually discussed business, too. In fact, they'd ended up cutting lunch short, forgoing a taste of what she'd always heard were the truly inspired desserts at the Julien because of the appointment Reed had made for her to look at warehouse space in the waterfront area near Four Point Channel. But somehow, despite their good intentions, they'd walked right past the exit to the parking garage and headed for the reception desk, where Reed used his gold card and his clout to secure one of the hotel's famous loft suites without benefit of a reservation. They'd fallen into each other's arms in the empty elevator, necking like a couple of frenzied teenagers as it ascended to their assigned floor, then made their way down the hall in a swelter of heat and anticipation. In their room, several glorious, passion-filled hours slipped by before either one of them remembered the Realtor who'd been going to show them the warehouse property. Reed had called and smoothed things over with the Realtor, and then, while Zoe showered, he ordered up champagne and lobster and a sampler tray of the desserts from room service. They ate their feast in bed, then feasted on each other, and didn't leave the room until checkout time the next day.

Friday had been the same. Flowers. Another superb meal at another fabulously romantic restaurant. Another missed appointment. Another night of unforgettable sex.

Zoe had never been happier or more miserable in her entire life.

She felt like a sex toy. A mindless bimbo at the mercy of her hormones.

She didn't like the feeling one little bit.

Especially when it was her own darn fault.

She was the one who'd initiated the relationship, after all. She'd provoked him, that day in Moira's parlor. She'd tracked him down at the rugby field. She'd asked him to kiss her. She'd asked him to go to bed with her, too, then boldly challenged him to that game of strip marbles when he'd hesitated. It had seemed like a good idea at the time.

She'd been so sure she could handle it. So sure she wouldn't get all stupid and sappy and sentimental. So sure she wouldn't fall in love.

"Fool," she muttered, disgruntled and disgusted with herself. "Silly, stupid fool."

Eddie glanced into the rearview mirror at the sound of her voice. "Excuse me?"

"Nothing." Zoe shook her head at him. "Just thinking out loud," she said, wishing she could tell him to turn around and take her home, that she'd changed her mind about going to Moira Sullivan's cocktail party.

But she didn't. Couldn't. Precisely because it *was* Moira Sullivan's party, and it was being given in honor of New Moon. If nothing else, Zoe had an obligation to go, and she always met her obligations. Besides, she wanted to go. Of course she wanted to go. They were celebrating her success, after all, the expansion of New Moon, the thing she'd been working toward since her junior year in college. Only a silly, simpering, simpleminded idiot would even think of letting a...a tawdry sexual relationship get in the way of business, the way she'd been doing the last two days. Only a silly, simpering, simpleminded idiot would have let herself get involved in a tawdry sexual relationship with her financial advisor in the first place. Well, not tawdry, exactly—the last three days had been too romantic, too special, too beautiful to be called tawdry—but unwise, certainly. Yes, definitely unwise.

Well, it was over, she decided. Completely, utterly over. It had to be, because the next time he took her into his arms, the next time he made love to her as if it was all he ever wanted to do in the world, the next time she came apart beneath him, she wouldn't be able to keep from uttering those three foolish, fateful words that would ruin everything. *I love you.* He hadn't signed on for that. Wouldn't want it. Well, neither did she.

And that's why it had to be over.

It should have never started in the first place, of course, but that was water under the bridge now.

She would go to Moira's party, Zoe decided, and to the charity benefit for Mass General afterward, too. She'd meet new people, establish business contacts among the movers and shakers of Boston society. She'd even enjoy herself, by God. But afterward…well, afterward, she was going home. Alone. There would be no repeat of what had happened on the floor in the den of his Back Bay town house, she told herself as the sleek black Jag glided to a stop at the curb in front of Moira's Beacon Hill mansion. There would be no midnight rendezvous at some discreet hotel after the charity ball was over, she warned herself as the rear passenger door of the Jag swung open. There would absolutely be no—

"Zoe," Reed said as he extended his hand to her through the open door. "Welcome."

He was wearing black tie—understated, elegant and devastatingly sexy black tie—and smiling down at her as if she were the first, the only woman in the world. Zoe's mind went blank and she promptly forgot every reason she'd just given herself for ending their affair before the night was over.

"Reed," she murmured, her smile wide and soft and beatific as she reached up to place her hand in his.

He drew her out of the car, thinking as she stepped onto the sidewalk beside him that she was more beautiful each time he saw her. She was wearing a bronze-colored, 1930s-style, silk charmeuse evening gown that was nearly, but not quite, cloth-of-gold. It was slim fitting and bias cut so that it skimmed along every luscious curve and hollow of her voluptuous body, from the softly draped neckline of the bodice to the flowing floor-length hem. A rich, silk-lined velvet stole, the same color as the dress, was elegantly draped across her bare shoulders, and she'd gathered her flaming curls into a loose mass atop her head in an artless style that seemed just on the verge of tumbling down. Her only ornaments, aside from her own glorious coloring and spectacular figure, were the glittering crystal-and-topaz teardrops dangling from her ears. Even her hands, usually adorned with half a dozen narrow rings, were bare except for the subdued gleam of the copper-colored polish that slicked her nails.

She looked like a screen goddess from Hollywood's golden era and smelled, Reed thought, all but closing his eyes as he breathed her in, like somebody's' sweet old maiden aunt. It was incongruous and intriguing and intoxicating. He wanted to gather her up in his arms and kiss her until they were both breathless. He settled for brushing his lips across her fingertips.

"You're looking especially beautiful tonight," he murmured as he tucked her hand into the crook of his elbow and led her across the sidewalk and up the steps to where Moira waited in the open front door.

Zoe looked up at him from under the sweep of her auburn lashes, about to tell him that he was looking especially beautiful, too, when Moira swooped down the remaining two steps and enfolded her in a warm Chanel-scented hug.

"Zoe, my dear. Welcome." She touched her softly lined cheek to Zoe's porcelain smooth one, then stepped back, taking both of Zoe's hands in hers, and surveyed her guest. "Oh, you look wonderful. Just like Rita Hayworth in her prime, only prettier."

"The dress is all right, then?" Zoe said, relieved.

She hadn't been a hundred percent sure it was quite the thing for a charity benefit at the Isabella Stewart Gardner Museum with Boston's uppercrust. After all, she'd found it in her favorite antique clothing store in the South End. But if Moira said it was all right...

"It's beautiful," Moira assured her. "You're beautiful. Isn't she, Reed?"

"Exquisite," Reed agreed, but neither Moira...nor Zoe...was really listening.

"I do hope it wasn't too much of an imposition, asking you to get here without benefit of Reed's escort," Moira said. "But he's my host tonight, you know, and I needed him here to help receive."

"It was no imposition at all," Zoe assured her as they ascended the remaining steps and entered the foyer. There was a bouquet of fresh flowers on the center table and lighted candles in the wall sconces. The low hum of conversation was just audible over the soft strains of classical music coming from the parlor. They paused there as Reed lifted the velvet stole from her shoulders and handed it to a uniformed maid to hang up.

"Now, then, let's go in and meet the rest of my guests, shall we?" Moira tucked her hand into the crook of Zoe's elbow and steered her across the marble foyer and through the double doors into the parlor, leaving Reed standing stock-still, staring at the smooth expanse of Zoe's nearly bare back.

There was a crackling fire in the Adam hearth in the parlor, and lighted candles in polished silver candlesticks on the mantel and the sideboard. Tastefully extravagant arrangements of white flowers—roses, freesias, bleeding hearts and baby's breath—were arranged around the room, delicately perfuming the air with their scent. Two more uniformed women circulated among the two dozen or so well-heeled guests, passing silver trays of canapés and flutes of champagne. The men all wore black tie. The women were hardly more colorful, or less elegant; there was a lot of tasteful black and pearls, the discreet twinkle of diamonds, an occasional flash of ivory satin or ice-blue silk, and one brave soul in mint green chiffon that revealed a modest hint of cleavage.

Resisting the urge to turn tail and run, Zoe lifted her chin instead and followed her hostess around the room to be introduced to the rest of her guests. These people were the movers and shakers of Boston society, she reminded herself as she smiled and made small talk, the very people she would need to cultivate to make New Moon the success she knew it could be. Her knees might be shaking beneath the flowing bronze silk of her gown, but these people would never know it.

"You remember Katherine Hightower, don't you, Zoe?" Moira said as they approached the formidable old dowager. "I think you met her niece Margaret, too, that day at the hospital when Reed's secretary had her darling baby boy."

"Yes, of course," Zoe said politely, struggling, suddenly, against the inane urge to tug the bodice of her dress higher on her chest. It was perfectly modest, by any standard; she'd just have to remember not to turn her back on the old biddy. "It's a pleasure to see you again, Mrs. Hightower," she lied blandly. "Miss Hightower."

"I understand you and Moira have gone into business together," Katherine Hightower said when Moira excused herself to greet another guest.

"Moira has invested in New Moon, yes," Zoe said. "We signed the agreements a few days ago."

"Cosmetics." Katherine Hightower sniffed disdainfully. "A frivolous business. You do know, don't you, young woman, that the vast majority of such businesses fail miserably within the first year?"

Zoe's chin lifted a notch higher. "Mine won't," she said.

"That's telling her, darlin'," said an unfamiliar voice in her ear.

Zoe turned her head toward the owner of the voice and found herself nearly eyeball-to-eyeball with a golden Apollo of a man. He was lean and loose-limbed, with a shock of thick blond hair that fell over his forehead and a knowing twinkle in eyes the color of a summer sky. He wore his tuxedo with a casual air, and his slow, sweet smile was an invitation to a myriad of sinful pleasures.

"You've got to stand up to the old girl or she'll grind you into dust," he advised, grinning unrepentantly when Katherine Hightower tried to glare him into submission.

"My grandnephew. By marriage," she said with another disgruntled sniff, but the disapproval in her voice was belied by the glint of approval in her eyes.

Even Katherine Hightower, it seemed, wasn't impervious to the wicked appeal of such a charming rogue.

"Jesse de Vallerin," said the rogue, "and my wife—" he slipped his arm around the waist of a stunning woman in a slim column of rich ivory satin as she came up to join the group "—Kate," he said, and bent his head to kiss her bare shoulder. "Kate, darlin', this pretty lady is Miz Zoe Moon. She's the one made that hand cream you've been ravin' about.''

"I've been looking forward to meeting you," Kate de Vallerin said as they shook hands. "I'd like to talk to you about selling your products in my shop down in New Orleans. Early next week, perhaps, before Jesse and I head back home?"

As they stood talking business and making an appointment to meet the following Monday, a corner of Zoe's mind was busy putting two and two together. *Kate is her great-niece.... When Kate and I announced our engagement... The bride-to-be ran off three days before the wedding and married someone else.*

Without a doubt, Kate de Vallerin—elegant, understated, refined Kate de Vallerin—was the woman Reed had once been engaged to. She was the woman he'd wanted to marry. He'd said he wasn't sorry to have lost her, implied he no longer cared that she'd run off and married another man. But as he stood across the room by the fireplace, talking to Moira and a sleek blond, Reed kept glancing their way. And the looks he was giving Jesse de Vallerin were definitely sparked with the green-eyed monster.

"Yes," Jesse said, noticing that Zoe's attention wasn't entirely on the conversation they were having. "The whole scandalous story is true."

"I beg your pardon?"

"I really did snatch Kate practically out from under the nose of our illustrious host. I'm pretty sure he's gotten over it, but Aunt Katherine still hasn't completely forgiven me." His grin flashed when Katherine glared down her nose at him. "I keep hoping that if Alicia snags him, she'll finally let me off the hook for marryin' her favorite grandniece and keepin' her down in New Orleans.''

"Alicia?" Zoe murmured.

Jesse tilted his head toward the group in front of the fireplace. "The tall cool glass of water in the black dress," he said, indicating the young blond woman conversing with Reed and Moira. "She's another great-niece. Aunt Katherine thinks she'll do nicely for Reed. Don't you, Aunt Katherine?"

"Yes, I do." Katherine Hightower's gaze rested on Zoe for a long moment, as if making sure she understood. "Reed and Alicia are suitable in every way."

FROM WHERE HE STOOD shaking hands and making small talk, Reed discreetly scanned the faces of the party guests as they filed in through the open doors of the Tapestry Room on the second floor of the Isabella Stewart Gardner Museum.

"Where's Zoe?" he whispered, leaning down to kiss his great-grandmother's cheek as she came even with him in the receiving line. "Didn't she ride over with you?"

Moira shook her head. "She asked Eddie to take her home shortly after you left with Katherine and Alicia to come over here."

"She *what?*" The sharp rise in volume caused several heads to turn. Reed lowered his voice. "Why?"

"She said she had a beastly headache coming on and needed to lie down before it got worse," Moira said as she started to move along the receiving line.

Reed curled his fingers around her elbow, heedless of the holdup he was causing. "And you just let her go?"

"Well, really, Reed. I could hardly insist she come with me when she wasn't feeling well, could I?"

"No." He let her arm slip from his grasp. "Of course not."

"I do hope it's nothing serious." The dulcet voice, rife with spurious concern, came from Alicia Hightower, who stood directly to Reed's left in the receiving line.

"I hope so, too," Reed muttered, wondering what the hell had happened since he'd left Moira's house that made Zoe change her mind about coming to the benefit.

The possibility that something had happened *before* he left occurred to him, too. He hadn't been as attentive as he might have been, partly because his duties as host kept him busy circulating, partly because every time he got close enough to touch her, he wanted to. Since it really · wouldn't do to start groping his great-grandmother's guest of honor, he'd kept his distance.

But Zoe wasn't the type to succumb to a headache because she was miffed at being ignored. There had to be something more to it than that. Something that had hurt her feelings or—

"You hope what isn't serious?" Katherine Hightower demanded from her place on Alicia's other side.

"Moira's little protégée went home with a headache," Alicia said sweetly. "She won't be joining us, after all."

"Won't she?" Katherine Hightower's solemn expression couldn't quite hide the note of satisfaction in her voice. "How…distressing. I'll have to remember to ask Moira to convey our regrets at her absence."

"Please don't bother, Aunt Katherine," Reed said. "I'll convey them myself." He inclined his head slightly, bowing to each woman in turn. "If you'll excuse me, ladies?" he said politely, and stepped out of the receiving line.

"Well, of all the..." Katherine Hightower rapped her gold-headed cane against the floor in frustration and rounded on her young relative. "You certainly played that one all wrong," she said irritably. "He's gotten away again."

THE NORTH END on a Saturday night was a happening place, making the parking situation even more impossible than usual. Reed dealt with the problem by tossing his keys to the red-coated valet in front of the Ristorante Marcella, then wended his way through the cocktail tables that had been set up outside to accommodate the throng of patrons waiting to sample Mama Marcella's cooking.

The laneway between the restaurant and the building next door was silent compared to the busy, bustling street, and shadowed with wavering patches of light that shone down from the windows on the second floors of both buildings. Reed paused a moment at the mouth of the alley, letting his eyes adjust to the difference in light.

"So you have a fight with our Zoe, yes?" said a voice from somewhere above his head.

Reed looked up to see the wizened old woman from the bakery staring down at him from one of those second-story windows. "A fight with Zoe?" he said "What makes you say that?"

Signora Umberto shrugged. "Zoe leaves here in your fancy black car, all dressed up so pretty. And then she comes back, alone, with her chin up in the air. And now you are come after her. Is a fight. You should have brought flowers," she advised. "Men should always bring flowers to say they are sorry."

Reed shook his head. "We didn't have a fight."

Signora Umberto shrugged again, then waved toward the gate at the bottom of the stairs. "Try and see," she invited him, and crossed her arms on the windowsill to watch the show.

It was a full five minutes before anyone bothered to answer the buzzer. Five long minutes in which the vague anxiety that had prompted him to abandon his post in the receiving line turned to a steadily growing irritation. And the longer she made him wait, the more irritated he became.

"Yes? Who is it?"

"Zoe?"

"No, this is Gina. Zoe, uh...isn't here."

"Is here," the old woman at the window said.

"I know she's up there." Reed's irritation was rapidly turning into annoyance. The emotion lent a snap to his voice that any employee of Sullivan Enterprises would have recognized as a harbinger of trouble. "I'd like to speak to her, please."

Gina repeated her assertion that Zoe wasn't there.

Annoyance turned into anger. He knew a brush-off when he heard one. What he didn't know was why. "I know she's up there," he said in a voice so deadly quiet it would have sent anyone who really knew him running for cover. Reed Sullivan IV didn't lose his temper often, but when he did, heads rolled. "And you can tell her from me, Miss Molinari, that I'm not leaving until I've spoken with her."

"I THINK HE MEANS IT," Gina reported a moment later, peering down at him from behind the curtain at Zoe's window. "He's just standing in the ally, looking at the ground."

"He's what?"

"Looking down at the... No, now he's picking something up and—"

A shower of pebbles hit the window. "Zoe!"

"Just ignore him," Zoe said. "He'll go away."

Another volley of pebbles hit the window.

"Tell him to stop that," Zoe ordered. "He's going to break the window."

Gina obligingly opened the window and told him to stop that.

"I want to speak to Zoe," Reed said. "And I'm not leaving until I do."

Gina drew her head back inside. "He says he's not leaving until you talk to him. I think he means it."

"Oh, for pity's sake." Zoe stalked to the window and leaned out. Old Mrs. Umberto waved at her from across the alley. Zoe pretended not to see her. "What do you want?" she demanded.

The anger inside him boiled over at her snooty tone. "I want to know why the hell you ran out on me," he demanded, forgetting that he never swore at—or in front of—women.

"I didn't run out on you. I had a headache."

His sneer was eloquent. "A convenient excuse."

"It's not an excuse. I did—do..." She put a hand to her forehead. "I do have a headache." It was almost true. Now.

"Liar."

"Lecher," Zoe countered, and slammed the window shut.

"Lecher?" he roared. "What the hell does that mean?"

"Is a man who is fast with the ladies," Signora Umberto said.

Reed ignored her.

"Zoe, dammit, come down here and tell me what the hell you mean by that."

Zoe had nursed her grievances—real and imagined—all the way home, building them up in her mind until Reed was a man who had manipulated her emotions for his own lustful purposes; a man who had taken advantage of her innocent passion; a man who'd deliberately made her fall in love with him and then, when she was hopelessly hooked, had callously discarded her for an icy blond Boston debutante with the right bloodlines. Zoe pushed up the window sash again and let him have the full brunt of her feminine fury.

"It means I refuse to be used as your sex toy any longer, that's what it means," she shouted. "It means it's over. Finished. Kaput. It means that from now on the only thing between us is business."

"Sex toy?" Reed shouted back. "Sex toy!"

His bellow of outrage caused several of the people who were waiting for a table at the Ristorante Marcella to move to the mouth of the alley to see what all the hollering was about.

"If anyone's been used as a sex toy, it's me," he charged indignantly, unaware of and unconcerned with his growing audience. "I tried to slow things down, remember? *You're* the one who insisted we have sex."

"I did not insis—" she began, and then stopped, because she had. And quite emphatically, too.

"And you're the one who wants to call it quits now that you have what you want," he accused.

"Now that I have what I want? What do you mean, now that I have what I—" She broke off suddenly, as his meaning got through to her. He meant the money, of course. "How dare you insinuate that I—that I would..." Words failed her. "Oh, go away," she cried, and slammed the window down so hard it shattered.

Reed had to jump out of the way to avoid the shower of falling glass.

"Oh, now see what you made me do!" Zoe wailed.

"What I made you do? I didn't make you do a—"

"Stop this noise instantly!" The speaker clapped her hands together sharply, like a teacher calling for order in a noisy classroom. "Instantly, I say, and tell me what is going on out here."

Zoe caught her breath in abject horror and shrank back from the window, out of sight. Reed turned to glare at the woman who'd dared interrupt what he considered a private discussion in spite of the fact that it was being held on a public street at top volume.

"Well?" Mama demanded imperiously, unimpressed with his glower. "I am waiting."

"Is a fight," Signora Umberto said, when neither of the principals answered.

"Yes, I heard that much for myself." Mama made a sweeping gesture with one arm. "So have all my customers heard, as well." She glanced at Reed again, and then up at the broken window. "Zoe."

Zoe reluctantly reappeared at the window. "Yes, Mama?"

"I would like you to tell me, please, why you and this young man are shouting at each other and disturbing my customers?"

"Well, I...he...it's..."

"It's my fault, Mrs. Molinari," Reed said, automatically stepping in to shield Zoe. "I lost my temper."

"And you are?"

"Reed Sullivan, ma'am."

"Ahh." Mama looked him up and down consideringly. "I begin to see. Yes." She nodded to herself. "I definitely begin to see."

Reed didn't know exactly what she was beginning to see, but he was pretty sure it didn't bode well for him. Zoe's surrogate grandmother already suspected him of being up to no good; the current situation could only serve to further confirm those suspicions.

"You are the one who hired a detective to investigate my Zoe."

"Yes, I am."

"And you are the one whose grandmama gave her the money for her business."

"Yes."

"And you are also the one she chooses for her first lover."

"And only," he said, before he realized what his statement would reveal. "First and only."

Mama smiled. "You are in love with her, then?"

"Yes, I am."

"And do you want to marry her?"

"Yes, ma'am. I do."

"Good. That is very good." Mama nodded once more, emphatically, and looked back up at the window where Zoe stood, straining to hear what was being said. "You will let this young man in," Mama instructed.

"But, Mama—"

"You will let him in," she said firmly, "and listen to what he has to say. And if you want to continue arguing, you will do so in such a way that it will not disturb my customers. Is that clear?"

"Yes, Mama."

GINA RETREATED to her own apartment, leaving Zoe to face Reed alone. She waited for him at the top of the stairs, barefoot, her hair still gathered up on top of her head, her glamorous silk evening gown replaced by a pink terry-cloth robe that should have clashed with her hair but didn't. Her crystal-and-topaz earrings still dangled from her ears. She didn't even wait for him to get halfway up the stairs before she started babbling.

"I'm sorry I called you a lecher. I didn't mean it. I was just mad, so I said the first thing that came into my head, is all. It's a bad habit of mine. Saying the first thing that comes into my head, I mean. I know you're not a lecher. And I did, um, initiate our, uh, our sexual relationship. I admit that. But it wasn't just sex."

She backed up a step, and then another, and another, retreating into her apartment as he advanced, stalking her. This was one woman—*the* one woman—who wasn't getting away. If he had to track her to the ends of the earth, he'd do it. Happily. Because this was the woman he wanted for all time.

"Well, okay, it *was* just sex, I guess," she admitted. "But it wasn't just sex in a bad way. I mean, I'm...I'm fond of you."

"Fond?"

"Well, more than fond, actually. That's probably the wrong word, anyway. What I meant to say was that I, um...well, you're a wonderful lover, you know, and I was naturally overwhelmed by the whole experience, being a virgin and all, I mean. So it's understandable that I'd be, well...infatuated with you."

"Infatuated?

"Oh, all right." She took a deep breath, squared her shoulders under the pink terry-cloth robe, lifted her chin and told the absolute truth. "I'm in love with you, okay? Are you happy now that you've made me say it? I'm madly, passionately, completely in love with you."

She said the words defiantly, belligerently even, as if she expected him to gloat or throw them back in her face. Or laugh at her hopeless naivete. But he just stood there, staring at her as if he'd been poleaxed. Her heart began to flutter wildly in her chest. Panic, she told herself. Embarrassment. Hysteria. It wasn't every day a woman made a fool of herself over a man. Or maybe it was.

"You don't have to worry," she assured him. "It isn't a permanent condition. I'll get over it. I'm sure I'll get over it. Eventually."

"I hope not," he said softly. "I hope to God you never get over it."

Zoe stood there for a moment, wide-eyed, staring. The sick, panicky fluttering in her chest took on a different character. Excitement. Fear. A wild impossible hope.

"I'm in love with you, too." He reached out and gently, slowly, enfolded her in his arms. "I'm madly, passionately, completely in love with you. And I'm quite sure I'm never going to get over it as long as I live."

"Never?" she breathed, almost...almost allowing herself to believe it might be true. Might be possible.

"Never," he vowed, and bent his head to kiss her.

And Zoe let herself believe it. Just for that moment. She parted her lips and accepted his kiss and let herself believe. And when he raised his head...

"Are you sure it's not just the sex?" she asked.

"Not just the sex?"

"Making us feel this way. Sex scrambles your mind. It makes you stupid and sappy and sentimental."

He smiled into her hair and cuddled her closer. "What's wrong with stupid and sappy and sentimental?"

"It doesn't last."

He drew back a bit to look down at her. "What makes you think it doesn't last?"

"Experience."

He grinned wolfishly. "You didn't have any experience before me."

"My mother's experience. She's been married six times, and she's had I don't know how many affairs. She's always falling in love and thinking this guy is *the* guy. Only he never is. Or he is for just a little while. And then she falls out of love. Until the next time. She'd already been married and divorced four times by the time she was my age."

"And how many times have you been married and divorced?"

"That's not the point. I've been very careful not to let myself get intimately involved with anyone."

"Until me."

"Until you," she agreed.

"So you've already broken your mother's pattern, then, haven't you?"

The way Zoe's eyes widened it was clear she'd never looked at it in quite that light. "Yes," she said slowly. "Yes, I guess I have."

"Well, then." He cocked an eyebrow at her. "What's the problem?"

"It can't be that easy."

"I don't see why not."

"What about the debutante?"

"What debutante?"

"Alicia."

Reed just shook his head. "She doesn't glitter."

"She doesn't what?"

"She doesn't glitter." He flicked one of her dangling earrings with his fingertip, setting it to swaying and sparkling in the light, then tenderly cupped his hands around her face and tilted it up to his. "I've always had a weakness for the ones that glitter," he said, and kissed her.

HARLEQUIN® *Blaze*™

presents...

Four erotic interludes that could occur
only during...

Sexy
CITY NIGHTS

EXPOSED! by *Julie Elizabeth Leto*
Blaze #4—August 2001
Looking for love in sizzling San Francisco...

BODY HEAT by *Carly Phillips*
Blaze #8—September 2001
Risking it all in decadent New York...

HEAT WAVES by *Janelle Denison*
Blaze #12—October 2001
Finding the ultimate fantasy in fiery Chicago...

L.A. CONFIDENTIAL by *Julie Kenner*
Blaze #16—November 2001
Living the dream in seductive Los Angeles...

SEXY CITY NIGHTS—
Where the heat escalates *after* dark!

And don't miss out on reading about naughty New Orleans
in ONE WICKED WEEKEND, a weekly online serial
by Julie Elizabeth Leto, available now at www.eHarlequin.com!

LOOK FOR OUR EXCITING

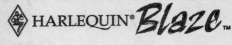
HARLEQUIN® *Blaze*™

RED-HOT READS

NEXT MONTH!

JUST A LITTLE SEX... by Miranda Lee
SLEEPING WITH THE ENEMY by Jamie Denton
THE WILD SIDE by Isabel Sharpe
HEAT WAVES by Janelle Denison

HARLEQUIN®
Makes any time special ®

Visit us at www.tryblaze.com   HBUSCOUPONSEPT

LOOK FOR OUR EXCITING

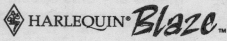

HARLEQUIN® *Blaze* ™

RED-HOT READS

NEXT MONTH!

Including:

JUST A LITTLE SEX... by Miranda Lee
SLEEPING WITH THE ENEMY by Jamie Denton
THE WILD SIDE by Isabel Sharpe
HEAT WAVES by Janelle Denison

HARLEQUIN®
Makes any time special ®

Visit us at www.tryblaze.com

HBCANCOUPONSEPT

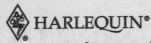